ROUGH JUSTICE

A SHRAP NELSON MYSTERY
BOOK 1

BIBA PEARCE

1

In the hours before dawn, the streets belonged to her.

Not to the hurried commuters, umbrellas angled against the rain, not the tourists with their expensive cameras and vacant smiles, not the workmen in their yellow hardhats, beefy hands wrapped around Styrofoam cups.

To her.

Shrap sat on the low concrete wall separating St Thomas's Hospital gardens from the South Bank and watched as the sun painted the Houses of Parliament a burnished gold. The river walk was empty. She glanced along it, then down the other way. There was nobody in sight.

The river rushed past, governed by man-made tides, unable to do what it wanted. The surface was still, but just beneath she could see flurries and eddies, a sure sign the undertow was strong and relentless.

A port authority patrol vessel appeared from around the bend, kicking up white water as it raced by. Two men hunched over the bulkhead in high-visibility jackets. Shrap wondered if they were going on a rescue mission. A hapless kayaker, perhaps?

Then it was quiet again.

The frosty chill in the air whispered winter was coming. She pulled her long coat around her and rubbed her hands. It would soon be her second winter on the street. Practically a lifetime.

She spun around at the crunch of boots on the gravel path behind her. Two police officers, a man and a woman, were approaching. Without thinking, Shrap slipped her hand into her leg pocket and withdrew her knife, then put her hand behind her back, over the wall.

She scowled as they smiled. Forced smiles, non-threatening, designed to reassure. She used to have a smile like that.

"Are you Shrap?" enquired the female copper, looking her up and down. She was in her mid-twenties. Pressed trousers, white shirt, shiny shoes. They both wore stab vests.

Shrap nodded warily.

"I'm Sergeant Baxter and this is Sergeant Willis. We'd like to ask you a few questions."

Willis stood further away from her than Baxter like he was afraid he'd catch something if he got too close. He had a pasty complexion, pale, judgmental eyes, and a bland expression that she found annoying.

"What about?"

"Do you know this man?" Baxter held up a grainy photograph taken from a CCTV camera of a white-haired man in his sixties, slightly stooped and lopsided, head down and to the side so that only part of his face was visible. He appeared to be in a hurry, his mouth pulled downwards in a misshapen O.

She nodded again. "What's he done?"

"What makes you think he's done something?"

Shrap gave them a hard look. "Why else would you be here?"

The woman paused.

"As it happens, we are trying to locate this man. Do you know where he is?"

Shrap frowned. "No, he moves around."

"When last did you see him?" asked the male officer.

Shrap shrugged. "Couple of days ago."

Baxter cleared her throat. "Would you mind accompanying us down to the station, ma'am?"

Ma'am. She hadn't been called that in a long time. "What for?"

"To answer some more questions about your friend."

"Who said he was my friend?"

"You seemed concerned about him." She flushed and glanced at the ground. "Apologies if I misunderstood."

She wasn't wrong. Doug was a friend. Shrap decided to stop giving her a hard time.

"I know him, that's all."

Baxter gave a little nod.

"Will you come with us?" asked the pasty-faced officer.

She dropped the knife into a flower bed to be retrieved later. The sunrise was ruined anyway. The moment was lost. She loved that short interval after daybreak when the world was doused in a rosy glow and anything seemed possible, before the glare became too bright and the cracks began to show.

"Yeah, I'll come."

She swung her long legs around and jumped off the wall.

"You carrying any weapons?" Pasty Face asked.

"No."

He glanced at his colleague, who flushed. "Mind if I pat you down?"

Rookie, still getting to grips with the job.

Shrap raised her arms. "Go ahead." Standard procedure. She got it. They didn't want any nasty surprises.

Baxter searched her for weapons, and finding none, gave a stiff nod. "Thank you, ma'am. If you'll come with us."

SOUTHWARK POLICE STATION was a ten-minute drive away. As she sat in the back of the patrol vehicle, Shrap tried to make sense of the situation.

What the hell had Doug done? Why were the police looking for him? The guy was a harmless old drunk. A vagrant nobody cared about. Unless you counted loitering, Doug hadn't committed a crime since he'd gone AWOL from the armed services twenty years ago.

The police car drew up outside and Baxter, who'd been sitting next to her, got out. "Follow me."

Pasty face, who was driving, didn't turn around.

Shrap got out and stared up at the mismatched building with its dark- and light-coloured bricks and concrete base. The cobalt-blue plaque above the door read *Metropolitan Police*. Attached to the wall above the entrance was an old-fashioned Victorian streetlamp, the glass the same reassuring blue.

Baxter pressed a buzzer and the door clicked open. Shrap had never been inside this building before, but all police stations looked the same. Bare lobby, harsh lighting, sombre-faced duty sergeants behind a smudged plexiglass screen desperate to knock off.

Baxter greeted the officer behind the desk and gestured for Shrap to follow her. They went through a revolving door and down a cold, unwelcoming corridor. At the other end was a large office, bustling with activity. Three police constables manned a long reception desk, computers hummed, and printers spat out charge and release forms. Somewhere, a radio crackled.

"D5 would like a drink of water," barked an overworked custody officer, appearing from a side door. "And DI Bailey is waiting for C2 in Interview Room 3."

A detainee shouted something obscene from inside one of the holding cells. The custody officer rolled her eyes. "He's still pissed."

"Hi, Gloria. Who's this?" The constable behind the desk gazed at her.

Baxter put a hand on Shrap's shoulder. "This woman has come in voluntarily. Detective Constable Trevelyan wants to interview her."

"Name?"

"Shrap," said Shrap.

"Surname?"

"Just Shrap." The constable arched a tired brow but wrote her name down, then checked the digital clock behind her and added the time. "Put her in Interview Room 2. They're finished in there now."

Baxter led her down a short flight of steps and along another passage. Everything was painted in a suffocating aquamarine. Shrap felt like she was swimming underwater.

"If you'll wait in here." Baxter opened a side door and gave her an awkward smile.

She went inside.

The smell of sweat and fear from the last inhabitant was so vivid, Shrap gripped the rim of the chair and closed her eyes. Déjà vu sucker-punched her in the gut.

She was on the other side of the table.

She was the one in charge, calling the shots. The interrogator, calmly and relentlessly breaking down her suspect. Finding cracks in their story, then prising them wide open.

But that was another life. Another person. Someone she couldn't relate to anymore. With a sigh, she sank down into the chair. It was bolted to the floor.

She didn't have to wait long.

"Thanks for coming in." A lanky man with an earnest face, curious eyes and unruly brown hair that he'd tried unsuccessfully to tame strode into the room. "I'm DC Trevelyan."

Shrap got up and held out her hand. He seemed surprised but shook it without hesitation.

"Please, sit."

She did so, keeping her eyes on him.

He wore a classy suit, middle of the range, probably from somewhere like Marks and Spencer, in a gun-metal grey. Not too cheap, but not hugely expensive either. A crisp white shirt and black tie completed the outfit. Sensible, smart, appropriate. He placed a manilla folder on the table, sat down and studied her.

"Is Shrap your real name?"

She stared back at him. "No."

When she didn't say anything else, he gave a curt nod, opened the folder and slid the same photograph the policewoman had shown her across the table. "I won't take up much of your time. I just have some questions about this man."

She studied it under the fluorescent light, looking for clues. No street names, no recognisable features. Doug stood beside a high brick wall; some cabling was visible overhead. Train lines? On the opposite side of the road stood a hulking grey building with dark basement windows. She couldn't remember seeing it anywhere.

Doug was a creature of habit, though. He wouldn't venture too far from his usual haunts.

"I believe you know him?"

"Yes, I do."

"Who do you know him as?"

So, they didn't have his name either. She wasn't sure she wanted to give it to them, not if they were going to arrest him. Although, to be fair, Doug could use a few nights in the nick. Warm, comfortable, fed and watered. Off the booze.

"What's he done?" she asked.

He frowned. "Could you answer the question, please?"

"I'm not sure I want to."

There was something about his face that she liked. The sincere, no-bullshit expression. The direct gaze.

"Why not?"

"Because he's my friend."

"And you don't want to rat out your friend?"

"How can I rat him out when I don't know what he's done?" Shrap kept her voice even.

Trevelyan studied her, taking in her dishevelled state, her grubby clothing, her short, boyish hair. His gaze lingered on the faint bruise beneath her left eye where that moron Nico had kicked her when he'd tripped over her the other night. Shrap wondered what opinions he was forming. Abused wife? Homeless drunk? Addict?

Shrap shifted in her seat. If she'd had some warning, she'd have showered and washed her hair. Maybe even got a change of clothes. Nobody was supposed to see her like this. That was the whole point. She wanted to be invisible.

Not much she could do about it now.

He leaned back in his chair. "Your friend may have witnessed a crime."

She wasn't expecting that. "What kind of crime?"

"I'm afraid I can't give you the details of an ongoing investigation."

Another standard response. How many times had she used that line herself?

"This where it happened?" She tapped the CCTV photo with her fingernail, conscious it was dirty and jagged. She put her hand back in her lap.

A pause.

"Yeah."

"Where is it?"

"Ufford Street, near Waterloo station. You know it?"

"No."

He gave a deep sigh and leaned forward, putting his arms on the table. "This is an informal discussion, and you seem like a smart person. It would be great if you could give us some information about your friend. We just want to ask him some questions, that's all."

That was never all.

There was a long pause.

If Doug had been caught on camera leaving a crime scene, he was a suspect, not a witness. At the very least, a person of interest.

Shrap stared at the folder, wishing she had X-ray vision. What was Doug supposed to have seen?

Once upon a time she had believed in the justice system.

Trevelyan turned his hands upwards on the table. A gesture of trust. "Look, I'm just trying to find out what happened."

She realised she still did.

"His first name is Doug," she said. "I have no idea what

his surname is, but he's an old vet. Grenadier Guards, I think. You should be able to find out from that."

He exhaled. "Thank you."

She waited while he opened the folder and scribbled inside. He had long fingers, and she watched his hand glide across the page as he wrote.

He glanced up at her. "When last did you see Doug?"

"Yesterday morning at the day centre."

His brown eyes narrowed. "Which day centre is that?"

She met his gaze. "The one that gave you my name."

He looked down at the file. "Webber Street?"

She didn't reply, it was all there in the file.

"What was he doing there?"

"Having breakfast. He's there most days." Shrap had also lent him a fiver, but she didn't tell the DC that.

"What time does he usually go?"

"Nine o'clock, when they open."

He checked his wristwatch, then reached into his pocket for his phone. "Excuse me a moment. I have to make a call." He got out of his seat and turned his back on her.

She'd expected the move. Baxter and her pasty-faced companion were being sent on another mission.

Shrap glanced up at the cameras. One mounted on the wall behind him, the other in the far corner. Recording their every move. Feeding it back to a server that anyone with the right clearance could access.

"Hello, this is DC Trevelyan. Can you get Sergeant Baxter for me?"

She leaned forward and surveyed the open folder.

His notes were scribbled inside the cover in a neat, slanted hand. She didn't bother with those; she already knew what he'd told her. What she wanted to see was the murder docket.

Victim's name. Photograph. Occupation.

Trevelyan issued the order. "The day centre. Yes. Nine o'clock."

She read it upside down. Slowly. Squinting to make out the name.

Bianca Rubik.

Blonde, sexy, short skirt, high heels. A soft face with hard eyes, and a seductive pout.

I can do things you only dream about.

Occupation: Sex worker.

Cause of death: Possible strangulation.

Which meant the post-mortem hadn't been done yet. She leaned back, arms folded across her chest.

Trevelyan hung up the call. "Right, where were we?"

2

"How long have you known Doug?" His tone was light, almost conversational.

"We met about a year ago."

On a station platform.

"Do you mind if I ask how?"

He stopped me jumping in front of a train.

"I'd seen him around. We got talking."

He glanced down at the folder, frowned, then shot her a hard look.

She stared blankly back. *What?*

He closed the folder and moved on, rubbing the stubble on his chin.

"Are you close?"

"Not especially."

Doug was the closest thing she had to a friend. When Shrap had moved out, she'd left her old life behind. None of her previous acquaintances would recognise her now. Dirty, bedraggled, undernourished. She looked like the homeless vagrant that she was. Just another ex-soldier unable to cope. A victim of the system.

"Okay." He took a measured breath. "Well, perhaps you can tell us where to find him? Where does he hang out? It's imperative that we talk to him."

"He didn't do it," Shrap said.

He looked up. "Do what?"

"Kill that girl." She gestured to the folder.

"You looked at the murder docket." It was a statement rather than a question. He'd known all along.

"I can read upside down."

Eyes narrowed. Mouth taut. Shoulders rigid.

It was his mistake for leaving it open and he knew it, even though he hadn't left the room, just turned his back for a moment.

"How do you know he didn't do it?"

"Doug's not like that. He's not violent. Besides, he's getting on a bit and has arthritis in both hands. He couldn't have strangled her, even if he'd wanted to."

Another pause, longer this time as he studied her. Curiosity mixed with annoyance.

"Do you mind if I ask what your profession was before..." He petered off, searching for the right words. What was the politically correct term for "gave up and became a bum"?

"Before I ended up on the street?"

He nodded, flushing slightly.

"I was in the armed forces."

"Like Doug?"

She stretched her arms out in front of her. It was suddenly very claustrophobic in here. The walls seemed to close in. "Yeah."

His gaze dropped to her forearm. "Is that where you got the tattoo?"

Shrap pulled down her sleeve. "Yeah."

He hesitated, about to say something, then decided against it. Too personal, maybe? They weren't here to interrogate her, after all.

"Let's go back to my original question," he said. She breathed a sigh of relief. "Where can we find Doug?"

"He usually sleeps under the railway bridge near Leake Street. If he's not there or at the day centre, I don't know where he is."

"Where does he go during the day?"

She spread his hands. "Where do any of us go? Doorways and hovels near the station, public gardens, homeless shelters... You don't need me to do your job for you."

His back straightened, his chin rose a few notches. "No, I do not, but your insight might be useful. You seem to know him better than most."

She admired his control, but then he'd been trained to handle all manner of insults. Her thinly veiled one wouldn't dent his cool.

"I'm sorry, I can't help you."

He sat in silence for a moment, his jaw flexing as he tensed, then he opened the folder and took out a card. "If you do see him, please let me know."

He wrote his mobile number on the back.

"You can get hold of me on that."

He slid it over the table toward her. Long fingers, strong hands. She hesitated for a moment, then picked it up.

"Okay."

"If your friend is innocent, he may have seen the perpetrator," he urged. "We still need to talk to him."

She knew the drill.

He stood up. She followed suit. He was at least a head

taller than her. They didn't shake hands again. Instead, he walked to the door and opened it, the folder tucked safely under his arm.

"Thank you for coming in, er, Shrap. This officer will show you out."

Like she'd had much of a choice.

She snorted, then waited until he left. His boots echoed down the oppressive corridor, fading as he got further away.

Then she followed the duty sergeant out.

BUDGE at the homeless shelter was surprised to see her.

"I'm sorry, Shrap." He avoided her gaze. "I didn't know it was in connection with a murder."

Bad news travelled fast.

"I understand," she said, even though it irked her that he'd given out her name, despite it being the right thing to do. "Has Doug been in?"

"Nobody has. Not with 'em sitting out there. All this food, going to waste." He shook his head.

Everyone had something to hide.

She grabbed some toast and a cuppa and stood in the doorway, surveying the police car. They weren't going to bring her in a second time.

I'm not afraid of you.

Encouraged by her defiance, a young kid of about eighteen shuffled in. He was so thin as to be almost emaciated.

Shrap smiled at him as he passed. She'd seen him around. New kid on the block. Sold naked pics of himself to strangers in Soho to survive. She supposed it was better than prostitution. This way, it was only his image that was being abused. Not his body. Same couldn't be said for his soul.

The kid fell on the toast like a starving hyena.

"Have another," said Budge. There was more than enough to go around today.

After that, a few more hungry stragglers scurried in. Nobody looked at the police vehicle, although everyone knew it was there. They should've sent an undercover crew or used an unmarked car from the police lot. That's what she would've done.

Jesus, Doug. Where are you?

Shrap finished her breakfast, then left the centre and walked in the direction of Waterloo station. A busy weekday, cars swirled around the bustling transport hub dropping off commuters, picking up business associates and out-of-towners. The pavements were crowded, people jostling for space, avoiding puddles and each other.

It wasn't raining, but it had been during the night. A steady, soaking drizzle that drove every rough sleeper undercover. The security guard at the Marriott let her bed down under the flapping awning at the delivery entrance when the weather turned bad. The sound always reminded her of the flag outside her ward at the military hospital in Afghanistan. She'd spent a morbid three weeks there after they'd found her unconscious on a frozen strip of dust north of Kabul.

You gave us a real scare, young lady.

You nearly didn't make it.

It would have been better if she hadn't.

She ought to have died with her team. Burned to a crisp when the IED exploded. Incinerated in a pressure-sensored heartbeat. Instead, she'd got to watch, an AK-47 pointed at her chest. Now she lived with their screams in her head, the blazing vision imprinted forever in her mind.

Doug wasn't under the railway bridge near Leake Street.

Shrap wasn't surprised. At night, after the bars and restaurants had closed and the city commuters had gone home to their Farrow & Ball living rooms, it was a quiet, sheltered place to sleep. Now, mid-morning, the pavements bustled with foot traffic.

Doug would be in the way. An inconvenience. People would step around his grubby sleeping bag or cross the street to avoid close contact.

Shrap walked through the Banksy Tunnel, as the Leake Street underpass was unofficially known. A twenty-something took Insta-worthy selfies against the graffitied background, while a businessman walked quickly through, his footsteps echoing ominously off walls that glared back at him.

A train rumbled overhead.

Doug wasn't on the other side, either. Sometimes he liked to sit on the low cement wall and watch the trains come in. But not today.

She put her hands on her hips and looked around. Where else might Doug have gone?

If he was scared, or if he thought the police were looking for him, he would go to ground. Off the beaten track. A different area, maybe.

Then again, Doug didn't like change. Change came with a warning.

This is my spot. Fuck off.

Or a beating. Doug couldn't handle another beating.

Strange he hadn't come to her, though. Despite the difference in sex and age, they'd become friends. No, not friends, but something. They knew each other's shame. It bound them together. Doug had talked her out of suicide, and she knew he was an alcoholic who'd lost everything due to his drinking.

Still, Doug must know she cared about him. Would help him. No questions asked.

Shrap walked in the direction of the London Eye, then along the South Bank towards the Jubilee Gardens. No sign of her friend.

"Seen Doug?" she asked Dicky, a tough old geezer who liked to draw the London landmarks on the back of discarded napkins. Some of them were quite good.

"Nah, mate. Haven't seen him for a few days."

Where the hell was he?

Was Doug mixed up in the murder of that sex worker? Had he seen something? She needed to find him and quickly, before his sorry arse got hauled in for questioning. A CCTV image was damning evidence. People had been convicted on less.

Maybe Doug had gone to the pop-up coffee shop in the Waterloo station car park. He'd get a decent coffee there and something to eat. He had the fiver she'd given him the day before – if he hadn't spent it on booze.

She crossed busy York Road and hurried up the street towards the parking lot. She hadn't got very far when she saw the flashing lights.

Shit.

It could be nothing, just a harmless smash and grab, but her gut told her otherwise. It was the feeling she got when something wasn't right, the same feeling she'd had the day their convoy set off from the army base in Kabul.

She broke into a run.

A police cordon had been set up at the back of the lot, near the railway line. There was a fire engine, an ambulance and two police vehicles parked haphazardly across the tarmac – never a good sign. The air was tinged with the smell of burning. Her gut heaved. She knew that smell – it was scorched human flesh.

Heart hammering, Shrap ducked under the cordon and dodged an officer who yelled for her to stop. She ran to where a group of firemen, policemen and two white-clad forensic technicians stood. On the ground, a blackened human form was twisted into the foetal position.

The ground bubbled with remnants of dirty foam. The firemen had obviously tried to hose him down, but they'd been too late. A third man, this time in blue coveralls, bent over the body. That would be the pathologist.

It was impossible to see who the victim was, since there was nothing left of the skin, hair or clothing. It had either melted or burned away. The victim lay on a blanket of smouldering ash. It could have been a sleeping bag – nylon burned fast – it was hard to tell.

The police officer touched her arm. "You know this guy?"

Shrap didn't reply.

She stared at the corpse, searching for a sign, anything that would tell her if this was Doug. The facial features were completely obliterated. She couldn't even gauge the height because the body had contracted under the immense heat.

"What happened?" she croaked.

"Accident." He nodded towards an empty whiskey bottle in the dead person's hand. "Idiot managed to set himself alight."

"There's something in his other hand," barked the pathologist. He pried it open and with a pair of tweezers, extracted something shrivelled and charred. "Looks like a five-pound note."

Shrap shut her eyes.

Oh, God.

The car park began to spin. Nausea rose like a wave.

"You can't be here, ma'am." A copper put a hand on her shoulder.

"I'm going."

She stumbled off between the rows of parked cars. When she got far enough away, she bent over and threw up.

3

T*hat smell.*
Shrap heaved until her stomach was empty.

For a moment, she was back in the desert. The car in front of them had just exploded in a terrifying fireball as the IED lifted it clear off the ground.

Soldiers screaming. A roaring in her ears. Deafening.

The passenger door of the burning vehicle opened, and a man emerged engulfed in flames.

Christ, Sam!

Shrap leaped from her vehicle to help but didn't get far.

"Get down!"

"On the ground!"

"On your knees!"

She was surrounded by robed warriors, AK-47s levelled at her head.

All she could do was watch as her friends burned.

Now this.

The same sense of helplessness she'd felt in the desert choked her, clutching at her throat, making it hard to breathe. She wretched some more.

Jesus, Doug.

She gripped the bonnet of a car, her entire body shaking. All she could see was Doug's charred corpse. She gulped at the air, forcing her lungs to expand.

Get a grip, soldier, she told herself, but her brain wasn't listening. It had given up months ago.

"Hey, you!" It was a different police officer. A superior voice.

They were looking for witnesses. An outer cordon would be erected, the car park closed and the murder squad called in.

He might even be there. Her presence would be suspicious.

Why didn't you call?

She had to get away.

As the uniformed officer approached, Shrap took off, ricocheting off the stationary cars. She banged her hip against a steel bumper but kept moving. Out of the car park... left... up the road.

Sirens coming closer.

She hurdled a low fence, tearing the bottom lining of her coat on the barbed wire. Stumbling on, she darted across a criss-cross of railway lines, heading for the grassy embankment on the other side.

A whistle sounded. Did they still use those?

Or was it from the platform?

The tracks vibrated, sizzling with electricity. She leaped onto the overgrown embankment and scurried up, ignoring the thistles and shrubs that tore at her hands and shins.

The shout of the pursuing police officer was drowned out by the train, as carriage after carriage sped past in a thudding motion blur.

Shrap ramped the low wall at the top and ran down the street. She risked a backwards glance. No one was following.

The train let out a loud hiss, then disappeared down the track. For a moment, Shrap wished she was on it. Racing away from the smell of death, from her memories.

A right turn and she was on a busy shopping street. People rushed at her; cars sped by. A moped hooted and she jumped back, heart hammering.

God, no. It was happening again.

She had to get control.

Her head felt fuzzy, like it was disconnected from her body. But then it always did during an attack. She stopped in a doorway and shut her eyes. If only everything would stop moving, just for a moment.

She concentrated on her breathing.

In-out. In-out.

Focus on little things, the therapist had told her. Back when she had one.

She stared at the cracks in the concrete. A leaf as it spun around, caught in an unseen gust of wind in the corner. Trapped.

Like her.

The peeling paint on the bottom of the once-glossy black door. An unidentifiable brown stain on the wall.

Her breathing slowed.

The world came back into focus.

The sounds behind her quietened to a manageable hum.

She rested her forehead against the door, absorbing the cool hardness. Just a few more moments.

She closed her eyes, forcing her body to relax. In the military, fear had its place, it sharpened her senses, invigorated her.

Now, it did the opposite.

She felt drained. Depleted. Foggy. Like she'd stopped moving but the world continued to spin on its axis around her.

She sank down onto the doorstep.

How could Doug be gone?

He was never gone. He'd been on the streets longer than anybody she knew. He was part of the landscape. Always there. Hovering in a doorway or under a bridge, minding his own business, a half-drunk bottle of scotch by his side.

Except, now he wasn't.

Hot tears pricked her eyes. She let them fall.

It didn't make any sense.

An accident?

No fucking way. Not Doug.

She sat with her head in her hands, watching as her tears mixed with the dirt in the doorway.

In order to set himself alight, Doug would have had to have spilled at least half a bottle of booze over himself, then set fire to it.

He didn't smoke.

Where had he got the matches? The lighter?

She thought about the police at the scene. If only she knew what they knew. In the old days, she'd be one of the first responders. The person they called when a soldier died under questionable circumstances. She'd had the power to investigate, to ask questions, to get to the truth.

Not anymore.

She sniffed and swiped at her tears. Now she was powerless. A homeless reject. A has-been. She'd opted out the day she'd left home. Left Trevor.

The sad truth was she'd never know how her friend had died.

Shrap took a rasping gasp. If only she'd found Doug sooner. She may have been able to prevent this – whatever *this* was – and he might still be alive.

Your friend may have witnessed a murder.

She peered out of the doorway. Shoppers carrying branded bags walked past giving her disgusted sideways glances. One woman even shook her head. Nobody wanted to get too close.

Was that why Doug had to die?

A chill crept up her spine and she pulled her coat tighter. What was the dead woman's name again?

Bianca Rubik.

Sex worker.

Had Doug seen who killed her?

It started raining again, big wet splodges that bounced off the pavement. Pedestrians scattered; umbrellas sprouted. Her shoes were quickly soaked.

Shrap didn't move.

The killer must have spotted Doug lurking in the shadows. He couldn't afford to leave a witness, even an unreliable one. Therefore, the doddering old man had to go. The killer had followed Doug to the parking lot. It would have been easy; Doug was old and decrepit. A washed-up alchy. He wouldn't have put up a fight.

Whiskey poured over his clothing and sleeping bag. A fallen cigarette. Stupid bastard passed out with it in his mouth.

The smell assailed her again. She took a deep breath and fought the rising nausea. She might never know exactly how or why Doug had died, but she did know one thing. It was no accident.

4

———

HOMELESS MAN MURDERS SEX WORKER screamed the headlines the next morning.

Shrap picked up the newspaper.

What the...?

Ignoring her pounding hangover, she squinted at the article.

"Hey, if you're going to read it, buy it," snapped the turbaned seller coming out of his kiosk.

Shrap fumbled in her pocket for a quid and handed it over. She got thirty pence back.

Homeless veteran Doug Romberg strangled sex worker Bianca Rubik near Waterloo station on Saturday night. He was caught on CCTV fleeing the scene. It is thought he suffers from mental health problems and could be dangerous.

Shrap hissed the air out of her lungs. What a load of crap.

Doug wasn't capable of strangling anyone, and he was one of the few people she knew who didn't suffer from mental health problems. His issue was the booze, but that didn't turn you into a murderer.

Idiots.

She clenched her fists. How dare they pin this on Doug? The old guy had never hurt anyone in his life.

Damn it, Doug. Why didn't you come to me?

Reeling, Shrap folded the newspaper under her arm and headed for the day centre. It had been a shitty night. Cold and blustery. The wind made the rain go everywhere. It seeped into your sleeping bag, blew into doorways and sprayed against walls.

Shrap didn't normally drink. Being drunk made her vulnerable, and being vulnerable meant she was more open to attack. Still, she'd had a few for Doug, then dozed till morning. The gritty, shrunken feeling behind her eyes reminded her of all-nighters in the army. On patrol. Watching, waiting for something to happen. Willing it to happen to end the boredom.

She got herself a brew and sat down to read. It was clear the article was pure supposition interspersed with one or two facts. The only things the journalist knew for sure were the victim's name, the alleged perpetrator and the manner in which she had died. Everything else was nonsense.

Bianca Rubik had been strangled, her body left on a deserted pavement behind the Old Vic theatre.

She glanced up. *That's* where the picture had been taken. Doug bed down there when the weather made his usual spot under the railway bridge too dank. There was an empty basement flat with an overhang that offered a decent bit of coverage.

Was that where he'd been the night he'd witnessed the murder?

The sex worker had been killed sometime after midnight. Shrap stored the facts away in her brain like case notes. Pity they didn't know the exact time of death.

The perpetrator, Doug Romberg, had been *caught on CCTV fleeing the scene* – running for his life, more like. And someone had leaked it to the press.

"Fuckin' 'ell, mate. I heard about Doug." A scrawny guy with a thick scab on the side of his face stopped next to her. "Did 'e really kill that prostitute?"

Shrap glared at him. "No, he bloody didn't."

"Okay, chill." The guy put his hands up in the air. "That's what they're saying."

"I know."

He shrugged and moved on.

Nobody knew Doug was dead yet. But when they did, it wouldn't come as too much of a shock. It was hard living on the street, people died all the time. Life was transient.

The door blew shut and she jumped. Damn wind. A scraggly, anorexically thin woman with bad skin had just walked in. Lexi, her name was. She hung out with her boyfriend Xavier, a brutal crackhead who doubled as her pimp when he needed cash for a score. They must have had a tiff, else she wouldn't be here, skulking around like she'd done something wrong.

Shrap caught her eye. She'd once helped patch her up when Xavier had given her a split lip and very nearly broken her nose.

Lexi grabbed some toast and a mug of coffee and sat down in the corner. She took a bite and winced, touching her jaw.

Shrap watched her for a moment, then picked up her tea and sauntered over. "Mind if I join you?"

Lexi glanced up in surprise. Her eyes said she minded, but Shrap sat down anyway.

"How are you, Lexi?"

Another shrug. Up close, she noticed a faint blue mark on her cheek, the size of a fist.

"Xav treating you okay?"

Lexi wrapped her hands around the mug. "He's in one of his moods."

"He do that?" Shrap nodded at the bruise.

"I deserved it. I gave him lip."

"That's not an excuse for him to take out his anger on you."

She shrugged.

That's just the way it was. She wouldn't leave him because even an abusive crack-addict pimp was better than nobody. This life was tough for a woman. You needed protection. She ought to know.

There was a long pause.

"Do you know a girl called Bianca Rubik?" Shrap broke the silence.

Lexi blinked at her several times. She was about to repeat the question when Lexi shook her head. "Nah, don't know anyone by that name."

"You sure? I think she works The Cut."

Another shake of her head.

"Okay, thanks. I'll leave you in peace."

She wanted to say that she should leave Xavier, that he was no good for her, but she'd be wasting her breath. Besides, it was none of her business how Lexi chose to live her life.

Look at her.

Most people would think she was mad giving up a comfortable home to live on the street, but they didn't understand. It was the only place she couldn't hear the screams in her head. The only place she felt sane. No one judging her. No one to see her shame. To witness her fear.

She left the centre and walked towards The Cut. Even the bright facade of the Old Vic with its twirly gables looked dull and pallid in the overcast, October light.

Shrap glanced up at the heavy clouds. It was going to piss down again.

She quickened her step, walking up The Cut to the theatre, behind which Bianca Rubik had been murdered.

There was the hulking grey building she'd seen on the grainy CCTV photograph. The bulging eye of the camera opposite glared down at her. A piece of police tape was still attached to the wall, flapping in the wind. She shivered, the street was a natural wind tunnel.

Shrap surveyed the buildings, mostly offices with the occasional residence squeezed in between. She found the one where Doug sometimes slept. The basement flat was still empty. Boarded-up windows, an industrial-sized lock on the front door, dead pot plants outside.

She went down the steps and looked around.

An empty whiskey bottle, an old Metro newspaper.

Remnants of Doug.

She shook her head, the heaviness crushing. She could almost see her friend sitting there, reading and drinking, sheltering from the rain.

A distant rumble of thunder made her glance up. From here, Doug wouldn't have been able to see the road, but more importantly, anyone coming down the road wouldn't have been able to see him.

If only he'd stayed put.

She pictured the scene. Bianca running, her heels echoing on the tarmac. Her pursuer close behind. Heavier footsteps, more determined. Gaining on her. A scream as he pounced.

Enough noise to startle an old drunk.

Shrap ascended the wrought-iron stairs, taking them one at a time like Doug would have done, gripping the railing for support. He'd have peeked over the top, seen the girl being strangled.

What did he do then?

Did he watch or try to save her?

Doug was old, his reactions slow. He would have known there was nothing he could do. Not against a stronger assailant. He'd have watched, shivering, feeling helpless.

When the killer had left, Doug would have rushed to check the body, just to make sure she wasn't still alive, that nothing could be done to save her. A hand on her neck, feeling for a pulse. Listening for a breath.

Realising she was dead, he'd scamper off into the night.

Had he been seen? Was the perpetrator watching?

Shrap looked back the way she'd come. Strange the killer hadn't been picked up on CCTV too. The camera was angled at the start of the road, behind the theatre. The killer must have fled the other way. The place where Bianca had been strangled was out of range too, otherwise they'd know Doug didn't do it.

She closed her eyes.

Why, Doug? Why did it have to be you?

5

Shrap wasn't the only one studying the crime scene. Gareth Trevelyan stared at the grainy image of the old man on his desktop computer. He'd watched the CCTV footage a dozen times but was still unsure as to what the old guy was doing there.

He looked scared. The fear palpable even in black and white. Was that because he'd seen who'd killed her, or because he'd realised what he'd done and was running away before someone called the police?

Was he a witness or a suspect?

Douglas Romberg.

Gareth thought back to the homeless woman. When he'd first walked into the interview room he'd thought she was a junkie, another young stray living on the streets. Then he'd noticed her eyes. Clear and startlingly blue. She was older than he'd expected too, maybe early thirties, and surprisingly articulate. She'd been right. Grenadier Guards. Twenty years of service. The Gulf War, Kosovo, Iraq, Afghanistan. By all accounts Romberg had had a successful military career.

Then one day, he'd walked away from his battalion at Observation Post Mest near the town of Yahya Kheyl in Paktika Province. His equipment was found neatly stacked, with his compass missing.

No note. No explanation.

He was court martialled in absentia for desertion and dismissed from Her Majesty's Service. He was sentenced to 154 days at the Military Corrective Training Centre, Colchester, which he never attended, and as far as he could see, the sentence was never implemented.

Romberg simply vanished. According to a statement by the MOD, it wasn't even certain he'd returned to the United Kingdom. Apparently, he'd told a member of his battalion that he was thinking about walking to India.

Not once during his two decades in the military had he ever been disciplined or accused of misbehaviour. Looking at his record, he'd been a model soldier.

What changed?

What had happened to make him walk off the base?

He sighed and scratched his chin. He'd probably never know. That was the frustrating thing about this job. Sometimes you just never knew.

There was no mention of Romberg again, until now. He'd successfully avoided the law for twenty years, and more recently had hidden in plain sight on the streets of London.

Gareth pulled up a photograph of Romberg in military uniform. He'd been a handsome man with sandy-brown hair and a craggy face. Kind eyes. Smiling eyes.

Perhaps he'd simply had enough of war?

Staring into those eyes, he shook his head. Something was telling him he wasn't their killer.

"Why would a man with no prior convictions, no history

of violence, who's lived peacefully for twenty years, suddenly murder a woman?" he said to Devi, his colleague at the station.

Devi Patel, a strait-laced detective sergeant with jet-black hair pulled back in an efficient ponytail, had been his first point of contact when he'd arrived from Kensington Police Station six months ago. She'd shown him the ropes, letting him tag along, do some of the grunt work. They weren't friends, but there was a growing respect there, and that's all he wanted. He could work with that.

"I don't know." She threw up her hands. "Maybe he cracked? Maybe he had mental health issues? Maybe she disrespected him? Who knows?"

He shook her head. "I just can't see it. Besides, he was old. It would take a strong man to hold a woman down and strangle her." He nodded at the image. "Stronger than him anyway."

"Do we have the post-mortem results back yet?" asked Devi.

"No, it's been scheduled for later today. Why?"

"He may not have strangled her with his hands. Weren't there ligature marks as well?"

"Hmm... I'm not sure." He pulled up the crime scene photographs. The victim lay on her back, one leg out at an angle as if she'd been trying to kick off her attacker when she'd died. She was slender, lithe.

"She's got excellent muscle tone," Gareth, who'd been into gymnastics as a teen, noted.

"So?"

"It looks like she works out. Unusual for a sex worker, don't you think?"

"Not really. Her body is her business. Not all of them are junkies."

Devi would know. She'd done a stint in SCD9, formerly the Vice Squad, before she'd joined CID. By all accounts, it wasn't an easy job.

Gareth nodded. "Okay, so let's take a closer look at her throat." He zoomed in as far as he could. The photographs were high resolution, and they got a clear look at the markings on her neck.

"Definitely ligature marks." Devi peered in. "Doesn't look like hands. A thick rope maybe."

"What about a chain?" Gareth studied the circular bruises around her neck. They were more prevalent at the front, where the pressure had been the greatest. Where he'd cut off her air supply and crushed her larynx.

"Could be. Let's wait and see what the PM report says."

"Fine." He sat back and looked up at her. "You're right. No jumping to conclusions."

Devi grinned. She knew patience wasn't his strong suit.

His mobile buzzed on the desk.

"I'll leave you to it." Devi walked away.

He stared at the number flashing on the phone.

Melanie.

His heart pounded and he felt a familiar tightening in his chest. Damn her. Damn her for having this effect on him. Four years he'd gone running every time she'd called. After work, weekends, even in the middle of the night, when he was on the way back from a domestic incident or a bar brawl and needed a release.

"You help me blot out the world, Gareth," she'd told him once. "You take away the ugliness and wipe it clean."

He could understand that. She was the same for him. Sort of.

If it hadn't been for Austin.

Gareth had never met Melanie's husband. He'd been

housebound, fighting cancer for the better part of their marriage. Mel loved him but the ongoing stress was wearing her down. "It's like an unexploded bomb that we're waiting to go off," she'd admitted once, after he'd gone back on chemotherapy. "I can't take it anymore."

He'd held her close and kissed away the pain.

"Don't ever leave me, Gareth."

But he had.

Austin was in remission. Again. While Gareth was happy for him – of course he was – he couldn't keep hanging on.

"He needs you, Mel," he'd said, the last time they were together. They'd met in the little wine bar down the road from his flat in Shepherd's Bush. His hands had been gripping his beer glass so hard he thought he'd crush it. "It's not fair on him. This. Us."

Her eyes had filled with tears.

"You're ending it?" She'd stared at him, incredulous. She'd got used to their arrangement. Relied on it, even.

"Yes, I think I am. I can't do this anymore. Not knowing if and when you'll ever be free. And I don't want to feel guilty all the time."

"But I need you, Gareth. We're good together."

They were. That was the problem.

He'd downed the beer, looked the women he loved in the eye and said, "I'm sorry, Mel. It's over."

And walked out of the bar.

And out of her life.

And out of a job.

Everything reminded him of her. He needed a fresh start.

Some would consider Southwark a step down, but not him. It was a step in the right direction. An act of self-preservation. No reference letter, no recommendation – Mel wasn't a very good loser. A horizontal move that did nothing for his career.

But the Met were desperate. They needed experienced police officers and he'd cut his teeth as a beat cop. It was an easy step to Detective Constable. God only knew they needed more of them down here. South London was no joke.

The phone rang off.

He took a deep, steadying breath. The calls were becoming less frequent. Soon, they'd stop altogether. He just had to stay strong.

GARETH READ through what they knew about the victim, Bianca Rubik. A Polish national who'd been in the country for six months.

Was that all?

He frowned. Even the media knew that much. He'd read it in the goddamn newspaper on the way to work.

Bianca lived in Shoreditch with another woman, also a sex worker. The flatmate had said Bianca "kept to herself, didn't do drugs and didn't have a boyfriend".

He flicked to the 'before' photograph of a tall, leggy blonde. Younger than the one lying in the gutter, but the same smooth skin, the same wide mouth and lithe body. She was gorgeous. Who'd want to strangle her? Who'd want to wipe out that young life?

Gareth felt a heaviness descend. There was so much ugliness in the world, sometimes it wore him down.

His gaze returned to the dark bruises around Bianca's neck. Her eyes staring vacantly at the night sky. Her mouth open in a silent scream. How must she have felt in those last few minutes as the breath was squeezed out of her? Helpless. Terrified. Frantic.

At least he was in a position to do something about it. He couldn't save Bianca, but he could make sure justice was served. "I'll find out who did this to you," Gareth murmured, too softly for anyone to hear. "I promise."

6

_____

No sooner had she left the scene of Bianca's murder when the heavens opened.

Commuters darted into the station, raincoats pulled tightly around them. Others took refuge in the pubs. The dullness deepened and the streetlights flickered on. Car headlights bounced off the wet asphalt, their beams interrupted by pedestrians running across the road to escape the deluge.

Shrap sheltered in the public library in Lambeth North. She often came here. It was warm and dry, and open until six. She liked the constant trickle of people, their comforting murmur, the sound of books being stamped and the rustle of pages. Anything but silence.

Gathering up all the news articles she could find on Bianca Rubik's death, she sat down to read, but they weren't any more enlightening than the _Mail_. Not much was known about her other than she was a Polish national who'd been in the country for only six months.

Shrap stayed as long as she could, but eventually the librarian began giving her loaded glances. A slender, nerdish man, he was often behind the counter, stamping books. What she liked about him was that he didn't treat her any differently to anyone else. He didn't speak much, only a few syllables and only when strictly necessary. He preferred a look to words. A classic introvert.

She took the hint and left, hoping the rain had stopped. It had.

As she walked up The Cut, she wondered what drove a young Polish girl to sell her body on the street. Was she desperate for cash? Had she tried to find a job but failed? Maybe she didn't speak English. You didn't need English to sell your soul.

Night fell and the dullness disappeared. Bars and pubs sprung to life. Music filled the air, along with the smell of grilled burgers. Her stomach rumbled. She went into a local grocery store and bought a sandwich and an apple, then ate it on a damp bench at the back of a pub. A man in a thread-bare T-shirt with needle marks in his arms tried to chat her up. She shut him down, stood up and walked back up the street.

What now? She could go back to the hotel awning with a bottle of cheap cider or keep looking for someone who knew Bianca. Doug was dead, what did it matter? Except she couldn't get that newspaper headline out of her mind.

HOMELESS MAN MURDERS SEX WORKER.

It wasn't right. Doug was no killer. She remembered that day on the platform, the warm blast of air as the train roared down the track, the eery calm that settled over her.

She was going to do it. She was going to put an end to the screams of her friends, the guilt that held her captive.

Blissful oblivion was only a screeching heartbeat away.

Then Doug's hand on her shoulder, pulling her back.

You don't want to do that, lass.

She owed it to Doug to find out what had happened. Doug had been there for her, now it was her turn. Her old friend wouldn't go down as a murderer – not on her watch. Not when she had the power to do something about it.

She looked up and down the street, torn between wanting to curl up and block out the night and doing what she knew she had to. Investigate.

It had been a while, and she had none of the resources she used to have. No backup team, no Trevor on comms, no weapons – other than her tactical folding knife, which she'd managed to retrieve from the flower bed. Just a burning desire to see justice done.

Was she mad? Was this ludicrous?

Probably, but still she stood there, watching the traffic race by, feeling the drizzle on her skin. She had to do this. Not only for Doug, but for Sam and the others who'd died in Kabul. The mates she couldn't save. They deserved justice too, and they hadn't got it.

Shrap tugged the collar of her old woollen coat up against the cold. She'd be damned if she'd sit in a corner rocking herself to sleep when she had an opportunity to do something worthwhile. Even if it scared the living crap out of her.

Slowly but surely the ladies of the night emerged, recognisable by their seductive clothing, provocative stances and forced smiles.

She approached a group of four women, although one was little more than a girl. Seventeen, eighteen? Wide eyes and red hair cascading down her back. Christ. Surely, she had better options.

None of them balked as she approached. A down-and-out junkie wasn't a threat. Not unless they thought she was going to rob them for a score.

"Hi," she said. The redhead gave her a curious look, while the others studied her with open distrust.

"Yeah?" said a woman in fishnet stockings with a face that said she'd seen it all. "What do you want?"

"I'm looking for a friend of mine. She's Polish. Doesn't speak much English. Her name's Bianca. Haven't seen her around, have you?"

Fishnets' eyes narrowed. "Nah, don't know 'er. That's what I told the coppers when they came asking."

"The police were here?"

"Yeah, for some reason they thought we'd know 'er." This woman in the fishnets was obviously the leader of the pack.

"That the dead girl?" The redhead had a high-pitched girly voice and a sparkly clip in her hair.

"That's the one. Her body was found behind the Old Vic," said the fourth woman, petite with dyed blonde hair. "She'd been strangled."

"Lord," whispered the redhead. "You hear of these things, but you don't think they're ever going to happen to you or someone you know."

"Working the streets can be dangerous," Shrap said, then bit her tongue. She didn't want to antagonise these women. They were just making a living.

Fishnet's gaze darkened. "That's why we got each other's back. Anyway, why do you care? It's no more dangerous than shoving a dirty needle in your arm." She didn't appreciate the scaremongering. They probably didn't want to be reminded of what could happen. That death was only one heavy-handed client away.

Shrap backed away. "You're right. Sorry to have bothered you."

She moved on, conscious of their stares burning into her back.

These girls knew their strip. If they said they didn't know Bianca, they didn't know her. That told her one of two things. That either Bianca Rubik didn't work in these parts, or she wasn't a hooker at all.

Eventually, after she'd spoken to nearly every sex worker in the vicinity, an older woman in a skirt two sizes too small, lingering outside a bar in Southwark, said she knew an exotic dancer called Bianca who worked at Whispers, a gentleman's club in the West End. "Polish, blonde, mid-twenties?"

"Sounds like it could be my friend." Then again, it might not. Bianca was a fairly common name.

"Your friend's got a keeper," the woman called after her. "The owner of the club, some dodgy Russian geezer. Ain't gonna take to kindly to a nice-looking dyke like yourself muscling in on his territory."

Shrap nearly grinned. "Thanks for the warning."

WHISPERS WAS SITUATED in a historic London building that looked like it once might have been a theatre of some sort. Elaborate and imposing, it seemed wrong that the ground floor was dedicated to adult entertainment.

The entrance was a dark doorway in the Baroque facade beneath a black awning that read *Bar and Gentlemen's Club*. A red velvet rope hung across the entrance, operated by a bulky bouncer in a black T-shirt designed to show off his biceps. He obviously didn't feel the cold.

Shrap sank into a doorway across the road. The bouncer didn't give her a second glance, simply looked through her like she wasn't there. Perfect.

The deep thud of dance music could be heard from inside. It was nearly one a.m., and the strip club was in full swing. A middle-aged punter walked in, nodding to the bouncer. A regular.

A few moments later, a hesitant man in his thirties hovered outside the door. The bouncer said something to him and unclipped the rope, enticing him in. With a furtive look behind him, he darted inside.

A quarter of an hour later, a group of men staggered out, jostling and laughing. One guy with thick rugby player's thighs under a ballet tutu was being supported by his mates. A stag do. Cabs were called and the drunk men dispersed.

Shrap pretended to pass out. Drugs or exhaustion, it didn't matter. The doorway was dry and wide, allowing her to curl into a ball and be swallowed by the shadow. She kept her eyes half open, peering across the road at the strip club. A few more punters entered, a few left. No one piqued her interest.

Three o'clock.

The streets had quietened considerably. Normal party-goers had gone home, while a couple of stragglers waited for night buses. The only cars on the road were taxis.

A high-pitched laugh roused her, and she looked up as several girls appeared from around the side. They were slim and leggy, long overcoats hiding lithe, dancers' bodies. Pole dancing was hard work. Shrap had tried it once for a laugh and her stomach muscles had ached for days afterwards.

Two of the women got into an unmarked car, probably an Uber, while the other three split up. She watched a brunette saunter toward the bus stop and then perch on the seat while she checked her phone.

Another disappeared up a dark side street, her heels echoing long after she'd been absorbed by the buildings.

The last woman, a platinum-blonde in a blue faux-fur jacket paused outside the entrance chatting amiably to the bouncer.

Shrap watched her. Who was she waiting for? A lift? Or someone inside?

Five minutes later, a stocky man in torn jeans and a black T-shirt with a white logo on it emerged. He was pulling on a puffer jacket, but not before Shrap glimpsed the tattoos snaking up both arms.

She squinted, trying to make out his features in the streetlight. A wide forehead, high, Slavic cheekbones and a cruel mouth. He swaggered rather than walked. Was this the dodgy Russian geezer? The one the woman from Southwark had warned her about.

If so, he didn't look particularly cut up about his girl-friend's death. It had been forty-eight hours since Bianca's body had been discovered and he'd already moved on to the next one.

The blonde laughed and lit a cigarette, blowing the smoke into the cold night air. No prizes for guessing his type then.

They walked towards a silver Mercedes parked further down the road. The man got in behind the wheel, while the blonde climbed into the passenger seat. Music pulsed from inside, and then they were off, speeding down the road. Shrap watched until the car turned a corner and the brake lights disappeared.

Things wound down pretty quickly after that. The few remaining customers were shooed out, the doors locked and the bouncer disappeared inside, taking his rope with him. Shortly afterwards, he reappeared from the staff entrance, dressed in a puffer jacket and accompanied by a tall, fit-looking man in a leather jacket. Barman, maybe?

It was late and Shrap was warm in her sleeping bag, so she decided to stay where she was. Nobody had come to kick her out, so she figured she was safe until daybreak.

As she drifted off, she thought about Bianca. Had she worked at the club the night she was killed? If so, she must have left early. The papers had said she'd died sometime after midnight.

That could mean four in the morning, but she doubted it. Doug would have been comatose by then. A parade of elephants couldn't wake him after he'd polished off a bottle of Bells. And what was she doing across the river in Waterloo, when the strip club was in the West End?

A night bus pulled up and the doors wheezed open. The waiting dancer climbed on. Perhaps she'd got it wrong. Maybe the woman in Southwark had been mistaken and it was another Bianca who worked here. She could even be the girl in the blue coat.

Too many questions, but they'd have to wait for another day.

It would be light in a few hours. She had to get some shuteye as her day began early.

7

A loud rumble woke Shrap just before dawn. She started, her pulse hurtling into overdrive, adrenaline kicking in. The street seemed to vibrate as the rumbling got louder.

What the hell?

A tank? Were they under attack? She looked wildly around her and reached for her rifle. Except it wasn't there. There was no time to go for her knife. She crouched back in terror as a street sweeper truck rolled past.

It took a moment for her brain to register this wasn't a threat.

Thank fuck!

She exhaled slowly and collapsed back against the wall, her heart hammering. She watched the sweeper as it slid down the street, collecting litter and leaves from the gutter with its circular brushes. Eventually, it snaked off around a corner.

Jesus, her heart was going like a semi-automatic. She took a few more deep, slow breaths until she was able to move. Then she rolled up her sleeping bag and shoved it into her rucksack. Her hands fumbled with the buckles.

Shit.

The shakes could last for hours after an episode like this. A random sound, something she associated with her past, would set her off and she was pretty much useless until she calmed down.

She glanced up and down the empty street. At least nobody was around to witness it. No one to tell her she needed help or to get a grip. She knew Trevor had only been trying to help, but his constant worrying had made things worse.

"I just want my sassy, confident girlfriend back," he'd tell her, imploring her to see someone.

Didn't he think she wanted that too? That this affliction was ruining her life as much as it was his?

Sassy, confident girlfriend.

Ha! What a joke.

She'd never be that person again. That woman had died on a frigid roadside somewhere north of Kabul. The woman who'd recovered and come home was someone entirely different.

She glanced at her grubby image in the shop window, then turned away, swinging her rucksack onto her back. This was who she was now. Invisible. Her existence pared down to a point where she could cope with it.

It was just the way it had to be.

She used the portaloos across the road from a construction site, then splashed icy water onto her face. It stung but woke her up. She'd shower later at the day centre. One thing that'd been ingrained into her in the military was cleanliness, and she couldn't go more than two days without showering. It was both a blessing and a curse.

She emerged into a scarlet dawn. The pink sky reflected off the newer chrome-and-glass buildings and soaked into the brick and stone of the older ones. She'd never paid much attention to the sunrise before. Always rushing to a briefing or a new assignment, or bleary-eyed and groggy from lack of sleep. Now she got to watch it unfurl, degree by degree, captivated by the stillness, the pureness of a new day, like she was witnessing the start of something really special.

Until reality intruded and the spell was broken.

The strip club wouldn't open for some time, so she made her way back to Waterloo, enjoying the clean, empty streets and the crisp, autumn air.

As she walked, her thoughts returned to the dead girl. Had she been a dancer at Whispers? And if so, was she tied up with the dodgy Russian? Was it something her boss was into that had got her killed? Was he the guy who'd followed Doug to the car park and set him alight?

Marching towards the Embankment with her rucksack on her back, thinking about the victim – she almost felt normal again. She could be back in the military police, investigating a case. For the first time in almost two years, she felt a frisson of excitement. She had a purpose. She'd always been good at surveillance, even in the old days. Holed up for hours at forward observation posts, waiting for the enemy to make a move. No one at the club would suspect a rough sleeper, let alone a woman who looked like a crackhead, to be keeping tabs on them.

As she stepped onto Hungerford Bridge and gazed out at the Thames shimmering in front of her, she made a decision. She'd watch the club and see what transpired. If it was the wrong Bianca, or she couldn't find anything suspicious, she'd try a different tack.

But as it stood now, the police had it all wrong. Doug hadn't killed her, neither had he set himself on fire in a tragic accident – somehow, Shrap had to find a way to prove that. She owed him that much.

BY MIDDAY, she was back outside the club. Her doorway was in use. Busy shoppers in high heels stomped in and then re-emerged with designer carrier bags and expensive smiles.

Shrap took up a position against a wall between shops, making sure she could see the front as well as the staff entrance. She'd left her rucksack in a locker at the day centre in case she had to follow anyone. There was nothing in it she needed during the day.

She'd eaten, showered and dressed into the same old clothes – her sturdy combat pants she'd bought from an army surplus store, her dark fleece-lined hoodie and a black, wool coat that had once been smart but was now ripped and tatty. It was the warmest thing she owned and did a pretty decent job at keeping out the cold.

She had one change of clothes in her rucksack, and she alternated every few days. Milton, the old East Ender who ran the laundromat on The Cut, took pity on her and let her change in the back.

To anyone watching, she looked like the same apathetic junkie who'd been there the night before. She even had a two-litre bottle of cheap cider beside her for effect. She'd work her way through it during the day. It would be easy enough to pour some into the gutter when no one was looking.

The strip club was still closed, both the front and side doors locked and bolted. A corrugated iron roller door covered the front, while a no-nonsense industrial-sized padlock secured the side.

A sign beside the staff door said *CCTV in operation*, but she couldn't see any. The only camera was above the front door, at the main entrance. The sign at the side must be for effect, to warn off anyone tempted to break in.

Interesting.

At one thirty, the same silver Merc she'd seen yesterday pulled up. The cocky Russian got out, as did a broad tank of a man with square shoulders and an easy, controlled gait. Ex-military.

Why did the dodgy Russian need military-grade protection?

They opened up and went inside, using the staff entrance. Shrap expected the front door to stay closed for some time yet. The club officially opened at seven o'clock.

She was right. Nothing happened for several hours, and then just before three o'clock, another car pulled up. A BMW this time. Convertible. Metallic blue. Leather interior. Gangster rap blaring from inside. Out of habit, she memorised the licence plate number.

She'd expected the occupants to get out, but they just sat there. The minutes ticked by. Shrap frowned. What were they up to?

The sound of another engine made her glance up. A grey Ford trundled up the road. Slowly, purposefully, the right cruising speed for a drive-by. In the military, she'd be taking cover round about now. Her breath caught in her throat as her pulse skyrocketed, and she rested her hand on the blade in the pocket of her cargo pants, forcing herself to remain calm. This was London, not Kabul.

She waited. The car came closer, the window slid down.

She half expected to see a gun appear, except the man in the passenger seat was holding an envelope.

Strange.

It was thick too, packed with what she guessed was cash.

The Ford slowed to a halt. An arm emerged from the BMW and the envelope exchanged hands. The window slid up and the Ford moved off. Not a word was uttered.

Shrap watched as it accelerated down the road.

Two men in jeans, puffer jackets and an eye-watering amount of bling got out of the stationary BMW. Average heights, slender builds, expensive shoes and designer facial hair. One wore a maroon cap, the other a grey beanie.

Maroon Cap had been driving. The other one had taken the envelope and was now slipping it inside his jacket pocket. They were young, early thirties, sporting an arrogance that comes with sudden and unexpected wealth. Their jackets were open. Shrap caught a glimpse of the butt of a handgun. Suddenly, dodgy took on a whole new meaning.

Were these guys connected with the club? Was that handover a payment for something? Drugs? Guns? Girls? Was it blood money? Had Bianca been involved with them somehow? Was that why she was dead?

She sniffed in frustration. Too many questions. No answers. Not yet.

The men strode up to the staff entrance and Grey Beanie pressed a buzzer. The door opened and they went inside. Easy access, no questions asked. They were definitely connected to the club somehow.

Shrap took a swig of cider making sure to dribble some down her chin and ignored the disgusted glances of a couple of passers-by. With a hiccup, she lounged back against the wall, gaze pinned on the door.

An hour and twenty minutes later, they all came out. First the two gangsters, followed by the Russian and his henchman.

Voices drifted across the road.

No, not Russian. The woman in Southwark had been wrong about that.

Eastern European? Serbian? Albanian, maybe? She was pretty good with languages and knew a smattering of most after being stationed in Germany, Cyprus, Bosnia and finally, Afghanistan.

Maroon Cap and the club owner shook hands, three short movements, changing grip each time. There was an association there. Same country, culture or gang.

Shrap caught a flash of gold as Maroon Cap's sleeve rode up.

Nice watch.

The BMW, designer clothes, gold watch – not to mention the thick envelope. These two were into something, and she was betting it wasn't legal. They turned to get into their car when the club owner called after them. It sounded like he'd said, "*Shihemi sonte.*"

Sonte meant "tonight" in Albanian. Were they coming back tonight? Was something going down later?

Maroon Cap grinned and gave him a thumbs-up.

It was on. Whatever it was.

8

Gareth Trevelyan ignored the flashing red man and dashed across the road, weaving between cars.

Shit.

The briefing had started ten minutes ago. DCI Burrows would not be impressed.

He flashed his ID card at the duty sergeant and sprinted up the stairs, taking them two at a time. No time to wait for the lift. Panting, he threw open the department doors, tossed his rucksack at his desk and slipped into the back of the briefing room.

The door creaked, announcing his arrival. Heads turned. Burrows glanced up, frowned and muttered, "Thanks for joining us, DC Trevelyan."

"Sorry," he wheezed. "My neighbour had a fall, I..."

Burrows held up a hand. Not interested.

He bottled it.

His DCI carried on with the briefing.

A colleague threw him a sympathetic look. Burrows was

a stickler for procedure. It was like he got some perverse kick out of showing up those who weren't as pedantic as he was.

God forbid he stop to help his elderly neighbour who'd fallen outside the apartment block and quite possibly fractured her hip. Trevelyan took a deep breath and focused on what the DCI was saying.

"The post-mortem results on the murdered sex worker are back. Cause of death was strangulation, as we thought, but there was also some foreign DNA found on the body."

Trevelyan perked up. This was news. Would it lead them to the killer?

"We've run it through the database and didn't find a match. However, when we ran it through the MOD database, we did."

The Ministry of Defence?

An image of the grubby, homeless woman with the piercing blue eyes flew into his head. She was ex-military. So was her friend, the rough sleeper seen running away from the crime scene.

DCI Burrows was saying, "It belonged to a veteran by the name of Douglas Romberg."

It was him.

He has arthritis in both hands. He couldn't have strangled her, even if he'd wanted to.

"He was discharged in 2003 which was..." Burrows paused.

"Twenty years ago," cut in someone from the front. There were a few muted snorts.

"Yes, thank you."

He'd looked much older, but then he supposed living on the street would do that to you.

"There's more." Burrows thrust out his chest, a smug

look on his face. "The same DNA was on the corpse of a man burned to death in Waterloo station car park two days ago."

"Found on him, or it was him?" Trevelyan raised his voice.

The SIO's eyes narrowed. "He was too badly burned for a thorough DNA analysis, but the pathologist's report suggests it was him."

Stunned, Trevelyan leaned back against the wall. "The old homeless guy we saw on CCTV at the crime scene is dead?"

"Yes, DC Trevelyan. It appears so. What's your point?"

He didn't know if he had one. Not yet.

"It seems like a hell of a coincidence, don't you think? He strangles a sex worker one night, then is murdered the next."

"He wasn't murdered," a DS piped up. "He either committed suicide or it was an accident. They aren't sure which."

He stared at the DS. "He committed suicide by setting himself alight?"

The sergeant shrugged. "More likely he fell asleep with a cigarette in his hand. The thing is, he was soaked in whiskey from an empty bottle still in his hand, which suggests he poured it over himself."

"Or he was murdered."

Heads turned to study him.

"What?" He stared back. "Anyone could have poured a stimulant over him and made it look like an accident."

There was a momentary silence.

"That's not our case." Burrows said. "The team working on that enquiry will update us if they find any evidence of foul play."

And he had to be content with that.

Burrows went on to talk about the victim. "She was twenty-seven years old and from a place called Pruszków near Warsaw. Her parents are understandably devastated at the news of her death. They couldn't think of anyone who would have wanted to hurt her, but they admitted they didn't know much about her life in England. In fact, they didn't know she was a sex worker. She'd told them she was employed as a dancer."

Gareth thought about the muscular legs. "Are we sure she wasn't?" he blurted out.

"The flatmate confirmed she was a prostitute," said a female sergeant next to her. "I spoke to her myself."

Gareth pressed his lips together and nodded. When would he learn to keep his mouth shut?

"Sorry." He turned back to the front and listened to Burrows drone on.

"Ballsy move, speaking up like that." Devi fell into step beside him as they filed out of the incident room a few minutes later.

He shrugged. "The two deaths could be connected."

Devi walked with him back to his desk. "They're saying he suffered from mental health issues, killed her and then topped himself."

He scoffed. "What if he didn't do it? What if he saw who did, and they killed him for it?"

Devi raised her eyebrows. "I'd be careful with that theory," she said after a short pause. "His DNA is all over the dead girl. It's a slam dunk."

"Burrows isn't interested anyway." He mimicked his deep monotone. "Not our case."

Devi grinned, then glanced over her shoulder. "Zane helps out on Cruickshank's team from time to time. He has access to their files. I'm sure he'll keep you updated if you ask him."

"Cruickshank is heading up the inquiry into the homeless guy's death?"

"Yep."

He didn't know him, but he'd seen him around. A short, stocky man with a Liverpudlian accent. He seemed capable.

"Thanks Devi." He smiled and eased into his chair.

"Always happy to help."

Zane had been surprised when he'd cornered him in the canteen later that day.

"Sure, I'll keep you posted," he'd said. "The official inquiry is tomorrow morning, but based on the evidence, it looks like it'll be ruled death by misadventure."

TREVELYAN SPENT the rest of the afternoon reading the forensic reports on Bianca Rubik. On paper, it certainly seemed like the old guy, Doug, had done it. His fingerprints and DNA were on her clothing as well as in her hair. Then there was the CCTV evidence.

He knew Burrows. The DCI wouldn't look for anyone else. Like Devi had said, this was a slam dunk – and the department needed those. Their closure rate was appalling.

Rumour had it that Detective Superintendent Ridgeway had received a phone call from the Police Commissioner only last week telling him to get it up or heads were going to roll.

They needed to be seen to be fighting crime in the borough. Southwark had one of the worst crime rates in London. Knife crime was through the roof and now they were getting shootings too. Youngsters, in their teens and twenties. God only knew where they were getting the weapons from.

He might be new here, but he wasn't naive enough to think the SIO would query a case that could net him a sure win. Doug Romberg was going down for the murder of Bianca Rubik. At least the poor guy wasn't around to see it.

9

An hour before opening, a slender guy in a leather jacket, tight blue jeans and trainers stepped off the bus and walked across the road towards the club. He took small, ladylike steps, a subtle swing of the hips, and he pulled on a cigarette like he was starved of nicotine.

Even from across the road, Shrap could see the glint of the diamanté earring in his left ear and the dark nail polish on his fingers. Was that a little tremor?

She watched as he fished a crumpled tissue out of his pocket and dabbed at his eyes.

That was her opening.

She took a deep breath, ran her tongue over her teeth to make sure she didn't have lipstick on them and plastered a smile on her face. Who would have thought being normal could be so hard?

"Excuse me," she called out.

The guy turned around.

"I'm sorry to bother you, but—"

"If you're here for the bar job, you'll have to speak to

Peter. He's the manager." His kohled eyes scanned her up and down. She'd showered and changed at the day centre, much to the amusement of the staff, who said they hardly recognised her. Even the tattoo on her forearm was invisible, thanks to the stage make-up she'd found at a dance and theatre shop in the West End. Funny how her homeless persona had become the real Shrap, and making herself look like she used to meant she was unrecognisable. It showed just how long she'd been on the street.

On her way to the club, she'd bought a pair of tight, skinny jeans and a glittery, pink T-shirt from a discount store. At a second-hand shop she'd found a pair of four-inch heeled boots, well-used and scuffed at the toes, but she'd managed to touch them up with a permanent marker and a good spit and polish.

It felt weird buying clothes. She hadn't used her debit card in nearly three months, not since she'd had to get a new pair of trainers because the others had holes in them and every time it rained her socks got soaked.

Living on the street meant she had to conserve what little cash she had. Her army pension covered the basics, and she gave Budge at the centre some money every month because she knew how tight their budget was. She'd thought about selling the *Big Issue* but couldn't stand the thought of interacting with all those people. If she'd wanted human interaction, she'd have stayed in the real world.

Besides, she never knew when the terror would strike. It could happen at any time. A backfiring car exhaust, a rumbling bus, fireworks. And she was right back there, on that fucking road, watching her mates die.

She'd left her backpack and tatty ski-jacket in a locker at Waterloo station. It was open later than the day centre and she'd need it after the sun set.

"Oh, right. No, I'm a friend of Bianca's," she told him. "Did you know her?"

"Bianca?" He blinked at her.

"Yes, you know, the girl who was—"

"I know," he cut her off. The cigarette was burning down between his fingers. "I knew her, yes." More softly. His gaze softened, just for a moment. "She was my friend."

Shrap nodded and let a moment pass. A heartbeat of shared grief. "I'm trying to find out what happened. The police won't tell me anything."

He shrugged. "That's not unusual. I don't think they know anyway."

Shrap was surprised. "Were they here?"

"God, no. It's just what I read in the papers They said she was a prostitute." He snorted.

"They always get things wrong."

"I mean, as if. She was the best dancer at the club. Classically trained. I told her once, honey, it's a travesty you working here. You're better than this. But do you think she listened to me?" He shook his head, earring flashing in the dusky light. "Nope. She knew better. She always knew better. And now look what's happened." He gave a sniff.

It was clear this guy had known Bianca fairly well.

"When did you meet her?" she asked.

"Six months ago. When she arrived in England." He studied her, frowning at the used shoes, tacky in the pool of streetlight. "How about you?"

"We were at the same hostel," she said. "Before she moved on. My boyfriend's Eastern European... I liked her. We became close. Had each other's backs, you know?"

He gave a nod. "She was a decent person. Sometimes we'd go out after closing to wind down. She was fun. Clever, too. Fiz was crazy about her."

"Fiz?" She stared at him blankly.

"Fiz Xhafa. He owns the place." He waved at the building with his hand.

"Ah, the tattooed guy in the silver Mercedes."

He smirked. "You've noticed?"

She shrugged, as if that was obvious.

"Can't say I blame you. Who doesn't like a bad boy, eh? Rich as Croesus too." Arrogant, cocky, aggressive. She knew the type.

"He Albanian?" she asked, thinking about the word she'd heard.

"Yeah, I think so. I remember him talking about it once. Why? You interested, darling?"

"No, I was just wondering what Bianca saw in him."

"Oh, they weren't together." He blew a vicious fume of smoke skyward. "Not for lack of trying on his part, though. But Bianca wasn't like that. This was just business for her."

"Do you think he could have had anything to do with her death?"

A pause. Another heavy drag.

"I don't think so." He exhaled, turning his head so he didn't blow smoke into her face. "He had no reason to."

"What about jealousy?"

He shrugged. "I don't know. He's never short of attention. Listen, darling, I'd love to stay and chat, but I have to get to work."

She stared at the entrance. "Oh, okay. I was hoping to talk about Bianca a bit more. It helps, you know, to talk to someone who knew her."

He shrugged. "We open in an hour."

Go in. Her?

She hadn't set foot in a bar or restaurant since she'd left home. She didn't know if she could. Anxiety clutched at her chest, suffocating her. No need to go inside, not yet. She did want to speak to the barman some more, but it could wait.

"Do you know where she lived? I heard she had a flat-mate. Maybe I can talk to her."

"In Shoreditch. I can't remember the road, but it's the one with the park and the newsagent on the corner." He grinned. "Bright pink house, hard to miss."

"Pink house. Got it." She smiled. "Thanks for your help. It was good meeting you, er...?"

"Alex."

"It was good meeting you, Alex."

He tossed his cigarette butt on the ground, crushing it underfoot. "Hey, if you're looking for work... How about that bar job? I could use a friend on the inside. It'll be fun. Free cocktails." He winked.

Not a chance.

"Maybe."

He gave a quick nod and turned towards the staff door. She watched him tap in his code.

*8745#

He didn't seem to care that she was watching.

"See ya, darling." And he was gone.

SHOREDITCH WAS RIDDLED with small parks and newsagents. Shrap put the A to Z down and asked the shopkeeper if he knew of a pink house. He didn't.

Hard to miss, he'd said.

Yeah, right.

She tried the next one, and then the next one. Eventually, a customer overheard and pointed her in the right direction.

There it was. She stared at the double-storey house

blushing in the streetlamps that ran down the road. Rightly so. Hard to believe that someone actually chose to paint their house this colour.

It was a decent neighbourhood with neat, terraced houses all squished together. Tomorrow must be rubbish collection day, because there was an assortment of bins out on the street. Strange place for an exotic dancer to live. She'd have thought she'd go for something more budget, but then what did she know? Maybe stripping paid better than she thought.

She knocked on the door.

It was opened by a striking mixed-race woman in her early twenties. She spoke with an Afro-Caribbean accent.

"You here for the room?"

"No, sorry. I'm a friend of Bianca's. I was hoping we could talk."

Her eyes narrowed. "A friend? How come I never seen you before?"

"We used to live together, when Bianca first got to the UK." It was always best to stick with the same story. Consistency was everything in undercover work.

The woman frowned. "You're not with the police, are you? 'Cos I already spoken to them. I got nothing more to say."

Not anymore.

"Do I look like I'm with the police?"

If this woman had seen her a couple of hours ago before she'd cleaned up, she wouldn't have asked that.

She shrugged. "You never know these days."

Good point.

Shrap slouched onto one hip. "Okay, well, I'm not. Her parents want to know what happened to her, and I said I'd help them. It would mean a lot to them if I could ask you some questions."

"Her parents?"

"Yeah, they're in the UK. I'm trying to help them out. Bianca was good to me, you know?" The lie came more easily this time.

The flatmate's eyes darted up and down the street. "Okay."

They stepped out onto the pavement.

"I'm Shaz." Close enough, fewer questions.

"Rona." They shook, tentatively.

"Did you know Bianca long?"

The flatmate wrapped her arms around herself. They were thin. Too thin. "A couple of months. She was great. Clever. Wanted to be a solicitor one day."

"Oh?" That was news.

"Yeah, she was studying and everything."

"You mean she was at university?"

"It was some correspondence course. Open University, I think. Something like that anyway."

Shrap raised her eyebrow. Bianca Rubik had gone up in her estimation.

"Was she seeing anyone, do you know?"

A pause.

"She didn't have a steady boyfriend. I told the police that."

Shrap glanced up at her. "What about that club owner? Fiz, wasn't it?"

Rona gave a little shrug. "He was into her, all right, but she turned him down. She wasn't like that, you know."

That was the second time she'd heard that about Bianca.

"I heard they were seeing each other."

The woman scoffed. "B didn't sleep around. She had

goals. Big ones. She wanted to study, then bring her kid over."

"Kid?" The word was out before she could stop it.

Rona frowned. "How come you didn't know about her kid? Thought you was friends."

"You know B. She kept things like that to herself."

A resigned shrug. "I guess so. I only know 'cos she had a photo of him in her bedroom. Sweet little thing." Tears sprang to her eyes, but she blinked them away.

"Oh yeah, I saw the photo. I just assumed it was her nephew or something." Shrap noticed Rona's fingers were bitten to the core.

"Nah, she was saving up. When she wasn't working, she was in her room studying. She didn't go out or nothing."

"Her parents thought she might be into drugs, but I say no way."

Rona nodded in agreement. "She was real classy. I believed her that she'd be a solicitor one day. I could see her in a black coat with a wig on her head."

She gave a sad smile. Shrap felt her pain.

"It's a tragedy," she said.

And it was.

Bianca Rubik was nothing like she'd expected. Bright. Ambitious. Focused. She had a little boy and big dreams. They'd been crushed that night someone had strangled her and left her in a gutter. She clenched her fists. The same person who'd killed Doug.

"I told her that guy was no good."

"Who? Her boss?"

"Yeah, the scumbag. He came here in ripped jeans and a tight T-shirt and strutted around like he owned the place. Drove up in his fancy car, music blaring. All the neighbours heard him. I said to her, 'Girl, he's into some bad shit. I can tell.' I mean, anyone who drives around in a swanky convertible and wears a Rolex is into something illegal, unless he's a fucking investment banker. And he ain't one of them." She rolled her eyes. "But she never listened. Said he was good to her, and she needed the work."

Shrap's pulse increased.

"Do you think he had something to do with her death?"

Rona shrugged. "I don't know. Maybe."

They talked for a few more minutes, but Bianca's flatmate didn't know anything more about this Xhafa guy. Shrap thanked her and said she had to go.

"Tell her parents I'm sorry," Rona said, before she closed the door. "And I hope the cops catch whoever did this."

The police wouldn't. She knew that for a fact. They had Doug to pin it on. A homeless guy with no alibi, caught on CCTV at the crime scene. Why would they look anywhere else?

"Don't worry, I'm working on it," she murmured as she walked away.

10

It was nearly nine when Shrap got back to Covent Garden. She stifled a yawn; it had been a long day. Usually, she was curled up in a doorway by now, shutting out the world.

How about that bar job?

Shit.

If she were really investigating this case, she'd go to the club. Ask for an interview, check out Xhafa and those two gangster buddies of his who may or may not make an appearance, and pump Alex, the bartender in need of a friend, for more information.

Yet she stood outside, staring at the place.

The bouncer was back in the same tight, black T-shirt, his biceps bulging. *Don't fuck with me.* The entrance was lit from within, attracting punters with its not-so-subtle rose-tinted glow. A glossy poster of a stunning model promised untold delights.

As she watched, several men walked in. Some in groups, but mostly alone.

She glanced at her reflection in a store window and

grimaced. Her eyes were beginning to itch and the lipstick she'd applied earlier had almost worn off. She couldn't pretend for much longer. If she was going to go in, she had to do it now.

Fuck it. May as well get this over with while she looked the part.

Taking a deep breath, she crossed the road and entered the club.

SHRAP NODDED to the bouncer and walked through the door into a scarlet tunnel. She felt like she'd just entered the mouth of a lion. Her pulse throbbed in her ears as she walked through it, mingling with the beat of the music.

Claustrophobia gripped her. The tunnel seemed to swirl. Bloody hell, what was she doing? The temptation to turn around and run was so strong she could barely force herself to keep moving forward.

Finally, she emerged into a large lounge with booths around the edge and smaller circular tables in the middle. The walls were a dark burgundy and she stood on a carpet the colour of blood. Her heart beat frantically in her chest. She was actually doing this.

Elaborate chandeliers hung from the ceiling, dripping with fake crystals. There were low, silk-covered lamps on the tables and a frisky anticipation in the air.

Everything was designed to stir the emotions, and hers did not need stirring. They were already on high alert most of the time anyway. Hypervigilance, she'd read, when she'd got home from Afghanistan and googled her condition. Back in the days when she actually thought she could defeat it.

The lights dimmed and a spotlight captured the stage.

The music changed, pounding out of strategically placed loudspeakers. It reverberated through her body. She put a hand against the wall and froze. This was a mistake. The air was thick, making it hard to breathe. The bile started to rise. She was about to turn and run when two punters walked in behind her. She was in the way.

Then, she caught sight of Alex and propelled herself forward.

She could do this. She had to do this. For Doug.

Heart racing, she took a seat at the bar. There were some other men standing there, all of whom turned to check her out, eyes flickering with interest.

"You decided to go for it after all." Alex gave a smug grin.

"I did." Gripping the counter, she inhaled, then let it out slowly. Just breathe.

"Peter's over there." He nodded to a booth at the back where a man dressed in black jeans and a leather jacket was talking to a bunch of guys at a table. She hadn't noticed them when she'd walked in. The booth was in a dark spot, and with the spotlight on the stage it was hard to see clearly. Four guys sat at the table: Xhafa, the two from the blue BMW and a third whose back was to her.

"Looks busy."

"Yeah, have a drink first. The first act's about to begin, then there's a break. I'll get him for you then."

She forced a smile. "Thanks."

"What can I get you?"

"Chardonnay."

"I'll make it a large."

It was too loud to talk, so she sat back and waited for her senses to adjust and the nausea to fade. The music changed tempo and became beat-heavy, almost rap-like. The first dancer appeared. Lithe, sensual and dark-skinned, she glistened as she strode across the stage and down the ramp that extended into the middle of the room. There was a pole at the end.

She had luminous yellow ribbons in her long, dark hair that matched her bikini-style top and four-inch heels. How could she walk in those things, let alone dance?

Shrap had never been to a strip club before, although some of her army mates had. The woman began to gyrate on the floor in front of the pole. She performed a series of staccato, jerky moves, her body snaking in an almost mesmerising rhythm. Her hips went one way, her torso the other, her head another still. The long hair whipped from side to side and all around, the luminous streaks catching the light.

The men in the room were mesmerised, and she hadn't touched the pole yet.

"Good, isn't she?" shouted the bartender, handing her the wine. "That's Jasmine."

"Very." Her throat was dry and tasted of fear. She took a gulp.

After doing a series of complicated turns and landing in the splits, the dancer pulled herself up using the pole.

Then the show really began.

The tension in the room mounted as she whirled around it, going upside down and using her knees to grip as well as her hands. Shrap could see the muscles flexing in her slender arms.

The beat seemed to get stuck in her chest and she hovered at the edge of panic. If her palms sweated any more, she'd drop the wine glass.

One hour, then she could leave. That should do it. Except right now, an hour seemed like eternity. She took another sip and glanced around. In the stage lights she could make out a bottle of champagne on the table, and one on ice next to it.

"Big night?"

Alex shrugged. "Always, with those guys."

"Who are they, do you know?"

"Friends, I think. They're here a lot."

The exotic dancer slid down the pole and bounced at the bottom for a while, then spun around and wiggled her behind at the crowd. There was muted clapping and some jeering from the group at the back.

Shrap frowned, but the look on the dancer's face was pure pro. She smiled and performed, milking it for all it was worth. The beat escalated and she did a few more dazzling spins on the pole, then executed a crazy backbend into a standing position and threw her hips out as the music came to an abrupt halt.

More muted clapping. Hardly a reflection of her talent.

She didn't seem to care. With a provocative grin and a flick of her hair, she strutted back down the ramp and vanished into the wings.

"She could be a professional dancer," she told Alex.

"She is," Alex replied. "Stripping pays more."

Seriously?

The lower-key background music came back on. Thank God. Now she could hear herself think.

"What's your name?" Alex asked.

"Shaz." She stuck to her previous legend. "Sharron."

"I'll just get Peter for you."

"Wait."

He stopped. "Yeah?"

"What's he like, your boss?"

"Who? Peter?"

"No, Fiz."

A pause. "I told you, he's not a friendly guy."

"Dangerous?"

A shrug.

"Violent?"

"Never with the girls, although he's got a nasty temper. I wouldn't want to get on his bad side. Once he punched a punter who got physical with Bianca. Mick had to pull him off the guy. Smashed his face to a pulp. No one went near her after that."

"Mick?"

"Mikael. Fiz's bodyguard. He's the big Russian guy at the next-door table."

Shrap studied the mountain of a man who'd been at Xhafa's side earlier that day. He was drinking a bottle of water, a newspaper open on the table in front of him. As if sensing her gaze, he looked up. A practised glance, a quick once-over, then he turned away. No threat here. Just another hopeful looking for a job.

"Why the security detail?" Shrap turned back to Alex.

"Dunno." He rolled his eyes. "Don't want to know."

Shrap watched as Xhafa threw back his head and laughed, simultaneously slamming his fist down on the table. A lot of pent-up aggression there.

Maroon Cap reached for the champagne and refilled everyone's glass.

Would a club like this pay for a top-of-the-line Mercedes convertible, a gold Rolex and endless champagne? It was a classy joint, as far as strip clubs went, but that kind of cash? She didn't think so. And what about that deal that went down outside earlier? Was that Xhafa's money? Or something else entirely?

Xhafa was into some dodgy shit and Shrap wanted to

know what it was. Club owners didn't normally require around-the-clock protection.

When she'd been in the military police, she'd heard about the Albanian gangs. Young, ruthless and violent. Was Xhafa affiliated to one of them? Were these two guys? And where did Bianca fit in?

Maybe it was time she found out.

Taking a deep breath, she nodded to Alex. "Okay, now or never, right?"

In response, he beckoned Peter over. The man in black nodded and strode toward them. Shrap bit her lip. This was actually happening.

11

"You bartended before?" Peter asked. His eyes roamed around the room. Never still. It was disconcerting.

"Of course."

After school. Before she'd joined the military.

"Where've you worked?"

"Sports Café," she said, rolling venues off the top of her head. She knew their doorways pretty well, if not the interiors. "Hard Rock, Tiger Tiger."

He sniffed. "Got a CV?"

"Not on me. Alex just told me about the vacant position. I can drop it off tomorrow."

The moving eyes rested on her for the briefest of moments. A shiver shot through her. Would he see her for what she was? Less than a human. Not worthy of any job, even this one.

"Tomorrow's fine."

He didn't.

She exhaled. Her disguise had held.

"Alex is due a break soon. Why don't you fill in for him and we'll give you a trial run?"

She gulped. "What? Now?"

"Yeah, now." His gaze narrowed. "You want the job, don't you?"

"Sure. No problem." She grit her teeth. It was like riding a bike, right?

Alex would show her how the till worked. She could do this. It was going to be okay. Half an hour, max, and she'd be out of here. Back in the drizzle. Back in the place where none of this mattered.

Alex threw her a knowing smile when she told him what Peter had said. "Good work! Come round and I'll show you the ropes. It's not hard. Any idiot can tend bar."

She hoped he was right.

"Did you work last Saturday night?" she asked, as he showed her the basics.

"I work every night, except Sundays."

"Do you remember if Fiz was here?"

"Yeah, I think so." His eyes drifted over to where he was sitting. "He was definitely here when I finished my shift, around four."

"Could he have gone out during the course of the evening without you knowing?"

"I suppose so. He's usually in his office but..." He shrugged.

"What about Mikael? Is he always here?"

"Not always. He comes and goes."

The next dancer strutted on and the music changed. This time it was a sultrier Latin number, which wasn't so grating on her nerves. A striking Spanish-looking girl, she wore silver hot pants with a barely-there bra top that was nothing more than two tiny triangles over her nipples. A complicated criss-crossing of silver straps covered the upper half of her back.

From behind the bar, Shrap took the opportunity to study Mick. The bodyguard didn't give the gorgeous Spanish dancer more than a cursory glance before he went back to his crossword, or whatever it was he was doing. He had a pen in his hand and was looking down at the newspaper. Every now and then, he'd scan the room and check on the table beside him.

He was alert, well trained. Ex-Russian military, most likely. Now a mercenary, a gun for hire. Although, he could probably do a lot of damage with his bare fists too.

Had Mikael strangled Bianca on that deserted road? His beefy hands squeezing the life out of her, destroying her future and depriving a young boy of his mother?

The sultry black woman from the first dance appeared from behind a pair of red velvet curtains. She sauntered up to the bar. Even from behind the counter, she could smell her perfume. It wasn't cheap. What Alex said must be true. Stripping paid more. The dancer's face was heavily made up and she had eyelashes that couldn't possibly be real. She leaned forward. "You're new?"

"Trial period." Shrap forced a smile. "Can I get you something?" Did the dancers get free drinks? She didn't know.

"Yeah, give me a lime and soda."

Perhaps they weren't allowed to drink on the job.

"Sure." She managed that, although her hands were shaking. She breathed out, forcing herself to relax. The dancer didn't notice. She'd moved on to a punter who was nursing a whiskey while he checked her out.

"You want a private dance, handsome? Just you and me?"

Her voice was just the right kind of husky. She fingered his shirt collar.

"How much?"

Jasmine leaned over and whispered in his ear.

He shook his head.

Shrap watched the exchange, the crushing reality of her situation hitting home. What the hell was she doing here? She wasn't ready for this. She could barely cope on the street, let alone in a strip joint where she was supposed to serve drinks to desperate, lonely men while investigating potential suspects.

Fuck. She had to calm down or the terror would take hold and ruin everything.

Grey Beanie beckoned to Jasmine. She sauntered over, wearing her practised smile like a mask. He smacked her on the bottom, a little too hard for Shrap's liking. The dancer wasn't fazed. She bent over, laughed at something he said, then he got up to follow her.

She'd found a willing customer.

Shrap watched as they disappeared behind the velvet curtain.

"Did Bianca give private dances?" she asked Alex, when he got back from his break. He smelled of cigarette smoke.

"All the girls do," he replied, as if she were talking about getting a manicure. "It's how they make their money."

"Was Bianca popular?"

"God, yeah. The punters loved her. All that blonde hair." He grinned. "She was any straight guy's wet dream."

"Did she have a problem with anyone? Any of the customers give her a hard time?"

"Not that I know of. Besides, Fiz would have seen them off if they did. He was obsessed with her."

"Obsessed is a strong word."

He glanced at his boss. "When Bianca was around, he had no time for anyone else. He watched all her routines. His eyes would follow her as she walked around the room. It was creepy."

"How did Bianca handle that?"

Alex shrugged. "She didn't mind, or so she said. I think she was flattered, and it meant she always had a job. There's a high turnover of girls here. Fiz pays well, but he only hires the best and the schedule is harsh."

"Was she seeing anyone, do you know? A boyfriend?"

"Nah." He gave a nervous laugh. "I don't think Fiz would have liked that."

Too scared of him or of losing her job?

"What about regulars? Anyone she saw often?"

"Yeah, all the girls have regulars, but Bianca was a pro. It was strictly business with her. She never got close to anyone."

So she'd heard. She wasn't like that.

It looked like Xhafa and his mates were settling in for a long night. Shrap wiped her hands on her jeans and walked back to the other side of the bar. It was over.

"Leaving already?" Alex looked disappointed.

"Yeah, sorry. I've got to go."

He nodded. "Good job. I'll tell Pete you did okay."

"Thanks."

She wouldn't be coming back here.

"See ya, Glitter Girl."

Shrap managed a smile, then turned to leave. She only just stopped herself from running. She couldn't get out of there fast enough.

12

After leaving the club, Shrap walked past the blue BMW parked across the road and disappeared around the corner, out of the bouncer's line of sight.

Whatever Xhafa was into had something to do with those two guys. Their visit this afternoon hadn't been a social call.

She'd already decided that if the Albanians made an appearance tonight, she'd follow them home. The cash payment, the flashy car, the connection with the strip club... it was all pointing to organised crime. Then there was Bianca. An exotic dancer who'd caught the eye of her boss. Had she seen too much? Is that what had got her killed?

To find out what these guys were up to, she needed to know where they operated from. Then she could set up some sort of surveillance. That's what she'd do in the old days, anyway.

It was more difficult now. She had no phone, no vehicle, and no backup. But there was a payphone at the end of this road.

She dug into her pocket for change and made a call.

Twenty minutes later a red Toyota Prius pulled up. It wasn't the best colour vehicle for a tail, but she didn't have a choice. Hopefully, it wouldn't be as noticeable in the dark.

A big, athletic guy in jeans and a hoodie got out of the car. "Yoh, girl. Look at you!"

Shrap grimaced. "Yeah, I had to go somewhere."

They hugged.

Her friend looked around. "Where? Here?"

"Club up the street."

Music wafted out from a couple of bars, and in one restaurant they could see customers eating through the well-lit glass windows.

He arched an eyebrow. "What you into?"

"Let's get in, I'll tell you."

They climbed back in the car. Frank was an old mate, they'd done basic training together, but then gone on to different regiments. Frank had been out for some time, driving an Uber to make ends meet. There weren't many well-paying jobs for ex-servicemen around. Whenever Shrap needed a lift, which was rare, Frank was her go-to guy.

"I need to tail two guys at the club," she said. "I think they might have something to do with Doug's murder."

"Doug, your old mate? I heard he committed suicide, set himself on fire or some shit."

"No. That's a bullshit story made up by the police. He didn't smoke."

Frank looked worried. "And you think these guys did it?"

"I don't know. I think they might have something to do with it."

Frank started the car and did a U-turn. "Are you sure you

should be doing this, Shrap? Isn't it the police's job to find out who killed him?"

"I was police, remember?"

"That was a while ago. No offence, but you've moved on since then."

Moved backwards, more like.

She hesitated. "I know, but this is important."

Frank didn't keep on at her. "Where's this club?"

"There. On the left."

"Whispers? A strip joint? *That's* where you've been?"

"Yeah." She didn't explain about Bianca Rubik. Frank didn't need to know. Questioning Alex and then the bar trial had worn her out. She wasn't used to so much conversation.

"Okay, so who are we waiting for?"

"Two Albanian guys. That's their car there. The BMW. I saw them receive an envelope of cash – at least it looked like cash – earlier today. I'm thinking drugs."

Frank took in the high-performance vehicle and gave a low whistle.

"Now I know you should leave well alone. Those motherfucking gangsters take no prisoners."

"I'm not messing with them, I'm tailing them."

Frank shook his head.

"I can give you till four a.m., then I gotta get back. I've got an airport transfer booked for five thirty."

"Thanks, mate. I owe you."

"No, you don't. You know that."

Shrap fell silent. They never talked about what had happened back at the academy. Just like they never talked about what Shrap had become. About the terrors that had driven her out of her own home and onto the street.

Frank got it. And even if he didn't, he respected Shrap's

need for space. Her desire to handle this on her own. In private.

It was nearly one in the morning now. Shrap leaned back and closed her eyes, but she couldn't sleep. She was too wired. She had to keep reminding herself why she was doing this.

For Doug.

The old guy didn't deserve to go down as a murderer who'd taken the easy way out.

He was her friend, he deserved justice. She wouldn't sit by and let him take the blame when she could do something about it. She'd been powerless in Kabul; she wasn't power-less now. Close to it, but she wasn't out of the running just yet. There was still something she could do. Doug... Bianca... It all started here. She was sure of it.

Frank nodded off, snoring gently next to her. Shrap, used to sleeping with half an eye open, managed to doze, enjoying the warmth of the car and the comfy seat.

At three o'clock the remaining punters left the club.

Closing time.

"Hey, Frank. Time to go." She nudged her mate.

Frank rubbed his eyes and sat up.

Maroon Cap, Grey Beanie and their friend were the last to leave. Xhafa saw them out himself, followed closely by big Mick. They shook hands. Secret handshake, shoulder bump. Hit and miss since they were so drunk.

"Gangster style," muttered Frank.

Maroon Cap stumbled into the passenger seat, Grey Beanie climbed into the back and the friend drove. That's why he'd come along. The designated driver. He didn't look entirely sober either, but the others too pissed to notice.

They pulled away from the curb, Xhafa watching.

Frank followed, keeping his distance.

They drove north out of the city, through Whitechapel and towards Canning Town. The further out they got, the less traffic there was, until it was only them and the car in front of them.

"Pull back," cautioned Shrap, as they approached a dark but sizable housing estate.

"Don't worry, I ain't going in there. This is the end of the line for me, mate."

They switched off the lights and watched as the BMW drove in. Shrap focused on the taillights for as long as possible. Then the world went dark.

"Now what?" Frank glanced at her.

Shrap looked up. There was, or rather there had been a security camera at the entrance, but it had been destroyed and the pole pockmarked with bullet holes.

A clear message. Don't spy on us.

She put her hand on the door handle.

"Hey, wait. You can't go in there."

"Might as well have a gander," she replied. "We've come this far."

Frank looked at the time on the dash. "I can't wait, mate. I've got to get back."

The drive had taken thirty-five minutes, and with another thirty-five to get back, Shrap couldn't ask much more of her friend.

"Okay, thanks." She opened the door.

Frank stared at her like she was mad. "Fuck it. I'll stay. I can't let you go in there alone."

"I'm just going to have a sniff around. You head back, I'll be okay."

"How are you going to get back?"

"I'll get the train tomorrow morning."

"Do you even know where we are?"

"Yeah, I saw a sign a couple of miles back. Barking station isn't that far away." She sounded more confident than she felt, but then Frank knew she could take care of herself. She'd kicked his arse a couple of times.

"Okay, if you're sure, but I don't like it."

"I'm sure. Bugger off. Thanks for the lift." She knew her friend was worried about her.

Frank gave her a last look, then put the car into reverse. Shrap got out and watched as he performed a three-point turn then took off up the road.

THE SPRAWLING ESTATE was a mishmash of brown brick buildings, concrete blocks and parking lots. At this time of night, there was no activity. The roads were deathly quiet. Even gangsters had to sleep.

Shrap stuck to the shadows, avoiding well-lit areas and tracking the route that the blue BMW had taken. It was cold and damp and she wished she had her coat, but she was still in her ridiculous pink T-shirt, which offered nothing in the way of protection.

Suddenly Waterloo seemed a long way away.

A concrete court had been turned into a football pitch with nets at both ends. It sat in darkness, a punctured ball discarded in one corner.

She passed a torrent of obscene graffiti on a low wall. Skulls and lurid faces stared down at her through hollow eyes. It was a warning.

Go home.

She continued around the corner to where the taillights had disappeared. And there it was. Parked at the foot of a dirty brick high-rise jabbing the dark sky. The blue convertible. Except now the hood was up. She put her hand on the bonnet, still warm. The engine ticked quietly as it cooled down.

She studied the building. Was this where the gangsters lived? Why here, when they supposedly had all this money? Was it a hood thing? Gang HQ? A rubbish skip outside let off the sweet, putrid aroma of decaying food.

Glancing up, she saw the windows were in darkness, the residents asleep. The activities of the evening, the boisterous youths, the troublemakers had all quietened down and gone home. Even the three guys she'd followed had called it a night.

She inspected the base of the building. A permanently open entrance, no doors, just a walkway to a lift that was out of order. Cold, concrete steps to the side led upwards into the bowels. The smell from the bins was overpowering.

After taking a last look around, Shrap headed back to the entrance. Sticking around wasn't a good idea. Soon it would be sunrise, and the estate would come to life. First the manual labourers and shift workers would get up, then the mothers and their kids, followed by the night owls and those that operate under the cloak of darkness.

She didn't get very far before a young, black youth let off a low whistle.

Shrap spun around.

In this 'normal' disguise, she had no cover. As a crack addict bum she could have made a case for herself. It was a mistake, she'd wandered off her usual route, she was high, crazy. But in her glittery clothes, made-up, and wearing four-inch heels, she was exposed.

Make that fucked.

"Who are you?" the kid asked.

She didn't reply.

Sixteen, maybe seventeen. Slender. About sixty kilos. She could take him if she acted now. The first rule of attack was to go in hard, don't give your opponent time to react.

She took a step towards the youth when a man appeared behind him. Then two, and before she knew it, she was surrounded. Shit. This was not good. A blade glinted as it caught the light.

She lifted her hands. "I was just leaving."

"What you doing here, bitch?" demanded another guy. Older this time, harder.

Her gaze dropped to the weapon in his hand. That was some serious hardware.

"I was looking for someone, but I've got the wrong place."

Scowls of disbelief interspersed with a few curious glances, appreciative even. Then, at the back, she saw a grey beanie. Crap.

The circle parted.

He wore the same T-shirt, but track pants instead of jeans, and he'd lost the jacket and the bling.

"Who the fuck are you?" His hot breath assaulted the cold night air.

"I'm nobody." At least that much was true. "I was just leaving."

She turned around, then felt a rough hand grip her T-shirt, jerking her back. "Not so fast, *putanë.*" His accent was strong. She fell onto the ground. There was a murmur of laughter.

"You know what happens to girls like you in places like this?" Snorts of agreement from his cronies.

"I-I'm looking for Solly. He said he'd set me up."

"She's just a skanky ho," one of the younger men said. "Probably off her tits."

Grey Beanie grunted.

"Nice tits," another guy smirked.

More sniggers.

Thank God she'd covered her military tattoo, else things could have been a lot worse. Shrap tried to get up, but a well-placed boot sent her sprawling back onto the filthy ground.

It was worth one last-ditch attempt. "Solly said—"

"There's no Solly here," growled Grey Beanie, who sounded remarkably sober for one who'd been so drunk barely an hour ago.

He gave her a last lingering look, muttered something to one of the other guys, then strolled towards the building without a backwards glance.

Shrap braced.

No surprise what was going to happen next.

13

She was handcuffed to a chair in a squalid room in the Taliban compound. She'd spent all night in a freezing cold cell with the screams of her dying colleagues in her head.

She knew what was coming.

"Who are you with?" a turbaned official asked.

"British army," she managed to rasp out. "We were transporting..."

That's as far as she got before they launched into her. Fists pounded her face and boots kicked her shins. The fact she was a woman made no difference. Their hatred wasn't defined by gender. The chair fell over, breaking her wrist. She screamed in pain. The chair splintered beneath her and somehow, she managed to get her hands free.

But the kicks kept on coming. She covered her face and head and curled up into a ball, but it did little good.

The laughing and jeering of her torturers echoed in the background. It sounded like a competition, a dare or a bet. Who can do the most damage?

The soundtrack to her shame.

The beating carried on and on. Her captors didn't ask any more questions. They weren't interested. Their aim was to inflict as much pain as possible. She was convinced she was going to die.

THE AIR WAS KNOCKED out of her, then she felt a crunch as a boot connected with her ribs. Pain flashed through her brain, releasing a rush of adrenaline.

Then, she'd been tied up, powerless to protect herself. That wasn't the case now, and she wasn't going down without a fight.

Shrap grabbed the leg that was kicking her, holding on tight. He lashed out with a knife, slicing her arm.

Fuck, that hurt. She used the pain to give her strength and pulled her assailant down on top of her. He grunted but laughed it off. Two others held her down while he straddled her. His eyes weren't smiling. "Keep still, you bitch. It'll hurt less."

"My turn next," jeered another voice.

Not if I can help it.

She twisted out of their grasp, then rammed her palm upwards into her assailant's face. He howled as his nose snapped. Not waiting for the others to react, she scrambled to her feet and charged after Grey Beanie. The bastard was going to pay. For feeding her to the dogs, for Doug, for being a fucking gangster.

She tore after him, shrugging off the hands that grabbed at her. Her target was about to disappear into the building, when Shrap jumped on him from behind. He twisted around, trying to shove her off, but she'd wrapped her legs around his waist and clung on while squeezing her arms around his neck. Shrap may have been on the street for a year, but she hadn't forgotten how to fight, and unlike these fuckers, had absolutely nothing to lose.

He made a choking sound and dropped to his knees, then his stomach. She released him, then landed several hard punches to the face. Snot mixed with blood dripped onto the dirty ground.

There was a loud shout and rush of warm air. The stunned gang had woken up, spurred into action by her frenzied assault. A blow landed on the back of her neck. It was a hard, metallic object, probably the butt of a gun. Her eyes glazed over, vision blurring. A second blow sent her reeling, and she fell forward onto her target.

The background noise became static. A steady hum in her ears. Multiple hands gripped her shoulders, tearing her T-shirt and pulling her off the man beneath her. Her face connected with cold concrete. She smelled muddy water and oil slicks. Another kick to the ribs, and more to the stomach, then she blacked out.

THE SOFT PITTER-PATTER of rain massaged her aching face. She opened her eyes, blinked against the wet, then closed them again.

Fuck, she hurt.

The events of last night came rushing back and she groaned. Jesus, they'd given her a right beating. Tentatively, she pressed between her legs. Thankfully, everything felt intact. They must have given up on the idea of sexual assault once she'd passed out. Not much fun when your target couldn't respond.

Pain sliced through her head, making her wince. Still, if she could move, it was going to be okay.

She'd had worse.

It had taken a medevac team to scrape her off the pavement after the Taliban had discarded her. They'd thrown her out of a moving vehicle onto an icy road outside Kabul. Left her to die of her injuries or freeze to death, whichever came first.

If it wasn't for the Dutch aid workers who'd found her, she wouldn't be here right now.

She tried again, opening her eyes and waiting for her vision to clear. Thankfully it did, and she rolled onto her side, grimacing against the pain.

She pushed herself into a sitting position and took stock. Where was she?

It looked to be some sort of derelict warehouse. Crumbling concrete pillars, broken wooden beams, dusty, pockmarked ground. The rain was coming from a gaping hole in the roof directly above her, which was why she was sitting in a wet puddle.

She tried to twist onto her knees, but the sharp pain in her left side caused her to collapse back down again. It hurt to breathe.

She rolled over instead, so she was under cover. Her arm throbbed, but it wasn't as bad as her ribs. She glanced down and saw the slash from the knife. Dried blood crusted over her skin. At least it wasn't a bullet. She lay staring up at the ceiling, or what was left of it, taking shallow breaths and testing different areas of her body.

Why had they spared her? Was it because she was a woman?

LIFE WAS cheap on these estates, but hers wasn't worth shit. Not worth the hassle. Dump the crackhead and let her crawl back to where she came from.

Good enough.

It took Shrap an hour to crawl out of the abandoned construction site to civilisation. She held her damaged ribs, teeth clenched against the pain. Her head ached and dried blood had crusted down the side of her neck and on her T-shirt. Although that may not be hers. She had a vague recollection of palming her would-be rapist in the nose.

She hoped it hurt.

Shrap passed a house with a washing line out back. Someone had forgotten to bring in the laundry. The clothes were wet, but so was she. She grabbed a dripping jumper and pulled it on. It hid the blood.

Now, to find the train station.

She followed the early morning dribble of people to a high street, and at the end she spotted the welcoming parallel red lines of the British Rail symbol. She had no change from the twenty she'd gone out with last night – bastards must have taken it – so she ducked under the barrier and proceeded onto the platform. There wasn't anyone around checking.

Luckily, she'd left her wallet and bank card in the station locker, so the Albanian gangsters wouldn't have found any identification on her. They'd have no clue who she was, or what she was doing there. Other than looking for the mysterious Solly. The only thing that could potentially have given her away was her tattoo, but the stage make-up had done its job and stayed on.

The train rushed into the station and came to a standstill. The doors opened. She got on and took a seat in the middle carriage where she could spot a conductor if he or she came down the aisle. It was warm inside and the gentle motions of the train made her eyes close. She felt like she was floating, the pain began to dull.

"This station is Waterloo," came the tinny voice through the speakers, jolting her awake. "Change here for the Bakerloo and Jubilee lines and mainline railways."

She opened her eyes. Passengers were disembarking, while more waited on the platform to board. There was the general chatter of commuters, the flick of turnstiles, the sound of heels on the platform. In the background, a whistle blew.

She sighed in relief. She was home.

"Jesus, Shrap." Budge rushed over to her when she finally stumbled into the day centre. "What the hell happened to you?"

"You should see the other guy," she grimaced, although it was plainly obvious that she'd been the losing party. She ignored the knowing stares of the others. Violence was commonplace on the street. A kick from a stranger, a territorial beef for no other reason than you were in their spot, being pissed on. It happened to all of them.

"Come, let's get you fixed up. Tessa is here until midday."

"Let me take a shower first." She had to get this dirt and grime off her.

"Go and see her afterwards. She's in my office." Tessa was a junior doctor, who as far as Shrap could tell, was volunteering at the centre as part of her degree. Pro bono community service. She wasn't complaining.

Shrap stood under the hot shower for a long time, filtering the events of last night.

Xhafa and his party. Drinking and whoring away their ill-gotten gains.

Alex. Keeping to himself behind the bar. Not seeing too much.

Frank. Who'd be worried about her.

The ride to the estate.

The beating.

That last part was a blur, not helped by her foggy brain. She felt the base of her skull and winced.

Wankers.

Still, it could have been worse. It could always be worse.

Yep, it had been foolish entering the estate, but she'd discovered two important things. The Albanian gang ran that place, it was their base of operations and she doubted even the cops went in. Secondly, and no surprises here, they were very bad men. Those weren't toy guns the gang members had been carrying. She'd clocked a Skorpion sub-machine gun before she'd blacked out.

Which begged the question: What was Xhafa's business with them? Drugs? Girls? Weapons? All of the above?

Then there was the victim. Everything she'd discovered about Bianca Rubik told her she was a determined, ambitious person. A dancer and a mother. Soon to be a lawyer. Had she found out what Xhafa was into and said something to him? Had she threatened to go to the police?

Shrap winced as the water sliced over the broken skin on her forearm and ran off her damaged ribs. Stinging. Cleansing. Washing away any sign of them.

She'd collected her backpack from the locker when she'd arrived at Waterloo station, so she changed into her old, comfortable clothes and immediately felt better.

Back to her old self. Back to normal.

"Take a seat," Tessa told her when she hobbled into Budge's office. The junior doctor was here twice a week, but usually administered painkillers and patched up grazes and the odd cut. Nothing like this.

Her eyes widened as Shrap lifted her top. "You need to go to a hospital," she said, straight away. Shrap's entire side had turned purple. Tessa touched her ribs with a gloved hand, making her wince. "Definitely fractured."

The centre had large windows in keeping with the Georgian style of the building, and Shrap squinted against the light. It wasn't doing her head any favours.

"Look at me?"

Shrap turned to face the junior doctor, who made her headache worse by shining a torch into them. "You also may have a concussion."

That would explain the blurry vision.

"You need to rest. Have you got someplace safe to stay?" she asked gently.

She meant well.

"Yeah," Shrap lied.

She nodded, not quite believing her.

"Let me look at your arm." Tessa opened a medical kit and took out some cotton wool swabs and disinfectant.

Tessa dabbed the long, jagged cut on her forearm with disinfectant.

Shrap sucked in her breath. "Fuck, that stings."

"I'm going to wrap this up tight," Tessa said. "But you'll probably need a few stitches."

Shrap gave a tired nod. Her head was pounding, far worse than her arm. Funny how the visible injuries weren't always the worst.

"Looks like you gave as good as you got." There was a note of respect in Tessa's voice as she inspected her grazed, bruised knuckles before dabbing them too.

She snorted. Not nearly enough, but it would have to do. She wasn't going back.

She had something else in mind.

14

Gareth stared at the computer screen in front of him. He'd pulled up a photograph of Bianca Rubik and positioned it beside one of Doug Romberg from his army days.

They both had brown eyes, but while Bianca's were clear and smiling, Doug's were haunted and empty. It was the last photograph taken before he'd gone AWOL. Somehow, he'd made his way back into the country and vanished off the grid.

"What happened to you?" he whispered. "Why did you kill her?"

There was no apparent motive and since the guy was dead, they couldn't ask him. He sighed in frustration. Perhaps he was just a crazy old man with a dark soul.

Yet, he couldn't get away from what Doug's homeless friend had said.

He couldn't have killed her, even if he'd wanted to.

"Want to grab a coffee?" Devi stopped in front of his desk.

He glanced up, surprised. *Oh, yeah.* It was lunchtime and

the squad room had cleared out. Two officers who he vaguely knew were waiting for her at the door.

She looked at him expectantly. He wanted to keep going through the files, but he must make more of an effort socially.

"Sure," he smiled, feeling his face crack.

"Great."

He grabbed his jacket and they headed for the stairs. "You know Maisie and Graham, don't you?"

"Yeah, hi."

They smiled back.

The normal office banter ensued, and he asked polite questions and smiled and nodded in all the appropriate places.

"Where were you before Southwark, Gareth?" asked Maisie, once they were seated inside Starbucks with their lattes and toasted sandwiches.

"Kensington. I did two years there before transferring here."

"God, why did you move?" Graham asked. "Southwark's a bit of a step down, isn't it?"

Because I was in love with my boss.

He gave a vague smile. "I like the action."

Graham shook his head.

"Well, their loss is our gain," said Devi kindly.

More questions were asked. He told them what they wanted to know. He'd studied Criminal Justice at uni, joined the force as a police constable, then after two years on the beat, applied to CID, did the stint in Kensington, then transferred here. He was single, no kids and lived in Bermondsey.

They reciprocated. Graham had started a law degree then decided to go to police college instead, much to his parent's disgust. They still hadn't forgiven him.

Masie was engaged to a real estate agent. She displayed the ring proudly. At least a carat, set in a platinum band. The wedding was next June, and eight months might seem like a long time, but there was still so much to organise.

Devi was a surprise. She had two kids and a husband who worked at an electricity company in Elephant and Castle. She'd got married straight out of school and was about to take her Inspector's exam.

"How long do you have to work here before you can take it?" he asked.

"It depends. Usually a good few years, unless you get a commendation. There are some people who are fast-tracked. You've got a degree, so you might be one of them."

He gave another vague smile.

They were back in under an hour. He'd just sat down at his desk when the phone rang.

"DC Trevelyan," the voice said. "There's a letter for you at the front desk."

"Right, thanks."

He went back downstairs.

"Who dropped it off?" he asked the duty sergeant, a young officer who barely looked old enough to have a job.

"Some kid. Didn't leave a name."

A kid? That was weird.

He took the letter and opened it. It was an A4 piece of paper folded into an origami envelope. Cute.

One short, printed paragraph.

Fiz Xhafa, Whispers Club. Bianca Rubik's boss. Albanian gang connection.

It was unsigned.

"What did this kid look like?" He glanced up.

The duty sergeant shrugged. "About sixteen, black,

pulled up on a bicycle. He just said to give it to you, then he left. I had no reason to stop him."

He'd be on camera.

Trevelyan thanked him and went back upstairs.

The first thing he did was google Fiz Xhafa. When that didn't turn up any results, he tried Whispers Club.

Whispers Gentlemen's Club.

This discreet gentlemen's club in the heart of Covent Garden is a premier lap dancing venue with pole and table dancing. Watch our professional entertainers strut their stuff, whether it's in a private area or a VIP booth.

It was a strip joint.

He clicked on the link and studied images of the plush red-velvet interior, the intimate tables and the private booths. There was a stage in the front and an elevated runway in the middle encased in a subtle purple hue, the silver pole glistening in anticipation.

This was where Bianca Rubik had worked? They were under the impression she'd been a sex worker, but that was based on what she'd been found wearing, along with the testimony of her flatmate.

Trevelyan dug out Rona Sheraton's statement and read it carefully.

Idiots.

She hadn't said her flatmate was a sex worker. The police had asked whether she was, and Rona hadn't corrected them. That was entirely different.

Reading on, it became obvious Rona hadn't said much at all. In fact, the only thing she'd actually confirmed was her flatmate's full name.

Who were the interviewing sergeants? DS Heely and DS Brenner.

Graham and Maisie.

Great.

Eyes on the screen, he picked up the phone and dialled the club. A raspy voice said, "Hello?"

It was mid-afternoon, they wouldn't be open yet.

"Hello, this is DC Trevelyan from Southwark Police Station. Who am I speaking to?"

"This is Peter. I'm the manager here."

"Peter, I'm phoning to confirm that Bianca Rubik was employed as a dancer at your establishment?"

A pause.

"Yes, she was. We're very sorry to have lost her."

"Of course. Thank you very much."

He hung up.

What to do? He could – *should* – take this to the SIO, but he'd ask where the information came from and he'd have to divulge he got it from an anonymous note. There'd be questions. Who'd sent the note? Why him?

Yet, what was the alternative? Pretend he'd come by the information himself? Bianca Rubik wasn't on social media. There was no evidence in her room that she was an exotic dancer.

Or was there?

He pulled up the evidence log of the search of Bianca's room and browsed through the contents. It was shorter than expected. Bianca didn't have a lot of stuff or not everything had been deemed important.

But then, the cops conducting the search had been looking for links to whomever might have killed her. A jealous lover. An angry pimp. A violent client. They weren't listing personal items or effects.

There was no way around it, he had to tell Burrows.

Taking a deep breath, he picked up the note and walked across the squad room to the guvnor's office.

"Come," barked Burrows, in response to his knock. Why did he always have to sound so sanctimonious?

He entered.

"What is it, Trevelyan?"

He took a seat opposite him, ignoring his impatient expression.

"I've just received this, sir." He put the origami envelope on the desk. He'd folded it up again so the SIO could see the full effect.

Burrows stared at it.

"What is it?"

"An anonymous note, sir. It's in connection with the Bianca Rubik murder."

He picked it up and turned it over, studying it. "Seriously? Who dropped it off?"

"Some kid. The duty sergeant gave a vague description, but he'll be on the CCTV in the lobby."

The SIO grunted and opened the envelope. Trevelyan watched his eyes flicker across the page. Twice.

"She was a stripper?"

"A dancer, sir. I've confirmed it with the club. She wasn't a sex worker."

He frowned. "But the flatmate…"

"Rona Sheraton didn't actually confirm she was a sex worker. The detectives interviewing her made that assumption and she didn't correct them. I've just read her statement."

"Shit." He glanced up at him.

"Shall I go and see her? There might be more she neglected to tell us."

Burrows studied him, pursing his lips. "Hold off on that for now, constable. It might not be necessary."

"But sir..." He couldn't believe he wasn't going to follow it up.

"The case is as good as closed, Trevelyan. The old guy did it. His DNA was all over the victim and he was seen fleeing from the scene."

"I know, sir, but don't you think it's worth exploring? This guy, this Xhafa character, has ties to an Albanian gang. He doesn't have form, but he is on an NCA watchlist. Bianca may have been killed because of something he was into."

"Alleged ties. We don't know if we can trust whoever wrote that note."

He had a point.

"Still," he pushed, "we should at least bring him in for questioning. Based on this tip-off, we'd be neglecting our duty if we didn't question every possible suspect."

The SIO hesitated.

Trevelyan knew what he was thinking. Why open this can of worms when you don't have to? When there's a suspect in the bag? Another gold star next to his name?

"Okay," he said finally. "Let's bring Xhafa in for questioning, but if we don't get anything from him, I'm not going to waste anymore of the department's budget. The case will be closed."

"Fine." That's all he wanted. A chance to check him out. "I'll send Uniform to pick him up."

15

Shrap watched as two police cars roared up to the club entrance. Four uniformed officers hopped out, chests pumped, stern expressions on their faces. They were ready for battle.

She smiled.

Trevelyan had got her note.

"No, sir. Just you." The officer held a protesting Xhafa by the arm, as his bodyguard attempted to come with him.

Two other officers barred his way.

"Call my solicitor," Xhafa called, as he was shepherded into the waiting police car. "Get him to meet me at the station."

The burly Russian gave a quick nod and strode back inside.

He'd need one. Shrap was betting the strip club owner had a dark and shady past. At the very least, the police should find his connection with the Albanian gangsters.

She walked back to Southwark and took up a reconnaissance position in an alley opposite the police station. Xhafa had been there for almost an hour.

"Everything go okay?" she asked Luke, the kid who'd delivered the note for her and who she'd asked to keep an eye on the place.

"Yeah, Shrap. They brought him in, like you said. He's still there."

They fist-bumped, and she handed the kid a fiver. He gave a wide grin and disappeared among the backstreets. His mother worked at a homeless shelter, even though they were barely better off than she was. She tried to help the kid out when she could.

Shrap eased herself down on the pavement, wincing as her head throbbed and her ribs complained. She hoped the police were giving Xhafa a thorough going-over.

It certainly took long enough. Almost three hours later, when Shrap was stiff with cold, the Albanian was released. She could sense the fury emanating off him as he marched out of the police station accompanied by his solicitor, an athletic, middle-aged man in a sharp suit with a hungry gaze. A fighter. But in the courtroom.

He had his work cut out for him with Xhafa as a client.

The two men hailed a taxi and jumped in.

Shrap took the bus back to Covent Garden. Her head was killing her, and the thought of walking was too much. She needed to sleep.

The cab dropped her off outside the shelter where Luke's mum worked. She wasn't on duty, but a haggard woman whose life story was etched into the lines on her face admitted her and assigned her a bed. The woman's name was Cyndi, but everyone called her Cyn.

Xhafa would have to wait.

Shrap hadn't felt this rough since her military days. There were a few nights after an op where she'd crashed out in her bunk, unable to function a moment longer, her head pounding from the sound of rifle fire and exploding grenades.

This was one of those times.

She took two paracetamol that she'd got off the junior doctor and collapsed. It was early, so not many people were here yet. It would fill up later as the temperature dropped and the weather worsened.

Until then, she was dead to the world.

SHRAP WOKE to the sound of raised female voices. Two junkies were fighting over a bed.

"Fuck off, I got here first."

"This is my bed, you skank. You fuck off."

Shrap groaned and turned over, then gasped as a piercing pain shot through her side. Fucking broken rib. At least her head had stopped pounding.

She blocked out the escalating fight and squeezed her eyes shut. This was why she didn't use the shelter. This wasn't her problem. Cyn would send someone up to sort it out.

Then she heard the flick of a switchblade.

Shit.

She opened her eyes.

Sinewy body, long unwashed hair and glazed eyes. The woman swayed drunkenly, bolstered by crack-induced bravado, oblivious to the threat facing her. The other woman was slightly more sober and angry as a hornet. She grasped a knife in her hand, and shifted her weight from side to side, poised for attack. Her back was to Shrap.

Slowly, Shrap sat up. Neither woman acknowledged her. Still invisible.

Until she didn't want to be.

The first woman threw a slurred insult at the knife-wielder, who lurched forward. Shrap launched off the bed and grabbed her wrist.

"What the—?"

The woman spun around, but Shrap had bent her arm so far back it was about to snap. She screamed in agony.

"Drop the knife," Shrap hissed.

"You're breaking my fucking arm!"

"I said, drop it."

There was a dull clunk as the weapon hit the ground. The glazed eyes of the first woman fell on it, but before she could make a move, Shrap put her foot on it. She'd slept fully clothed with her boots on. Old habits. Never knew when you had to make a quick exit.

She released the would-be attacker, sending her sprawling forwards, and picked up the knife. Just then Cyn burst into the room followed by an overweight guy called Len, who despite appearances was as strong as an ox.

Shrap handed him the knife. "Belongs to this one."

The long-haired woman chose that moment to scuttle past the managers. She'd be finding alternative accommodation for the night.

Len took the remaining woman by her good arm and escorted her down the stairs.

Shrap climbed back onto the bed and closed her eyes. Cyn gave a nod of thanks and left the dorm. Around her, everyone got back to normal, like nothing had happened.

THE NEXT MORNING, she felt much better. It still hurt to take a deep breath and her arm was tender, but the inflammation had gone down, her head was clear and her vision was back to normal.

Thank God for that.

She resumed surveillance outside Whispers.

The day passed uneventfully. Xhafa came in around five, accompanied by big Mick. The club boss didn't seem any worse for wear after his stint in interrogation. The staff arrived. The dancers in their coats and trainers, faces clear of make-up. They could be going to any West End audition, rather than a strip club.

She saw Alex cross the road in his tight jeans and studded leather jacket. No cigarette this time. Peter the manager sauntered in, smartly dressed in a shirt and tie.

It was Friday. They had a busy night ahead.

Just before seven o'clock the bouncer appeared and laid down the red carpet and put up his gold rope. Music emanated from inside, a steady beat, faint but evocative. Shrap pictured the girls warming up on stage, perfecting their routines. It was nearly showtime.

She'd bought a sandwich and a Coke from a nearby off-licence, along with the obligatory two-litre bottle of cider. It was a Friday night, after all. She had to support the stereotype.

When she'd first started sleeping rough, she'd hoped to be ignored. Forgotten. She hadn't expected the insults, the kicks from passers-by, the hostile glances. She'd even been spat at once. That's when she'd learned to make herself scarce during the day and try to get some sleep at night, although she always kept half an eye open.

She was halfway through her supper when a VW Polo pulled up. An Asian woman and a tall, lanky man got out. She recognised the man. Trevelyan.

What was he doing here?

Off-duty recon on Xhafa?

The woman he'd brought with him seemed nervous, out

of place. First time at a strip club. She kept smoothing her miniskirt, like she was worried it was riding up, which it was. She screamed undercover cop. Xhafa would see right through them.

He looked the part, though, with his hair spikey with product. He wore denim jeans, a blue shirt and khaki jacket. Not too overdone, but enough to be believable. Pity his colleague had ruined it for him.

This was obviously her idea. If it had been his, he would have come alone. The bouncer gave them a dubious look, but let them in. Then he pulled out a two-way radio and spoke into it.

Busted.

They wouldn't pick up anything useful tonight. Xhafa would be on his best behaviour, if he even came out of his office.

This was not good news. It meant they had nothing. If Trevelyan had resorted to off-duty surveillance, he was desperate. It was a last-ditch attempt to get something on him, and it had failed before it had even got off the ground.

She shook her head and got up. There was no point in staying here now. Nothing was going to go down tonight. Swinging her backpack onto her back and cursing at the pain in her rib, she melted into the shadows.

16

S hrap stood on the south bank of the river and watched the sun rise behind the city skyline. Orange lasers shot between the concrete buildings, becoming more powerful by the second until they were blinding. The river turned gold. It was seven thirty or as close as damn it.

She'd been up for some time, waiting for this moment. It got later and later as the nights extended. She took a deep breath and felt the surge of anticipation that enveloped her when watching the dawn of a new day. The promise of a new beginning. Powerful in its simplicity. Just for the briefest moment, anything was possible.

A commuter hurried past, eyes downcast. Blind to the spectacle on the horizon. A bicycle whooshed by, bell ringing. *Coming through!*

Shrap stepped up to the railing. The molten water flowed by on its relentless journey. Surging upstream until the tides changed, and then it would stream back down again. A process on repeat.

She thought about Xhafa and his cronies, up to no good.

Trevelyan would have had a disappointing evening. The Albanian would have kept a low profile, warning his gangster friends to stay away. Nothing to see here.

She needed background information on the Albanian, something that would tell her what the club owner was up to.

Trevor.

The name conjured up a kaleidoscope of emotions. Affection, desire, but mostly guilt and regret.

Trevor had been her go-to guy for intelligence when she'd been in the military police. Quick, efficient, reliable, he'd been there for her. First in her ear, supporting her during ops, a calming voice in her head. Then in her life.

It had started with a friendly drink. Warm smiles, soft chestnut hair, a faint blush. "Would you like to come in for a night cap?"

They'd been inseparable after that. Shrap had spent every available moment between tours with him. Ecstatic hellos and tearful goodbyes.

Be careful. Look after yourself.

Then came Kabul.

She blinked. The orange glare had burned onto her retina. It replaced Trevor's face, wiped out his disappointment. "You need help, Shrap. It's nothing to be ashamed about."

But she was.

She hadn't been blown up by an IED. She hadn't lost a limb. She'd come home alive – unlike her colleagues. She was one of the lucky ones. What right did she have to feel like this?

She thought of Bianca Rubik lying in the gutter. Doug's charred body in the foetal position. The least she could do was find out who'd killed them.

And for that, she needed Trevor.

The mobile phone shop was run by a Pakistani called Ibrahim. According to people who knew, he didn't ask questions. Shrap hadn't needed a phone before, but she couldn't do what she had to without one. She bought a cheap, prepaid device and sim card, and strolled through Waterloo to the library to make the call.

"Hello?"

"Trevor, it's Shrap."

Silence. Nearly two years' worth of silence.

"Shrap. Good God. H-How are you?"

"I'm okay. Listen, I know it's been a while, but…"

"A while…?" A coarse laugh. "You could say that."

"Can we talk?"

Another pause.

"I'm not sure I want to. You made it pretty clear when you left that there was nothing left to say."

His words sliced through her. Guilt made her stomach clench.

"I know. I'm sorry. I was in a bad place. I couldn't… I didn't…" What could she say? Nothing excused what she'd done, how she'd left. "Please can we get together and talk? I need to see you. I want to… explain."

"There's no need. I've moved on. I'm married, Shrap."

She bent over, as if someone had punched her in the gut.

Trevor. *Her* Trevor. Married?

"Are you still there?"

"I'm here." A gasp, a croak. Her hand clutched the phone.

She inhaled, the cold air encasing her heart with icicles. It was only fair. Right, even. He deserved to be happy. Not crying over a loser like her. Not waking up to her nightmares, to her terror.

"I'd still like to see you, if at all possible. I don't want to leave things... as they are."

She couldn't. Not if she was going to ask for his help. He deserved an explanation. She should have done it before now, but she hadn't known what to say. She still didn't.

How could she explain... this? Would he even understand?

God, she missed him, but she was too late. A year ago, she might have had a chance, a shot at saving her relationship. Now he was with someone else. Happy. His memories of her fading like old photographs.

She couldn't go back now. Even if he had been willing. She was too damaged, too sullied. There was no place in society for her. It was better she remained in the shadows.

A sigh. She pictured him grinding his jaw, like he used to when he was thinking. "Okay, Shrap. One meeting but that's it. I don't want to drag this out."

One meeting to convince him to help her.

One meeting to put a lid on what they had. To shut it up and lock it away. Permanently.

"Thank you. Can you meet me tomorrow?"

Sunday.

"Where?"

"Borough Market?"

"Jeez, Shrap. That's a bit of a trek from Hemel Hempstead."

"I know. I'm sorry." All she seemed to be doing was apologising. "I'm living in London now."

"Don't you have transport?"

"No."

He hesitated. "I'll see you tomorrow at twelve. Will that work?"

"Perfect. Thanks Trevor."

"Goodbye, Shrap."

SHRAP WATCHED as he walked into the clearing. Familiar, yet different. Beige cargo trousers, a white shirt, black jacket unzipped.

Her mouth was dry, and she was more nervous than she'd been on their first date. What would he think of her now? She raked a hand through her short hair, conscious of how different it was to what he knew. To the woman he knew. Not out of place, though, around here. She'd bought yet another pair of jeans and wore a fresh T-shirt for the occasion. Same store as before. Discount prices. The skinny jeans were covered in blood and dirt and God only knew what else.

The phone in her pocket buzzed.

I'm here. Where are you?

She stepped out from behind a stall, the aroma of deep-fried falafels making her nauseous. There were people everywhere. Shoppers, tourists, wanderers, locals. Noise, conversations, braying laughs. It came at her from all directions.

She hurried over to Trevor.

"Hi."

He turned, his gaze resting on her face. "Shrap."

Suddenly the last few years disappeared. They were back in their kitchen, him pleading with her to get help, saying how much she meant to him.

She forced a smile. "Thanks for meeting me."

A nod. It wasn't a pleasure, but a task. It had to be done. To get this over with.

"Do you want to take a walk?" She needed to get away from the crowd.

"Sure."

She led him towards the bridge, under it and along the river. Suddenly, she could breathe again. The music and chatter faded behind them.

"Look, I'm sorry the way things ended," she began. "I wish it had been different."

That look. Regret mixed with pity.

"You could have said something."

"I know."

"You just left. You went out and didn't come back. I didn't know what had happened to you. I almost called the police."

"I left a note."

A snort. "Barely. One line saying you were sorry. What was I supposed to make of that? I thought you'd gone off to commit suicide."

She had.

It was Doug who'd saved her.

"It was only when I checked your bank statements and saw you were still withdrawing cash that I knew you were alive."

She hid a smile. "You ran a check on me?"

"Of course."

That was his job, after all. Soldiers, those missing in action, those gone AWOL, criminals, suspicious deaths, sometimes even the enemy. He ran them through the various systems and databases, building a profile, tracking movements, evaluating threats.

She ought to have expected it.

"Then you knew I was okay."

"No." He turned on her. "All I knew was you were alive and drawing a pension. I had no idea where you were or in what state." His eyes raked her over. "Or how close you were to the edge."

Too close.

"What happened to you?"

"I couldn't stand it anymore, trying to be normal. Trying to fit in and pretend like nothing was wrong. I kept seeing..." She shook her head. "It was too much. I had to leave, to get out and be by myself for a while. I thought if I was alone, I could make some sense of it."

"And did you?"

"No." Nothing made sense. She doubted it ever would.

"I'm sorry about what happened to Sam, to the others, but it wasn't your fault."

"I couldn't save them," she muttered.

"No." He reached out and touched her arm. "You couldn't. Those were bad men who blew up the convoy, who took you captive. Nothing you could have done would have prevented that. Why can't you see that?"

His touch was light, caring. The first touch she'd had in two years that wasn't violent. It felt strange, butterfly-like.

Heart-breaking.

"I know." Her rational mind knew, but she still couldn't stop the fear and panic every time she thought about it. The desperation. The need to help, to do something, yet not being able to. Of having a rifle pointed at her head, an eager finger on the trigger. Seconds to live.

On your knees! Don't do anything stupid.

"Anyway, I just wanted to say I'm sorry. I know I let you down, let us down."

The jaw popped, just briefly. Then it was gone again. "How are you now?"

"Better than I was," she said, after a beat. That much was true, at least.

"Good." He hesitated, unsure what else to say.

"Trevor, I need your help."

He stopped walking. "It's a bit late for that."

"Not that kind of help. Professional help."

He frowned. "I don't understand."

"I need you to look someone up for me."

He froze. The wind blew his hair back off his face, exposing his forehead. More lines than she remembered. That was probably her fault. A gull cried out overhead. "Is that why you asked to meet me? Because you need my help?"

"No."

Yes.

"I wanted to talk to you. To apologise. I should have contacted you sooner, but I didn't feel able to. Now..." She gave a little shrug.

"Now you need something, and you thought it would be a good time to apologise?" He turned away, neck tense. He could never hide his feelings. Not like her. "Jesus, Shrap."

"It's not like that."

"Really?" He took another look into her soul and knew. "It's exactly like that."

She hesitated. The wind was picking up, stronger now. A Coke can rattled down the path, jarring. "Can we sit down? I want to tell you something."

He glanced up and down the path like he wanted to stride off, then his shoulders slumped. "Okay, five minutes then I've got to go."

Five minutes to persuade him to help her.

They took a seat on a worn bench facing the river. Shrap gathered her thoughts. She wasn't good at sharing, never had been.

"When I left you, I was in a bad way. I'd been having

suicidal thoughts for weeks. I wanted to put an end to it, to stop the terror, to stop the images playing in a loop in my head."

He stared at her. "Why didn't you say something?"

She held up a hand and he fell silent.

"So, there I was standing on the platform at Hammersmith station, watching the trains whiz by and I thought, it would be so easy. One step and it would all be over. No more nightmares. No more hell."

His gaze hardened.

"I was about to do it, Trevor. I took a few steps forward. I'd planned it perfectly. The next train wasn't stopping at the station. It was a fast one. A split second of shock, not enough to even register pain, and then nothing. Game over."

She could feel the tears on her face, tugged at by the wind.

"The train was approaching. I felt the gust of wind that precedes it and took another step forward. I was about to jump off the platform when an arm reached out and grabbed me. A voice said, 'You don't want to do that, lass.'"

His eyes widened.

"This old guy, or at least I thought he was old, stopped me from killing myself. I was shaking, so he made me sit down while he gave me a talking to. Not fair on the train driver, he said." Shrap managed a weak smile. "Which is very true, if you think about it. They have to live with the trauma for the rest of their lives. It's not something you'd ever forget, is it? Running over a person. Then there's the mess, the paramedics, the clean-up crew, the inconvenience to passengers..." She faded out.

Trevor stared at her as if he didn't know who she was anymore.

"We went to a pub and got a drink. Turns out he'd been

in the military too, knew what I was going through. We talked. That night I slept on the street for the first time."

"You slept rough?"

Disbelief, shock. No one he knew slept rough. It was what other people did, vagrants and drug addicts. Something to look down on.

She nodded. She didn't say she'd never stopped. He didn't need to know that.

"Doug was my friend. He saved my life. And now he's dead."

Trevor gaped at her. "He's dead? The guy who saved you?"

"Yeah."

"What happened?"

"He was murdered. He witnessed a crime and was burned to death on the street, like he was nothing."

"I'm so sorry, Shrap." Trevor hesitated. "But what's this got to do with me?"

"I think I know who killed him, but I don't know why. I need you to do a search into this guy's background. I want to know what he's into, who his known associates are, the usual."

He shook her head. "Shouldn't you go to the police?"

"They're not interested. They've got it down as a tragic accident. An old drunk who dropped a fag and set himself alight."

He hesitated. "How do you know that isn't what happened?"

"He didn't smoke."

"Oh."

"Yeah. It was murder, and I want to get the guy who did this."

"What are you going to do when you find him?" he

asked, practical as ever. "You can't arrest him, you aren't that person anymore, Shrap. You have no jurisdiction here."

No, she definitely wasn't that person anymore. She was worse. She could do things she wasn't allowed to in the military police. There was a certain freedom in that.

"I wasn't planning on arresting him."

He studied her, his lips pressed together. Lips she used to kiss, but never would again. Someone else had that honour now.

"You won't do anything stupid, will you? I'm not going to help if you are."

"Of course not," she lied. "I'll build a case against him and take it to the cops. They can arrest him."

His sigh of relief was lost in the wind. He glanced down at his hands, then his wristwatch. Time was ticking on. He had somewhere to be.

"Okay, Shrap. I'll help you, but only this once, and only because this man saved your life. I owe him that much."

He owed him? Did that mean he still cared?

She touched his hand. "Thank you."

He stood up, letting her hand fall. "Text me his details, and I'll get on it as soon as I get to work tomorrow."

They gazed at each other and for a wild moment the urge to step forward into his arms was strong, but she couldn't do it. Not to him. She had to let him go. For good.

"Goodbye, Trevor," she said.

"Goodbye, Shrap."

She watched him walk away, his head down against the wind.

17

Gareth Trevelyan sat in a coffee shop on The Cut and cradled an Americano. The other night had been a complete waste of time. He hadn't even seen Xhafa, despite having stuck it out for over three hours.

It was a classy place and the dancers were good, no doubt about it. Too good for that joint. But then, it probably paid more than anywhere else. More than what he was earning, at any rate.

That made him snort.

He took a sip of his coffee and grimaced as it burned his tongue. As the caffeine was absorbed into his bloodstream, he began to feel more alert. Poor Devi. It had been her idea to stake out the strip club, but she'd been like a fish out of water. In retrospect, he'd have been better off going alone, but that would have sounded sleezy, so he'd agreed.

He sighed. Xhafa was a write-off. He may well be dodgy, but whether he was involved in Bianca Rubik's death, he had no idea. Burrows had been firm. Evidence doesn't lie. The case was now closed. High fives all round.

Outside, the sky dimmed as a cloud passed overhead. It

looked like it was going to rain again. He ought to be at home, fixing the boiler that was on the blink again, or having a lazy lie-in. Not here, looking for *her*.

The homeless veteran who'd known so much about Doug. She'd given her name as Shrap. Not her real name, and no surname. Impossible to trace. But that's what she'd intended.

She might look like a junkie, but it was her eyes that gave her away. Clear, piercingly blue, filled with a knowing glint he'd seen in senior detectives. A self-awareness that said she knew what she was talking about. Older than most young female runaways, but not rough-looking like she'd spent years on the street. The short hair was disconcerting, but he was betting she was mid-thirties, possibly younger. In the army, though, that could be a lifetime. He'd had an uncle who'd served, he knew the damage it could cause.

Was that what had happened to her? Was that why she was on the street?

The day centre had opened at nine, so that's where he'd started, except she hadn't been there. The guy in charge, Budge, hadn't seen her, and judging by the look he'd received when he'd asked, wouldn't tell him even if he had.

Now what? Cruise the streets looking for homeless women? Asking if anyone knew a Shrap? Not the most effective way of doing things, but it was a start. Part of him didn't even know why he was bothering. The case was closed. Except something didn't sit right, and he couldn't let it go. He'd promised himself a long time ago that he'd never be the kind of cop who took the easy way out. Closure rates, budgets and bonuses didn't matter to him. The truth did.

He glanced down at his jeans and fleece. Did he look normal enough or would they see through his attempt? Vagrants, criminals, those just this side of the law, they had a sixth sense about these things. He'd never quite managed to figure out how they knew, but they always did.

Shrap had said Doug used to hang out at the Leake Street tunnel, so perhaps that was a good place to try. He finished his coffee and shrugged on his hooded puffer jacket. The streets were strangely quiet, it being a Sunday, but the few people who were about walked with purpose, eager to get to their destination before it rained again.

He glanced up. Dark, flat-bottomed clouds drawing ever nearer. He had half an hour, if that. Hurrying, he made his way to the tunnel. It was empty. He looked on Google Maps and checked out the other underpasses in the area. Here he found a couple of homeless men.

"Do you know a woman called Shrap?"

Always the same answer. Suspicious eyes and a terse shake of the head.

How did they bloody know? Who's to say he didn't have good news for her? An inheritance. Free accommodation. News from her family, if she had one.

He walked back towards Waterloo station. A couple in sleeping bags sheltered under the arch.

Same question. Same answer.

This was a bloody waste of time. Nobody was going to help him.

It was a miracle Sergeant Baxter had found her in the first place, but then the guy at the day centre had told her where she was. He wasn't making that mistake again.

The Embankment.

He walked down to the river, past the London Eye and along the South Bank towards St Thomas's hospital. There were lots of people out, despite the weather. All wrapped up warm, taking pictures of the Thames, holding hands, sipping take-away coffees. No one was rushing here.

He was almost at Westminster Bridge when a big rain-drop hit his face. *Uh-oh.* He upped his pace, but before he got to the bridge, the heavens opened. Frantic, horizontal daggers pierced his skin.

Bugger.

He pulled his hood up and sprinted the last fifty metres. Panting, he looked around for somewhere to shelter when he saw an elderly man sitting on a bench, sketching. His dishevelled state led him to believe he was also homeless. Clearly talented, he had an artistic flick of the wrist and a roving eye that took in the rushing water under the bridge around the huge, concrete support columns.

Gareth walked over to him. "Mind if I sit?"

He grunted. "Suit yourself."

That was a first.

He sat down and took a peek at his sketch. To his surprise, he was drawing on a napkin with charcoal.

"That's very good," he remarked. And it was. Beyond the strong lines and lighter shading, he'd grasped the power of the Thames as it rushed by, and the energy surrounding the darker pillars holding up the bridge.

"Thank you."

"You should sell them."

The old guy chuckled. "Napkins don't sell, especially used ones."

He smiled. "Is that one used?"

The man shook his head. "Got this with me coffee this morning."

"Then I'll buy it."

He gawked at him.

Gareth took a ten pound note out of his pocket. "Here, how's this? I'm sure it'll be worth more one day."

With a shrug, the old guy handed over the sketch and pocketed the tenner.

"Will you sign it?"

Another chuckle. He took it back and scrawled his name in the bottom right corner.

"Dicky Lambert," he read.

"That's me."

"Thanks." He folded it carefully and put it into his jacket pocket. "Maybe you can use that to buy a sketch pad."

"Maybe." Another shrug.

He probably wouldn't. There were more important things to spend ten quid on when you were homeless. Like a hot meal, a night in a hostel, a new jumper or pair of shoes. Suddenly, he felt stupid.

He cleared her throat. "I wonder if you can help me, Dicky?"

The old guy rose a bushy eyebrow. "What you after?"

"A woman. Her name is Shrap."

The eyes narrowed. "What you want with her?"

His pulse quickened. "You know her?"

"Maybe. Who's asking?"

"My name's D—" He paused. "My name's Gareth. She helped me with something yesterday and I wanted to let her know the outcome."

"You police?"

"Yes, but I'm not going to arrest her or anything. I just want to tell her something. I think she'll want to know."

"Is it about Doug?"

"You know Doug?"

The old man gave a half nod and gazed out into the rain. "So sad, what happened. No way he set himself alight, you know. Geezer didn't smoke. Hadn't done for twenty odd years."

Gareth stared at him. "He didn't?"

"No, sir. Not since he passed out drunk with a fag in his hand and burned his house down. His missus died in the fire."

Bloody hell.

"For real?" He shook his head. "I had no idea."

"Not many people do. He liked to keep it to himself, did old Doug. I'm only telling you this so you know he didn't set himself on fire."

That ruled out an accident, then.

"What about suicide? Was he the type to pour whiskey all over himself and set himself alight on purpose?"

The old man scrunched up his face. "What? Is that what they're saying?"

Gareth gave a noncommittal shrug.

He snorted. "No way. Doug wouldn't do that. He wasn't the type."

"Did you know him well?"

"He was a friend."

"Seems like Doug had a few friends," he remarked.

"Yeah, he was a decent guy. He'll be missed."

Gareth fell silent. The rain was softening, the deluge turning into a steady drizzle. Still too wet to venture out. Sadness gripped him. "I'm sorry for your loss," he said.

The old guy nodded.

They sat in silence for a while, until the sun peeked out cautiously from behind a cloud. The river turned from slate grey to dusky blue and the world seemed brighter again.

"Well, thanks for talking to me." He patted his jacket pocket. "And for the sketch."

Another nod.

As he turned to go, the old guy said, "If you're looking

for Shrap, she's always down here for the sunrise. Never misses it."

"The sunrise?"

He shrugged. "Don't ask me. Too bloody early for my liking. But she's regular like clockwork. Something to do with getting up early in the forces. Can't shake the habit."

He smiled his thanks. "See you, Dicky."

He gave a toothless grin and held up a charcoal-smudged hand.

18

I t was Budge who first told her that DC Trevelyan had been looking for her.

"He came in yesterday, just after we opened. Told him I hadn't seen ya."

"Thanks, Budge."

"Not in any trouble, are ya?"

"No, it's about Doug."

His face crumpled. "Poor, sorry sod. Still, he survived longer than most."

Shrap got herself a slice of toast and a cup of tea and went to sit at the back, where she was least likely to be disturbed.

Budge had placed a copy of *The Times* on the table for her. The others went for *The Sun* or *The Mirror*, but she read *The Times*. It had nothing to do with anything other than habit. In the military, it was the only newspaper they could get, and she'd got used to it. Now it reminded her of the life she used to have, a thin strand of normality.

She looked for news on Doug or the murdered dancer.

Nothing. Their deaths were no longer newsworthy. It was as if they'd never existed.

She was halfway through Jeremy Clarkson's column when Dicky sauntered over. "Just the woman I wanted to see." He paused next to the table. "Met a nice copper yesterday who was asking about you."

Shrap glanced up. "Let me guess. About six four, auburn hair, big hazel eyes?"

Dicky grinned. "That's the one."

"Did he say what he wanted?"

"Something about Doug," he said. "Didn't say what."

Shrap gave a nod. "Thanks, mate."

"He bought one of me sketches."

Shrap arched an eyebrow.

"Ten quid. Thought I might buy meself some decent paper and try to sell a few. Might make a few bob."

"Worth a shot." Shrap smiled. "You're good enough."

He chuckled. "That's what he said."

He tottered over to the table to get himself some breakfast while Shrap went back to her article. Except she couldn't concentrate.

Trevelyan must have realised she'd sent the note. Now he wanted to know what she knew about Xhafa.

The truth was dismally little until Trevor got back to her. If he ever did. She'd given him her prepaid mobile number, which meant she had to keep the damn thing charged.

Pulling it out of her inside jacket pocket, she went over to Budge. "Mind if I charge this for a couple of hours? I'll come back and get it before noon."

He looked surprised. "You got yourself a phone now?"

"Temporarily. I'm expecting an important call."

"Alright, mate. Just don't forget to pick it up, else you'll have to wait till tomorrow."

"Thanks, you're a star."

He beamed at her. "For you, anything."

AFTER SHE'D FINISHED READING the paper, she washed, brushed her teeth and ventured out into the cold. It was a crisp, fresh day with a blue, cloudless sky punctuated only by the city high-rises and the odd gull circling overhead. The temperature this morning must have been in single digits. She'd woken up shivering. It was late October, so it was only going to get worse.

Still, it made for a beautiful sunrise.

She walked towards the railway station, deep in thought. Trevelyan obviously wanted something from her. He wouldn't have come to tell her of any developments in the case. The exchange of information didn't work both ways. She knew that first-hand.

But why was he interested? From what she could gather, the case was closed.

Doug murdered the girl, then killed himself. A drunkard with a history of poor mental health. Must be, since he was living on the streets.

The fact that he'd come looking intrigued her. Perhaps it was time she found out a bit more about the intrepid detective constable.

Shrap glanced up. Not realising it, she'd walked around the station to the car park where Doug had died. She hesitated. She hadn't been back here since that day.

It was in use, the police tape gone. Cars coming and going, the boom at the exit rising and falling. Shrap entered through the pedestrian gate. Since she was here, she may as well take another look.

She walked towards the railway line where Doug's body

had been found. Her breath quickened and she fought the rising nausea. It was still so vivid. She thought she could still smell burning in the frosty air, but that was impossible. It was her mind playing tricks. It did that a lot.

She stared at the patch of scarred ground where her friend had taken his last breath. Had he been awake when they'd come for him? Hopefully, he'd been out cold, oblivious to the horror that was about to befall him. Dulled to the pain.

She gagged and sucked cold air between her lips and down into her chest.

The police had been all over this spot, there was nothing to find. Except they hadn't treated it as a homicide. An unexplained death, maybe, but not murder. A murder detective thought very differently to one seeking merely to understand what was in front of him.

She walked around the scarred tarmac, first in a small circle, then expanding her circumference, her eyes glued to the ground. It was four metres out, next to the fence, that she found the cigarette butt.

Could be anyone's.

Could be the killer's.

Was this where the perpetrator had stood as he watched Doug burn?

Shrap picked it up, groaning at the pain in her side. Took a sniff.

Parliament.

She could just make out the logo and part of the word *ARLIAM* on the filter.

She placed the butt in her pocket. Pity she couldn't get it tested for DNA. But just by picking it up and pocketing it, she'd compromised any potential evidence. She wasn't a police officer anymore. She'd have to do without forensic analysis.

Luckily, she'd always been able to trust her gut. And right now, it was leading her back to Xhafa's club and its Albanian connections.

SHRAP PULLED her collar up and sank into the doorway opposite the strip club. Monday was a quiet night, not many punters out looking for a thrill. She didn't see any groups, only a few downtrodden single men.

Earlier, she'd seen the boss arrive, driven by his bodyguard, Big Mike. The silver merc was parked around the corner under a streetlight and in front of the fake CCTV sign.

At nine o'clock on the dot, a black SUV drove up and four men got out. Two in their forties, stocky and definitely packing. Bodyguards. The older two were in their midfifties, well-dressed and respectful to each other. The two younger men stood back and let the older men go first.

The bouncer gave a dutiful bow and released the golden rope. Important men. Business, not pleasure. She listened for accents, but their voices were swallowed by the beat from the club.

Five minutes later, there was a deep growl as the metallic-blue BMW sped up the street. It pulled over metres away. Neither occupant looked in Shrap's direction. She'd become part of the doorway.

She recognised Maroon Cap and Grey Beanie, still sporting a fat lip. Good. She hoped it hurt. Even though her arm was healing, her ribs ached every time she took a deep breath.

They performed their secret handshake with the

bouncer, who laughed at something one of them said, then let them enter. Tonight, they were dressed to impress. Black jeans, silk shirts and lots of bling. These guys weren't concerned with keeping a low profile.

No designated driver. They weren't getting drunk tonight.

Definitely business.

What Shrap wouldn't give to be a fly on the wall. She thought about Alex, serving behind the bar. He might know something, but she couldn't confront him like this. Not as the real her.

The two Albanians had left the hood of the convertible down. No need to worry, not with the bouncer directly across the road. But what if he were distracted?

Shrap slid out from her hiding place and snuck off down the road. It wasn't long before she came to a young woman in a short skirt and boob tube, despite the cold, standing on a street corner. Hollow eyes, fake blonde hair and a bony hip jutting out.

"Hi." She held up a fiver. "I need a favour."

The prostitute eyed her out. "That's not going to get you far."

"Not that kind of favour."

"What, then?"

Shrap explained what she wanted her to do and handed over the money. The young woman gave a lopsided grin and pocketed the cash.

Shrap went back to the doorway.

A short time later, she heard a piercing scream coming from around the corner. The bouncer's head shot up, then he darted into the side street to see what the trouble was.

Shrap leaped towards the car. She leaned over and looked inside, activating the perimeter sensor. The alarm was deafening. Heart pounding, she scanned the back seat. Nothing. She tried the glove compartment.

The girl had stopped screaming. The bouncer would hear the alarm and come running. She had seconds, if that.

She scrounged around, rifling through the items inside. A service logbook, receipts for the vehicle and accessories. Cash purchase. Warning sign number one. She spotted an elastic neoprene item at the back and pulled it out. An ankle holster for a gun, probably a Glock, with room for one magazine. Warning sign number two.

Was everybody here carrying a concealed weapon?

Warning sign number three came in the form of a discarded cigarette packet. She turned it over and her heart sank.

Stuyvesant.

BY THE TIME the bouncer returned, Shrap was nowhere near the car. She watched as he pulled out his phone and made a call. A few moments later, Grey Beanie appeared. He strode across the street to the BMW and disabled the alarm.

"Did you see anyone?" he asked the bouncer, who shrugged and shook his head. He wasn't about to say he'd been around the corner at the time.

The Albanian peered inside, pressed a button and the hood began to inch closed. Patting the bouncer on the back, he went back inside. False alarm.

Shrap let out an uneasy breath. She was shaking from the sudden burst of adrenalin and the siren was still ringing in her ears. She took a walk around the block to calm down, lifting her face to the cold air.

Maroon Cap or Grey Beanie could still have murdered Bianca.

The cigarette butt was only circumstantial. It could be used to back up a prosecution's case, but it wasn't real evidence. Any number of people could have left that discarded filter lying in the car park. It could have been flicked out of a car, or by a commuter fitting in a quick smoke before driving home.

She turned her attention back to the strip club. The Albanians were clearly using it to do business. Was Xhafa part of their gang, or was he just a willing participant? Perhaps it was in his best interests to accommodate them. The Albanian gangs' penchant for violence was well known.

What about the newcomers? The suits? Where did they fit in?

Shrap had done a lap of the block and was now walking back up towards the street in which the staff entrance was located. And the newcomer's SUV.

She peered through the windows, leaning close to see through the tint. It was neat and tidy. A hire car, perhaps. Walking around to the front, she saw a Hertz rental sign hanging from the rear-view mirror. A folded-up newspaper lay on the back seat. Shrap squinted as she read the headline.

Elezioni sindaco di Napoli.

Italian.

Were they connected to the two Albanians? They must be, otherwise why were they all here at the same time? Shrap was willing to bet the whole damn thing was related.

The most likely activity was drugs. The Albanians were getting quite a name for it. She began to put together a working theory. What role did the Italians play? Could they be suppliers? Older, more established? Or were they a new market for drugs going abroad?

Shrap didn't go back to the doorway opposite the club,

not with the BMW being so close by. The bouncer would get suspicious. Instead, she made her way back to Waterloo, enjoying the silence that curled over the city once she'd reached the Embankment.

The Thames glittered darkly beneath her as she walked over Hungerford Bridge. In the distance, the lights of the city flickered like fireflies. She made her way towards the station, then bypassed it and walked up The Cut. She considered going to her usual haunt behind the Marriott, but then decided against it.

She was closer to Doug's sleeping spot, the place where he'd witnessed the murder that had got him killed.

"Alright, love," came a throaty voice behind her.

She turned and saw Fishnets lounging against a wall, smoking.

"Yeah, you?"

She shrugged. "Bloody cold tonight."

In that outfit, it would be. "Yep. Look after yourself."

"Always do."

She turned into the side street. Five minutes later she was bedding down on the basement porch of the abandoned apartment. No one could see her from the street. For a homeless person, this was as safe as it got.

She picked up the newspaper, glanced at the headlines, then folded it up and put it to one side. *I'll get whoever did this to you, Doug*, she thought as she drifted off to sleep. *They won't get away with it.*

19

Shrap felt the inside pocket of her jacket vibrate and for a moment, couldn't work out what it was. Then she realised: the phone! It had been so long since she'd had one, and even longer since she'd received a call, that the sensation was completely foreign to her.

Fumbling, she answered it. "Trevor?"

Nobody else had this number.

"Hello, Shrap."

"Thanks for calling me back. I wasn't sure if you would." When he hadn't called yesterday, she'd assumed the worst.

"Neither was I, to be honest. Then I thought about what that man did for you, how he saved your life, and I couldn't refuse. He doesn't deserve to die like that."

"No, he doesn't."

"I did a full background check on Fiz Xhafa, real name Fisnik." A slight pause. "I think your friend got mixed up with some bad men."

"What did you find out?"

"You want me to email you the intel?"

"Yes, but give me a brief rundown."

"Okay. Xhafa is a Kosovan Albanian who arrived in this country as a teenager in early 2000s during the refugee crisis. He entered with his father, Albert, a hardened war veteran."

The Kosovo War.

Shrap exhaled. Xhafa would be no stranger to violence.

"Albert Xhafa started his career as a bouncer in Soho, which at that stage was the heart of the capital's sex industry. He quickly became a major player in the London vice scene and appeared on a number of law enforcement watch lists, including the National Crime Agency."

Shrap had read about this. "The Albanians took over the prostitution rackets."

"That's right."

It was crazy how easily they slipped back into their previous roles. Her in the field, him in her ear, feeding her intel vital to the investigation. It almost felt like they'd backtracked two years, to before her breakdown. Almost.

"They quickly got a reputation for being extremely violent – to the women, as well as anyone who got in their way."

She'd heard reports of unnecessary brutality dished out by the Albanian gangs. Women beaten for no apparent reason, in places where it wouldn't be immediately noticeable. The legs – that could be covered by stockings – the torso, the back.

Trevor continued. "Then, in 2004 Albert Xhafa was jailed for sex trafficking for twenty-three years. He served fifteen. According to the NCA, he left the country almost immediately and is now living on the Greek island of Corfu."

"No doubt funded by his son."

"Except, that was just the beginning," Trevor continued, getting into his stride. "The Albanian crime syndicate that had developed as a result of the sex trafficking moved into the drug trade. They began negotiating directly with the Colombian cartels and huge shipments of cocaine were arranged from South America. This allowed them to cut out the wholesalers, thereby reducing the price on the street."

"They sold a purer product for half the price," summed up Shrap.

"Exactly. The drug is now at its cheapest since the 1990s."

"Christ." She thought of the damage that was doing to the kids out there who could now afford a previously unobtainable narcotic.

"How do they bring it in?" she asked.

"They have control over Europe's ports," Trevor said. She heard clicking as he brought up a new screen. She pictured him sitting in his office at Military Intelligence, earphones on, talking to her like he had a thousand times before when she'd been in the field.

"There is evidence that the Albanian crime syndicate is collaborating with one of the most powerful Italian mafias, the 'Ndrangheta, who control mainland Europe's cocaine trade."

Italian mafia.

Shrap thought back to the two middle-aged men who'd arrived at the strip club last night along with their security detail. They were Italian. The sharp suits, the Mediterranean look, the hire car with the Naples newspaper on the back seat.

"Does that mean Xhafa is their link to the Albanian crime syndicate?" She thought out loud.

"Could be. Xhafa is a known associate of the syndicate,

although he's never been flagged as being part of it. He could be a facilitator, or he could be one of the top players, nobody seems to know."

"Either way, he's involved somehow."

His voice softened. "Whatever they're up to, it's not good. Be careful, Shrap. These guys don't mess around."

"I know."

Bianca Rubik hadn't stood a chance; neither had Doug.

"Right, well, I'll send through the rest of the file. It's got known associates and some background information on the syndicate, the Italian mafia and the Colombian cartels. Which email address do you want me to use?"

She hesitated. Could she even remember her password? She'd have to.

"My personal email. You still have it?"

"I'm sending it now."

"Thanks Trevor. I really mean it."

"I won't say it's been a pleasure, but I am glad we talked. You take care, Shrap."

"You too, and good luck with everything."

He hesitated.

"Goodbye, Shrap."

His voice had a note of finality in it. This was it. The end.

"Goodbye."

NEXT STOP, the library.

Shrap greeted the receptionist and took a seat at one of the computers. She logged onto her email provider and entered her details. To her relief, the password worked, and she was in.

A year of unanswered emails glared back at her. She

ignored them and clicked on the most recent one, from Trevor.

She read through what they'd discussed on the phone, only in more detail. Small groups affiliated to the Albanian-led syndicate scattered around the country imported and distributed the drug. They adhered to the traditional codes of *besa* – to keep promises – and *kanun* – the ancient blood feud laws. No one messed with them and they always delivered.

There was a special report on a London-based gang who'd produced a flashy recruitment video that they'd posted on Instagram showing off their fast cars, piles of cash and automatic weapons. Christ, was that even allowed?

The UK now had the highest number of young users in Europe, and more and more shipments were coming in thanks to the bumper cocaine production in South America.

Shrap exhaled. That was bad.

Rival gangs initially struggled to compete, until they began buying from the syndicate.

The document went on to list the syndicate's close-knit relationship with the Italian mafia, and the various ports in Europe where the drugs arrived via the direct "Colombian Express" route before crossing the Channel into the UK.

Shrap got to the end of the document and leaned back in her chair. If Xhafa was involved in the syndicate, perhaps Bianca had overheard or discovered something she wasn't supposed to. Studying law, she may have decided she couldn't keep quiet about their drug trafficking any longer. Maybe she'd felt compelled to go to the authorities.

They'd had an argument. She'd walked out, determined to do the right thing. Xhafa had sent his henchman after her, or those two thugs, Maroon Cap and Grey Beanie, who she now believed were violent low-level drug dealers.

A surge of adrenalin shot through her. She felt alive for the first time in years. She was getting closer to the truth, she knew it. Every instinct was telling her so.

The key was Bianca. If she could find out who killed her, she'd know who killed Doug.

20

"**A**lex?"

Shrap stood on the pavement and watched him turn, the studs on his jacket catching the light. He had dark rings under his eyes. The late nights were taking their toll.

Smoke curled between his fingers. One last puff before his shift began.

"Shaz!" He broke into a smile.

She wondered if he'd be smiling if he'd seen her an hour ago. She'd showered and applied a smattering of make-up again this morning, mumbling something about a job interview to Budge, who'd nodded approvingly. The new clothes were still in her locker, so she'd changed and run a comb through her hair, disguising the fact she'd slept on somebody's front porch.

Rather than the heels, she wore her army boots, but he didn't seem to notice that.

"How are you?"

He shrugged. "Okay. It'll be a quiet one tonight. The club doesn't get busy until midweek. What's up? You get the job?"

He wore a rainbow scarf around his neck to ward off the cold. His true colours.

"I turned it down. Don't think it's really my thing."

A disappointed frown. "That's a shame."

"Anyway, I was wondering if you could think back to the last time you saw Bianca."

His face clouded over. "Why?"

"I think someone might have followed her from the club."

Alex frowned, the cigarette slowly burning down. "You still trying to find out what happened?"

She nodded.

He sighed. "She left early, I remember that. Don't know why. She suddenly said she had to go and took off. Gave some flimsy excuse about not feeling well."

"Did she look sick?"

"No, the picture of health. Five minutes before that she'd given a private dance, and half an hour before that she'd been on stage performing. She didn't look ill to me."

"What made her leave?"

"I don't know. I suspected she'd had a row with Fiz, but I can't be sure. Sometimes they went at each other."

Shrap was surprised. "How did Fiz feel about that?"

He took a drag, then exhaled, eyes narrowed against the smoke. "He had a soft spot for Bianca. She was never disrespectful, but she did like a good argument. He humoured her."

Sounds like she would have made a great solicitor.

"He was never aggressive?"

He shook his head. "Nope. Fiz never touches the girls. If anything, he treats them like a business commodity, like you would racehorses or proper dancers, you know? They appreciate that. He's strict, don't get me wrong. If you're not here on time, you'd better have a jolly good excuse else you're out, but he's not violent."

Shrap arched an eyebrow. The Albanian gangsters didn't have the best reputation when it came to violence against women. She suspected Xhafa's two younger drug-dealing friends didn't share the same work ethic.

"He's smart, your boss."

He shrugged again. "I guess so. He does well out of it. Got a big house in Shoreditch. Drives a fancy car. But then the club's pretty classy, as far as these clubs go. The girls are well looked after, paid more than at most strip joints. No one's complaining."

"Is that why you work here? The money's good?"

He met his gaze. "Yeah, it's either this or a gay bar, and this pays better. Besides," he chuckled, "the punters leave me alone."

She shot him a sympathetic smile. That made sense. "Have you been to his house in Shoreditch?"

"No, Bianca told me. She's – sorry – she had been there a couple of times."

"He never invited you?"

"God no. I'm not his type."

Fair enough.

"Anyway, I'm guessing he's up to no good. I've seen the people who come in and out of here. Some drive hundred-thousand-pound cars, wear gold Rolexes and always pay in cash."

"Any idea what he's into?"

Alex looked her straight in the eye. "I told you, I don't want to know. I like my job, it pays well. That's enough for me."

She couldn't argue with that. "Okay, thanks."

There was a slight pause, then she said, "Is there security footage inside the club?"

He looked surprised. "Yeah, there are a couple of cameras. There's even one in the private cubicles, but don't spread that around. It's to protect the girls."

"So Bianca's last customer would be on camera?"

"Yes." His cigarette finally burned to the filter and he flicked it onto the ground. "Why do you ask?"

"I don't suppose you could take a look at it. Find out who he was?"

"Hell, no. Are you crazy? I'm not getting fired over this." He nodded to the club. "Look, I'd better get inside. My shift's about to start."

Shrap forced a grin. She'd overstepped the mark. It was wrong to ask Alex to snoop on his boss. "Sure, and thanks. I appreciate you talking with me."

He shot her an uneasy smile, then turned away. After a few steps, he stopped. "You know, you sound just like a cop, the way you ask questions. Are you sure you're not under-cover or something?"

"Nope. Just a girl trying to help her friend, that's all."

His gaze lingered, then he nodded. "If you're ever in the area, pop in for a drink. I'll give you one on the house." He scoffed. "Fiz can afford it."

She grinned, real this time.

"Thanks, I might just take you up on that."

Hell would freeze over before she set a foot back in that place, but he didn't need to know that.

"Shrap! Jesus, you clean up well." Jed stood at the front door of his council flat and looked her up and down. "You got a job or something?"

"Nah, just had a meeting, that's all. Felt like I should make a bit of an effort."

The technical whiz pursed his lips. "Suits you, girlfriend."

Shrap had met Jed shortly after she'd started sleeping rough. Jed had been walking back to his flat carrying a brand-new laptop when he'd been mugged by two opportunists who'd sought to make a tidy profit on eBay.

Shrap had intervened and saved the laptop, an item infinitely more precious to Jed than his own life. After that, Jed stopped whenever he saw Shrap on the street. Sometimes they had coffee. Jed was bright and witty, with a dry sense of humour, the kind of person Shrap had grown used to in the military. Under normal conditions, they'd probably have been friends. Jed often asked if he could do anything for her, although Shrap always refused. She had no need for technology, not anymore.

Shrap followed him into the flat. From the outside, it looked like any other council housing estate in London. Brown-brick, purpose-built blocks sprawled around a central quad and play area, mostly concrete, whatever greenery there was having died long ago.

They all had the same dismal feel about them, like this was the last resort. The place where dreams died and acceptance set in. It was hard to believe people were clamouring for these apartments, but then there just wasn't enough social housing in London. A town where everyone had given up.

She was a good one to talk.

Inside, however, you could be forgiven for thinking you were in the IT department of a tech start-up. The living room had been converted to an office/server room. A tower of machines purred quietly, raising the ambient temperature in the flat by at least five degrees.

The windows were open to cool the place down, not that you could see out of them past the mound of equipment stacked on do-it-yourself shelving units. The most luxurious thing in the room was Jed's desk chair. A plush, black-leather gaming chair designed for long hours at the controls.

Shrap once asked Jed what he did for a living, and the tech whiz had said something about data security for private companies. Shrap suspected, however, that Jed had a few very profitable little side-hustles that involved delving into dark places in which he wasn't meant to be.

"To what do I owe the honour?" Jed asked, grinning. He was wearing jogging bottoms and a jumper that looked like his grandma had knitted it. His hair was messy, and he hadn't shaved in a few days. "I'd offer you a beer or something, but I've run out. Had a big night last night. The new *Call of Duty* came out."

Shrap shivered. A war game would probably send her over the edge.

"Did you hear about Doug?" she asked the techie.

"That your mate? The old geezer I sometimes see you with?"

"That's him. Well, he died a couple of days ago. Murdered."

"Fucking hell. I'm sorry, Shrap. He seemed like a decent fellow."

"He was."

Jed frowned. "What you need from me?"

Shrap wouldn't be here unless she needed something – and she never needed anything, which meant her friend knew it was serious.

"A favour, but you're not going to like it."

"I owe you, remember."

"I need your help breaking into a club and downloading the security footage."

Jed's eyes widened behind his glasses. "What you into, Shrap?"

"Nothing dangerous," she lied. "It's to do with Doug's death. I'm trying to find out who was responsible."

"Ah." The techie studied her with newfound respect. "You doin' a bit of investigating, are ya?"

"Yeah. The police are saying it was an accident. That he fell asleep and dropped his cigarette, setting himself alight."

"Shit, is that what happened?"

"He burned to death, but someone helped him. He didn't smoke. No way he could have set himself on fire."

Jed shuffled uncomfortably. Shrap felt bad for putting him on the spot, but she didn't know anything about security cameras, or burglar alarms for that matter. She told Jed what she needed.

"You've got the building access code?" Jed asked.

Shrap nodded. She'd seen Alex type it in the first time they'd met. "Unless it's changed."

"I'll bring my codebreaker just in case. Some folks change their access codes on a weekly or monthly basis."

Shrap doubted that was the case at the strip club. It would be too hard with all the staff coming and going. "The place will be alarmed," she said.

"Don't worry, I've got a device for that too. What is it you want from the security cameras?"

"I'm looking for a private lap dance one of the girls gave a client. I've got the date and time. And then anything after that out front, when she was leaving."

"You tracing this girl's movements?"

"She was also killed," she said.

Jed paled. "Who are these guys, Shrap?"

"No one you want to know, trust me."

He swallowed. "You know I'm not good in real-life combat situations."

He was referring to the mugging. Jed might be one of the smartest guys she knew, but he wasn't a fighter. His domain was behind a computer, online. That's where he did the most damage.

"Don't worry, we won't encounter anyone. Nobody's there after hours."

"Okay, if you're sure."

"I'm sure."

"When do you want to do this?" Jed asked.

The club doesn't get busy until midweek.

Shrap grinned. "Got any plans tonight?"

21

I t was a cold, clear night. The streets were deserted, the
club having closed an hour earlier. It was sometime
after four in the morning. In another few hours, the
sky would lighten and the sun would start peeking through
the buildings.

Jed kept a nervous lookout while Shrap entered the
four-digit pin code into the pad on the wall next to the staff
entrance.

*8745#

It opened.

"Thank fuck," murmured Jed.

Shrap beckoned for him to follow. They couldn't see
each other's face thanks to the balaclavas. Shrap hadn't
asked Jed where he'd got them, or why he had them, but she
had to admit, they were useful. Just in case anyone surprised
them.

They went inside. As expected, the alarm system started
beeping. The keypad on the door was just an entry system,
not an alarm deactivator.

Jed removed the alarm system cover and clipped a hand-held device to the wires inside. He hit a few buttons and waited while the red numbers on the device ran through a sequence until it found the deactivation code.

"Bingo," whispered Jed.

Shrap exhaled. First hurdle over.

They moved further into the club, wading through the heavy darkness, the booths and tables hollow shadows. It smelled faintly of booze, lingering stage smoke and perspiration. Shrap clicked on a torch.

"Thank God," breathed Jed. "I couldn't see a thing."

Shrap led the way through a door to the left of the stage that she'd seen Xhafa come out of. A flight of stairs took them to an office with dark glass windows overlooking the club. Shrap hadn't noticed them before because of the spotlight and music pounding her senses into submission. Also, the lights would have masked the office above.

Had Xhafa sat here and watched Bianca as she strutted her stuff on stage?

Was this where he plotted to kill her, the girl he was obsessed with?

"I don't see any screens," murmured Jed.

At the back of the office was another door. Black and unassuming. It was locked. Shrap stood back and let Jed get to work. He took out a lock-picking set and gained entry in less than a minute.

"You should do that for a living," Shrap murmured.

"Don't have the balls," Jed sniffed. "Not good at this subterfuge stuff."

Unless it was on the dark net.

"Here we go." Jed took off his rucksack and sat down in front of the console. He pressed a power switch and three screens lit up. The first showed an image of the front of the club. That was the camera above the main entrance. It was recording a live feed, the current time displayed in the top right corner.

"These two aren't recording." Jed gestured to screens two and three. Two showed the tunnel entrance, the velvet throat of the lion, while three was divided into four mini screens, each displaying a small, red-lined cubicle. The private lap-dancing chambers.

"Can you bring up the evening of the third?" Shrap asked.

Jed's hands typed a command into the keyboard and the system hummed in response. Four new images popped up on screen three.

"What time?"

"Eight onwards." Shrap wasn't sure what time Bianca had performed her last lap dance. "Can you fast-forward it?"

Jed tripled the speed. The footage flew forward, the humans looking jerky and animated.

"Stop," she whispered as a woman with long blonde hair appeared in one of the rooms. "That's her."

Jed whistled. "She's alright, isn't she?"

Shrap didn't respond. Bianca had been a beautiful woman. Young, lush, exotic. These images were so different from the upside-down crime scene photograph she'd seen on Trevelyan's desk. She'd had an innocence about her that made you want to protect her, but a seductiveness that made men think of other things.

She could understand why the dancer was such a hit.

Even without sound, her body moved seamlessly as she straddled the man and danced over him. Close, but never touching.

The man's hands were around her waist, caressing her curves, clutching at her arse, but she wasn't perturbed. She smiled benignly and danced on. The perfect blend of sultry disinterestedness. The timestamp said 21.37.

"Keep going," Shrap urged, after Bianca had finished. They left the room, the next dancer came in. Same story. Practiced sensuality designed to entice. Expensive titillation.

"Fast-forward to the end of the evening."

Jed did so, the images of the dancing girls flying past in a hurried sequence of frames. At 23.23 Bianca appeared again.

"Hold it. That's her. Can you go back?"

Jed rewound it and played it at normal speed. They watched as a man came in. He was talking on the phone. Stocky, five ten or eleven, clean-shaven but with dark, bushy eyebrows that rose and fell as he talked. Bianca entered as he hung up and pushed him gently into the chair.

He leered at her, grabbed her waist and didn't let go until she'd finished.

Shrap found she was gritting her teeth.

Bianca seemed to be allowing this guy more leeway than the last. He reached up and fondled her breasts. She let him. Her expression didn't change. If anything, she leaned in closer and gave the best performance of the night.

Shrap frowned. What was it about this guy? Did she know him? Was he paying more?

The dance finished. The guy left the cubical. Bianca watched him go, then after a heartbeat, darted out after him.

"Switch to the main camera outside the club," hissed Shrap. "I want to see her leave."

"I'll have to pull it up." Jed checked the timestamp.

A moment later, Shrap was watching the stocky man leave. He walked out, hands in his pockets, jacket on and cap pulled low. It was definitely him.

No sign of Bianca.

"She'd use the staff exit," she muttered.

They could see a smidgeon of the side street from this angle, but only where it met the street the main entrance of the club was in. A shadow approached and they glimpsed the sleeve of a fake fur coat and red high-heel shoes in the corner of the frame.

"That's her." Shrap's pulse accelerated. "She left right after him."

"But why?" Jed shook his head. "I don't get it."

"Go back to the lap dance," Shrap said. "I want to check the part where he's on the phone."

"Before she comes in?"

"Yeah."

Jed wound it back. They stared at the screen. "Can you enlarge it?"

"Sure." He pressed a button and the quarter image enlarged to fill the whole screen.

"That's better." Shrap leaned in, watching carefully.

In walked the guy on the phone. He was talking rapidly, too fast to make out what he was saying. Shrap squinted at his mouth until he hung up.

"Was that 'See you tomorrow'?"

Jed rewound it again and watched closely.

"I'd say so." He glanced up at Shrap. "So what?"

Shrap frowned. "I don't know."

Then she pointed at the screen. "Look! See how the curtain is moving. She's there!"

"Who? The dancer?"

"Yeah, she's listening to his conversation. I'm sure of it."

"But why?"

"I don't know. Perhaps she didn't mean to, she was just there. He had paid for a lap dance, after all."

"True." Jed looked at her. "What does it mean?"

"She heard something on that phone call that caused

her to follow him. He leaves. She leaves immediately after-wards, making up some excuse about not feeling well."

"She looked pretty well to me," Jed smirked.

Shrap thought for a moment. "Can you play the lap dance?"

Jed let it play out.

"Pause it," said Shrap.

Jed did as he was instructed.

Shrap studied the guy's face, committing it to memory. Broad forehead; heavy eyebrows, almost meeting in the middle; dark eyes, close together. Then, she remembered she had a mobile phone. Pulling it out of her jacket pocket, she snapped a couple of shots of the guy.

"You going after him?" asked Jed.

"I need to find out who he is, and why Bianca followed him."

"Do you think he had something to do with her murder?" Jed's eyes were huge.

"Maybe." Shrap frowned. "What I do know is he was the last person to see her alive."

They were about to leave the CCTV room when Jed gripped Shrap's arm and pointed to screen one. "Look!"

A silver Mercedes had pulled up in front of the club. The door opened and Mikael, the big Russian, got out. He looked around, then reached behind his back and took out a handgun.

"Shit, there must be a sensor linked to his phone or something," said Shrap.

"What do we do?" Jed scrambled to pull on his rucksack, his face white.

"He's alone, that's good." Shrap thought hard. "Shut this stuff down. Quickly. Then, come with me. I've got an idea."

Jed's fingers flew over the keyboard and the images

disappeared. Then he hit the off switch and the screens faded to black.

"Now what?"

"Come on, let's go downstairs." As they headed for the door, Shrap flicked on the switch so Xhafa's office was flooded with light.

"What are you doing?" hissed Jed. "He'll know we were here."

Shrap ran down the stairs, the techie right behind her. "Trust me."

She pulled Jed into the wings of the stage where they were shrouded in curtains. "Don't move until he's gone upstairs to check the office."

Jed nodded.

They heard a series of beeps as the code was entered into the pad outside. The door hiccoughed open. The big Russian entered the club.

Silence as he crept into the interior. Shrap imagined he'd do a quick lap of the room, then look up and see the light on in the office. As expected, the stage door opened.

Footsteps on the stairs, only metres away. Neither Shrap nor Jed moved a muscle.

The office door creaked open, and Mikael was inside.

Shrap moved out from behind the curtain. "Now!" she mouthed to a terrified Jed.

They snuck out the open stage door, pushed open the staff exit and crept out onto the street.

"Oh, thank God," breathed Jed, once Shrap had closed the door behind them.

"Let's get out of here." Shrap took off down the street at a run. Jed followed, his rucksack rattling on his back.

That had been too damn close.

22

G areth stared moodily out of the window. He had work to do, he just couldn't bring himself to do it. His mind was still on Bianca Rubik, the dead club dancer. That case was now closed, thanks to DCI Burrows and his narrow-minded views.

It was pretty cut and dry when you looked at it. The old guy's DNA on the victim's body, caught fleeing from the scene on CCTV. On the surface, it was obvious. So why was he so restless?

He pulled up the case files again and scrolled through them, stopping when he got to DS Heely and DS Brenner's interview of Bianca's flatmate, Rona Sheraton. Thanks to them, they'd wrongly assumed Bianca was a sex worker.

There was no harm in going to speak to the woman. If the flatmate didn't have anything useful to add, he'd call it quits and accept the verdict.

Grabbing his jacket, he muttered something about a lunchtime appointment and left the building.

Rona Sheraton's house was a shocking pink. In the harsh light of day, it almost made his eyes water. It was in a good area, though, close to a park and on a leafy street with detached houses and bungalows. It felt very suburban, despite being close to the city.

Gareth had to ring twice and wait a couple of minutes before he got a response. In fact, he'd been about to turn away when the door opened and a sleepy voice said, "Can I help ya?"

He managed a smile. "Hi, are you Rona?"

A frown. "Who wants to know?"

"My name is Gareth Trevelyan. I'm looking into the murder of your flatmate, Bianca Rubik."

"I already spoke to the police."

"I know, and I'm sorry to disturb you again. It's just..." He stopped. How could he convince this woman who clearly didn't like or trust the police to talk to him? "It's just I don't feel like justice was done."

"You don't think the old guy topped himself either?"

Gareth was taken aback. "What makes you say that?"

"Her friend was here. The sexy one with the short hair. She was helping Bianca's parents find out what happened."

Now he was really confused. "Who?"

"I don't remember her name. Something short and snappy."

"Shrap?"

"Shaz – that was it. I liked her. She cared, you know?"

Shaz. Shrap. Close enough.

He frowned. She'd beaten him to it. He ought to have known she wouldn't let this go. A military policewoman. Loyal. Determined to prove her friend innocent. She'd sent the note about the Albanian; goodness knows what else she was doing.

But sexy?

"What was she wearing?" he asked the slim girl who'd

opened the door wider and was leaning against the frame. She wore a dressing gown wrapped around her shoulders, despite it being almost two o'clock in the afternoon, and her hair was tussled.

"Skinny jeans and pink, glittery top. Kick-ass boots too."

Really? Now that was interesting. Shrap had cleaned up to pay the flatmate a visit. Had she gone to the club too? Is that how she'd found out about the Albanian, Xhafa?

"You said she was helping Bianca's parents?" Rona was fishing in her pocket for a box of cigarettes. She found it, took one out and lit it.

Inhaling deeply. "Yeah, they used to live together when Bianca first got here. Don't think she'd seen her for a while though, because she asked if she was seeing someone."

"Was she seeing anyone?"

"No, like I told her, she didn't have a fella."

"What about her boss, Xhafa?"

Rona chuckled. "She asked that too. Nah, he tried it on a couple of times, but Bianca was having none of it. She had big dreams, that girl. She was studying. Law. Then she was gonna bring her kid over." Rona was proud of her late flatmate, it was evident in the way she spoke about her. Pride, tinged with sadness.

Gareth gave a sympathetic nod. He knew about Bianca's five-year-old son back in Poland. His team had broken the news to her family. But he hadn't known about the law degree.

"The dancing was just a temporary thing?"

"Yeah, it paid well. I'd do it too if I could dance. She made more than me and didn't have to deal with half the shit I have to."

Gareth grimaced. "I'm sorry."

Rona shrugged. "That's just the way it is. I grew up on a

council estate in Brixton. I ain't got no fancy degree. I tried modelling once, but I ain't got time to go to all them casting calls. That ain't gonna feed my baby girl, is it?"

"No, I suppose not."

She shrugged. "Still, it ain't that bad. I work my own hours. I'm my own boss. I don't have to rely on anyone else for work, and the pay is good. Plus, I get to spend time with my baby girl. Not many other jobs can say that, right? Can you say that about yours?"

Gareth couldn't.

He worked for a man he didn't respect, the hours were lousy, and the pay was even worse, but there was nothing else he'd rather do. He made a difference in people's lives, took bad guys off the street, got justice for victims of crime. That's what kept him going.

Everyone had their reasons.

The girl was puffing on her cigarette, a plume of smoke spiralling into the air. "Anything else you wanna know? Or can I go back inside now?"

"Just one thing. You said Bianca's boss tried it on with her. Was he angry that she rejected him?"

"Nah, I don't think so. He came round a couple of times. They talked. He left. It seemed pretty friendly-like."

"Was he ever violent towards her?"

"No, that was one of the reasons she liked working there. She said he was good to the girls, treated them right."

Gareth gnawed on his lip. Xhafa wasn't turning out to be a very likely suspect. What was Shrap after? Was it something Xhafa was into that had got Bianca killed? He'd heard about the Albanian drug gangs, everybody in the force had. Had Bianca somehow got herself mixed up in that?

"What did you think of him? This Xhafa?"

"I didn't know him, but from what Bianca said, he was

alright. Drove a fast car, liked a bit of bling, you know? I'd say he was up to some dodgy shit, but…" She shrugged.

"Did Bianca ever mention drugs or gangs or anything like that?"

Rona's eyes widened. "No way. She wasn't like that."

"I'm not asking if she was into it, I'm asking if she ever mentioned it, in connection with her boss or the club, perhaps?"

Rona shook her head, dispersing the smoke. "No, although I wouldn't put it past him."

"Okay. Thanks, Rona. You've been very helpful."

"I miss her," Rona said suddenly. "Bianca was my friend, and I miss her."

"I'm sorry for your loss." Gareth gave a tight nod, before turning and walking back to his car.

BACK AT THE POLICE STATION, Gareth went to see Zane, who'd worked on the investigation into the homeless guy's death. The inquest had ruled it misadventure, as expected. Doug Romberg had either burned himself to death in a tragic accident or committed suicide. Nobody cared which. He'd killed an innocent woman with a five-year-old kid. He deserved what he'd got.

"Hey, Zane. Can I see the post-mortem report on Doug Romberg?"

He glanced up. "Who?"

"The homeless guy. The burn victim."

"Oh, what you want that for?"

"Just tying up a loose end." He kept his voice light.

Zane shrugged. Most people thought him a little strange because he wasn't a joiner. He didn't hang out at the pub with them after work, didn't engage in office banter, kept to himself. Sometimes, this was an advantage. Like now.

Zane rifled through his inbox and pulled out a folder at the bottom. "Sorry, haven't got round to filing it yet."

"Perfect. Thanks."

He took it and went back to his desk. The sandwich he'd bought at the cafeteria was dry and tasteless, but he ate it anyway, washed down with a cup of tea. He couldn't stand the coffee around here.

Doug Romberg had been burned beyond recognition. DNA was used to confirm his identity, and it matched with that on the MOD database. Doug had been injured in combat and his medical records were on file. Lucky, otherwise they'd still have no clue who he was.

Cause of death was multi-organ failure due to severe burn damage. He cringed. What a way to go. He couldn't imagine the agony he must have gone through.

He read on. There was very little else they could find since the body was so badly damaged. However, when he got to the head section, he caught his breath.

The victim had a right occipital intracranial haemorrhage. Bleeding in the brain? How could that not be significant? He read on. Apparently this was not the cause of death.

Heart pounding, he picked up the phone. A few minutes later, he was put through to a Dr Liz Kramer, the Home Office pathologist who'd performed the post-mortem on Doug Romberg.

"Hello, Dr Kramer. My name is Detective Constable Trevelyan. I'm calling in connection with the post-mortem you did on a homeless man, Doug Romberg."

"Ah, the burn victim. Yes, I remember. How can I help

you?" She had a clipped, no-nonsense tone to her voice that Gareth appreciated. She didn't have time to waste either.

"I noticed you mentioned an intracranial haemorrhage in your report. I was wondering, would this be significant enough to render him unconscious?"

"Hang on a minute, let me pull up the report. You're lucky you caught me at my desk, I was about to go to the lab."

"Thank you," Gareth replied.

There was a faint clicking sound as the doctor accessed the computer file.

"Yes, that's right. In the right occipital lobe. Simply put, he suffered a blunt-force injury to the right side of his head, and to answer your question, yes, it was significant enough to cause a loss of consciousness."

He breathed out. "So, he was knocked out before he was burned alive?"

"He was indeed. Small mercies, eh?"

Gareth clenched his teeth. Why the hell hadn't anyone mentioned this? But he knew why. Because they wanted to wrap up the case. Neat and tidy, with a bow on top. This would have complicated things, led to more investigating, more resources. It was simpler to ignore it.

"Sorry, there's one more thing. Is there any indication of what caused this blunt-force trauma?"

"It would have been an object with a dull, firm surface. Something like a brick or a rock. A firm piece of wood would do it too. Unfortunately, the body was too badly burned to make out any more than that."

Gareth thanked the pathologist and hung up. He sat unmoving in his chair, his mind whirling. If Doug had been knocked out before he was burned, this wasn't an accident or suicide. It was murder.

23

Shrap took up a reconnaissance position behind an ancient oak in a small park diagonally opposite the club. She wanted to get eyes on Mikael, Xhafa's bodyguard, and this was when he usually arrived at the club.

It was bleak and overcast, and the damp seeped through the water-logged earth, squelching around her boots. The whole place smelled mulchy, like rotting leaves.

She also wanted to talk to Alex, so she'd donned what she was beginning to think of as her investigator's disguise. Transforming herself from the grubby waif into... some vague version of what she once was. She had to stop bombarding him outside the club, but there was no way she was going in there again, and she didn't know how else to contact him. He'd probably think her strange, but not half as strange as if he knew the truth. That most nights she slept under an awning behind the Marriott Hotel on Westminster Bridge.

She didn't have to wait long. At five o'clock, the Albanian's silver Merc pulled up, Mikael at the wheel. Xhafa was punctual, she'd give him that much. Shrap could see the henchman's broad outline filling the interior of the car.

The bodyguard got out, glanced up and down the road and opened the door for his boss. Xhafa walked around to the staff entrance. The front door wasn't open yet. No red carpet. No gold rope. That came later.

Mikael locked the car. A firm beep as the alarm was activated. Then he stood outside the club and lit up.

Shit, she was too far away to make out the design on the packet.

She focused on the Russian, waiting for him to finish his cigarette. Would he throw his butt on the ground? It started to drizzle. She pulled the collar of her jacket up around her neck and hunkered down. "Come on…" she muttered.

Eventually, the bodyguard flicked the butt away and went inside the club.

Shrap hurried across the road and picked it up before it got too wet. It had been smoked down to the filter, but a few blue letters were still visible on the one side: *RLIA*.

Parliament.

Bingo.

SHE WAS STILL HOLDING the cigarette when she heard heels on the pavement behind her. Spinning around, she saw Alex approach.

He stopped when he saw her. "Shrap?"

"I'm sorry, Alex, but I need to ask you a couple more questions. Do you mind?"

"About Bianca?"

"About one of her customers, actually." She took out her phone. It didn't take her long to pull up the only image she had in her picture gallery. "This guy. Do you know him?"

She held the phone towards him. He took it from her, frowning at the image.

"Hmm... I'm not sure. Maybe." He handed it back. "Who is he?"

"He's the man that Bianca followed the night she left so suddenly. The night she was killed."

Alex stared at her. "*She* followed *him* out?"

"Yeah, he left the club and she left immediately afterwards."

"How do you know this?" His eyes narrowed and he glanced at the phone again. "That's from the private booth. You've seen the video footage, haven't you?"

She didn't reply. "Do you remember him?"

He pursed his lips, unsure whether to answer. Unsure whether he could trust her now that she'd somehow got hold of the surveillance camera footage from the club.

"Please, Alex. It's important."

He tossed his head back. "Yeah, I remember him. He sat at the bar. Strange guy. Didn't talk much. Some of them are chatty, you know, but he didn't say a word. Just watched, drank, then paid for a private dance and left."

"Is he a regular?"

"Don't think so. Haven't seen him before."

"Did he pay cash?"

He sighed. "I don't know. I can't recall."

"Can you check?"

Alex gave her a stern look. "No, Miss Marple, I can't check. Once I've cashed up for the night, I give the till records to Pete. He gives them to Fiz. I can't go digging around in the office for card payments on the night Bianca died. Jesus. Are you trying to get me fired?"

Shrap raised a hand. "Okay, I'm sorry I asked."

He shook his head. "I don't know how you got hold of

that picture, but trust me, you don't want to mess with these guys. I know you're trying to find out what happened to Bianca, and I respect that, but be careful, Shaz. I mean it."

She forced a smile. "I will. You've been a great help, Alex."

He tilted his head to the side. "I like you, Shaz. You're crazy, but I like you. Let's go for a drink sometime. A proper one. I know this great place near Leicester Square."

"Sure."

She went through the motions and took down his number. She felt bad pretending, but what was she supposed to do? How could she explain her situation? The whole reason she was out here, roughing it, was because she wanted to avoid society. It wasn't voluntary. Given the choice, she'd much rather be normal. She'd much rather be with Trevor in their semi-detached Victorian terrace in Wandsworth. She might even have had his ring on her finger by now, not some other woman.

She swallowed. "Thanks."

He grinned. "Speak soon."

"Yeah. See you, Alex."

IT WAS close on four a.m. when Frank's Uber pulled into a loading zone behind the club. The mysterious customer whose face was ingrained in her memory hadn't made an appearance. Not that she expected him to.

"Alright, Shrap?" Frank didn't comment on her attire, her dishevelled appearance or the long, dirty coat wrapped around her.

"Yeah, thanks for coming." Shrap slid into the passenger seat.

"No worries, I'm on all night so it's no problem."

"This is a paying job," Shrap said. She didn't want Frank to feel she was using him. Once was okay, between friends, but not if it became a regular thing. Although, Shrap hoped this would be the last time.

"Forget it, mate. I'm not going to charge you. Besides, you've got to do it via the app. How'd that last trip turn out? You get back okay?" His gaze flickered over her bruised face. "I shouldn't have left you there alone."

"Fine." She was healing slowly. At least the bandages on her arm were hidden under her coat sleeve. Gesturing to the silver Merc parked up ahead, she said, "I need to find out where that vehicle goes."

"Sure thing." Frank knew better than to ask any more questions.

Close on ten minutes later, Mikael emerged from the club, followed by Xhafa. They walked towards the car, Xhafa carrying a leather briefcase. Taking work home with him?

The roads were quiet, so Frank stayed well back.

"Looks like we're heading towards Shoreditch," he muttered, as they stopped at a red light. The Merc had gone through, but it was a straight road and unless it turned off, they'd be able to catch up.

"Don't lose him," murmured Shrap.

"I won't."

The lights changed and Frank trod on the gas. The Merc turned a corner about half a mile down the road. Frank followed.

Another turn, another straight road, then they were in a small suburb with free-standing Georgian houses, leafy, well-lit streets, and expensive cars in the driveways.

"This is it," whispered Shrap as Frank turned the corner then slowed to a halt, cutting the lights. They watched as the two men got out.

Mikael kept an eye out as Xhafa unlocked the front door. They both went inside.

"Looks like the boss man likes to keep his personal bodyguard on the premises," said Frank. "It'll make it harder to get to him."

"It's not the boss man I'm after," grumbled Shrap.

Frank turned to her. "The big guy?"

"Yeah, he might be the one who took out Doug."

Frank studied her for a moment. "You do realise he's ex-military? Russian, most like. Ruthless motherfuckers, those guys."

"I know."

"I don't think he's the talking kind."

"No."

Frank hesitated, then said, "No offence, Shrap, but you're not fighting fit anymore. None of us are. Are you sure you know what you're doing?"

"I don't have a choice. The police aren't doing anything. They've already put it down as an accident." She gestured to the house. "I've got a couple of leads, but this guy is the most promising."

Frank contemplated this. "Let's say, for argument's sake, that this is your guy. That he did kill your friend. What are you going to do about it?"

Shrap turned to him. "Know where I can get a gun?"

24

Shemar "Shakes" Stevens ran a minicab company out of Kings Cross. His real business, however, was importing illegal firearms into the United Kingdom. He had various sources. Ex-military personnel, foreign nationals, antique dealers and thieves who stole weapons from licenced users.

His customers ranged from street gangs who wanted a weapon for protection or intimidation to hardened criminals who needed to get rid of used weapons and acquire new ones.

According to Frank, he had a workshop in his back garden in South London where he removed serial numbers, reactivated decommissioned guns and repurposed antique weapons for use.

"He's a hard man, Shrap. Doesn't give a fuck, if you know what I mean. He's just interested in doing business and doesn't care who with."

"How do you know him?" Shrap had asked.

"We did a stint together in Iraq. Same unit. Shitty conditions. Only four of us made it out. Shakes bailed after that.

Said there were better ways to earn a living. But he made a few contacts and put them to good use. He never did have many scruples. I'll put in a good word. He's paranoid, I suppose he has to be in his industry, so don't be surprised if he doesn't take to you straight away."

Shrap went up to the misted window and tapped. A woman pulled the glass aside. "Where to?"

"I'm here to see Shakes."

She frowned. "He expectin' you?"

"Yes, name's Shrap. I'm a friend of Frank's."

"One minute."

She shut the window with a slap and picked up her phone. Shrap saw her relay the information to Shakes, her eyes scanning her body as she did so. She felt decidedly vulnerable without her knife, but it was back in the locker with her other clothes. Frank had said not to bring it and she trusted Frank. After they'd found out where Xhafa lived, her friend had dropped her off in Waterloo, where she'd got a few hours' kip on Doug's porch before heading to the river to watch the sun come up. No matter how tired she was, she always made the sunrise.

She half-expected it not to come up at all if she wasn't there to see it.

This morning's had been spectacular. The dirty cloud cover had provided a sepia filter for an array of restless oranges, yellows and pinks that had forced their way through, dissolving onto the surface of the Thames.

She'd even taken a few snaps on her phone, not that she'd be keeping it. She had no reason to.

Trevor wouldn't be calling again.

Yet, for reasons she didn't want to analyse, she'd still asked Budge if she could charge it at the day centre.

"Shakes is comin'," said the woman behind the glass. "Five minutes."

The woman's idea of five minutes was vastly different to hers. Shrap was getting antsy by the time the corrugated-iron door opened. Customers had come and gone, and cab drivers had arrived and left.

"Got some ID?" growled a big, black man with a bald head and a gold tooth. Rough eyes scoured over her body, checking her out, looking for weapons.

Shrap shook her head. "Nope."

"Show me your left arm."

Frank had obviously told him about Shrap's tattoo as a way of identifying her. She lifted her sleeve, displaying the curved design weaving up her forearm. It was a rose coiled around a dagger. Alongside it read, *Where Right and Glory Lead*. The regimental motto of the Royal Engineers.

"How do you know Frank?" He had a deep, gravelly voice that would give Darth Vader a run for his money.

"We did our basic training together."

"Okay, come in. We'll talk."

He held the iron door open while Shrap slid past into a dank, smelly corridor. Before she could take another step, the weapon's dealer had her pinned to the wall.

"You don't mind if I search you, do you?"

Normally, this was where she'd kick him in the groin, except she needed him, so she gritted her teeth and raised her hands. "Go ahead." He wouldn't find anything.

Shakes patted her down. Shrap sucked in a breath when he ran his hands over her torso, but she managed not to wince. Eventually, he grunted and stood up. "Sorry, gotta check. You were military police, mate. I don't trust anyone in the police. Not even an attractive woman like yourself."

"Understood."

She would have done the same thing in Shakes' position. Even now, even with Frank vouching for her, Shrap
would have been hard-pressed to trust an ex-copper.

She looked around. The office where the woman sat was
to the right, and in front of her, a long corridor led to the
back of the building.

"Second door to the right." Shakes nodded toward the
dimness.

Shrap walked down the dark passage feeling Shakes'
gaze burn into her back. The interior smelled faintly of dope
and vomit. They walked into a makeshift office. It looked
like it had once been a kitchen. On the one side was a sink, a
fridge and a cooker. The countertops were covered in files
and folders, and the fridge, which was open, contained piles
more. Interesting filing cabinet.

"Take a seat," growled Shakes.

Shrap sat.

"Now, what do you want?"

"I'm looking for a handgun." Shrap told him the
specifics. She wasn't particular about the brand or model –
anything compact with reliable stopping power that could
be easily concealed would suffice. The man she was planning to confront could spot a bluff a mile away; it had to be
real, operational hardware. She hoped to hell she wouldn't
have to use it, but she needed the protection it would offer.
No chances.

"Ammo?" asked Shakes.

"Yeah, a full magazine at least, and two spares," she
replied. Better to have too much than too little.

Shakes nodded his understanding.

"When can you have it ready?"

"Come back Saturday."

They haggled over the price for a few minutes, then

Shrap stood up and left the same way she'd come in. It was as easy as that.

"THAT COPPER'S been here looking for you again," Budge told her when she went back to the day centre to fetch her phone. "You know, the detective."

"Oh yeah?"

"One of these days he's going to catch up with you." He looked worried.

"He just wants to talk," Shrap said. If he wanted to question her officially or make an arrest, he'd have brought another officer with him. For backup and to corroborate anything that might be said.

Shrap collected her phone, got something to eat and then helped Budge install a light bulb that had blown in the cooker in the kitchen. His aching back and protruding belly meant he couldn't get down there, and the couple of volunteers, mostly women, were too busy serving or treating the homeless to get around to DIY jobs.

"You're a star, Shrap." He broke into a smile. "I've been meaning to do that for days."

"Anytime, Budge."

"How are your ribs?"

"Much better," she said, even though they ached like hell at night and some mornings she couldn't move when she first woke up.

He nodded, not quite believing her.

SHRAP SPENT the rest of the day in the library reading the newspapers, then, just before five, made her way to Southwark police station. She took up a position at the bus stop, a block down from the squat brick building, and waited. Police detectives' hours were erratic, so she couldn't be sure what time Trevelyan would emerge from the building and head home. It didn't matter, she had nothing better to do.

It was closer to six when he finally left work. He emerged onto the street, rucksack over one shoulder, still doing up the zip on his jacket. His hair was messy, like he'd been running his fingers through it all day. He adjusted the straps of his rucksack then glanced up and down the street.

Borough tube station was to the right and Elephant and Castle to the left. Which way would he go?

He turned right.

She followed, hoodie up, as he walked down Borough High Street. In front of them, the Shard was lit up like a gold stiletto piercing the night sky. Shrap was expecting him to catch the tube, but instead, he kept walking, past Guy's Hospital, until he got to London Bridge, a good fifteen minutes from the police station. He didn't appear to be in a rush, and at one point he stopped at a newsagent and came out with a can of Coke and a newspaper. He slid the newspaper into his rucksack and drank the Coke as he walked the rest of the way.

He was an easy target to follow. Not once did he turn around or even seem aware of his surroundings. She could only surmise he must have been deep in thought.

Shrap followed him into the London Bridge Underground station, where he caught the Jubilee line westwards. She stood a carriage down, side on, hood up, and watched him in her peripheral vision. Only her profile was visible, not that he'd be able to see her through the afterwork crush.

She nearly lost him at Bermondsey when he got off the train. A surge of people pressed on and Shrap, who'd waited till the last minute to be sure he was getting off, had to push past them. He was disappearing up the escalator by the time she made it onto the platform.

Rushing, she spotted him exiting the station. She kept her distance, losing herself in the crowd. He crossed at the pedestrian crossing, before turning left and disappearing down a side street. She followed, head down, making sure there was plenty of distance between her and him. Nothing obvious.

Two-thirds of the way down, he stopped and shrugged a shoulder out of his rucksack. Reaching inside, he retrieved a set of keys, then climbed the four or five steps to his front door and inserted them.

In a heartbeat, Shrap was behind him.

"You were looking for me?"

25

Trevelyan nearly jumped out of his skin. "Holy shit, it's you."

"Yes, it's me. What do you want?"

"I wanted to talk to you." She'd startled him, but he hid it well. She could tell by the way he gripped the railing to steady himself. "Why are you ambushing me outside my house?"

"I wanted to be sure you were alone and away from the police station."

"Well, I am." He spread his hands. The key was still in the lock, but he hadn't opened the door. He wouldn't either, not while she was standing there.

"Is now a convenient time?" she asked.

He gave a dry laugh. "I suppose so. Do you want to take a walk?"

"No, let's sit."

They sat on the steps like teenagers, looking out over the street and the row of houses opposite. He took off his rucksack and sat down. She did the same, keeping at least half a metre of space between them. The railing dug into her shoulder, but it gave her something to lean against.

Trevelyan stretched his long legs out in front of him. Work shoes, scuffed and lacklustre. He wore black suit trousers, not expensive, the crease down the front faded and barely noticeable after a day at the station. She shifted her gaze from his thighs to his face.

"This is not entirely appropriate, Ms...?" He paused. "I'm sorry, I don't know your surname."

"Nelson," she said. She'd already decided she'd share her identity with him. It might give her some much-needed credibility since her current homeless situation wasn't doing her any favours in that respect. She wanted him to trust her – because she needed his help.

He gave a small nod. She knew he'd look her up as soon as he got into the station tomorrow. It was all there, laid out in incident reports, medical files and release papers. Her military history, her successes and her failures, and finally, her discharge. PTSD. In twenty-four hours, he'd know more about her than anyone else other than Trevor.

She flinched. It made her uncomfortable, him knowing. It went against everything she was trying to achieve. Anonymity, invisibility, being forgotten. Doug's death had pushed her out of her comfort zone. Still, she owed the old man her life. Nothing was too much to see his killer brought to justice.

She'd just have to deal with it. When this was over, she could lose herself again. Sink into the background where no one gave her a second glance.

"What is it you wanted to talk to me about?" she began. She'd get him talking then share a bit about what she knew, and hopefully he'd do what she wanted.

"I went to see Bianca Rubik's flatmate." He watched her,

gauging her response. "She said you'd been there, asking questions."

"So?"

"This is a police enquiry, Ms Nelson. You shouldn't be involving yourself."

She grunted. "I wouldn't if the police were doing their job properly."

He raised an eyebrow.

"They've pinned that girl's murder on my friend, Doug, who as I told you in our first meeting, couldn't have killed her. His hands were riddled with arthritis. He couldn't open a Coke can, let alone strangle someone."

He ground his jaw, causing the muscles at the sides to flex, drawing her eye. He had nice lips, full and sensual. She looked away.

"Did you know she was strangled with a rope or chain of some sort? Those weren't fingerprints around her neck."

She didn't. "It doesn't matter. He wouldn't have been able to grip it."

"What did Rona tell you?" he asked, changing the subject.

"Same thing as she told you, most likely. That Bianca was a trained dancer, she was studying for a law degree through correspondence and she had a kid in Poland." She changed position. Leaning against the railing was making her rib ache.

"She also said Bianca's boss fancied her, but Bianca wasn't interested. Do you believe her?"

"There's no reason not to. The barmaid at Whispers said the same thing. Fiz Xhafa had the hots for Bianca, but she wanted to keep things professional. The gig at the strip club was a means to an end for her."

"Except someone killed her, so she must have seen or

heard something she wasn't supposed to," Trevelyan said. "I watched the interview with Xhafa. He insisted he was at the club the whole time. We don't have anything on him."

"You don't believe Doug did it?" Shrap asked softly.

His shoulders slumped. "No, I don't. I looked at the post-mortem report on your friend and he was hit on the head before he was set alight. The injury was enough to render him unconscious."

Shrap was silent, thinking. "I thought as much. Doug didn't smoke, so I knew it was deliberate. He saw who murdered Bianca and tried to help her. That's what got him killed and that's why his DNA was on her body."

"And that's why he was seen running from the crime scene on the CCTV camera," finished Trevelyan.

Shrap met his gaze. "Exactly. Now tell me, what are you going to do about it?"

"Me?" He laughed. It was a quick, self-deprecating laugh. "There's nothing I *can* do. Not without evidence. The case is closed. Both cases, in fact. Bianca Rubik was killed by Doug Romberg and Doug Romberg died in a tragic accident."

Shrap's jaw muscles tensed. "You know that's bullshit."

"Yes, but my hands are tied. If I'm to go to my boss with a request to reopen the case, I'm going to need hard evidence. Irrefutable proof that Xhafa or someone else was involved."

"In other words," said Shrap. "You want me to help you find the culprit."

He leaned toward her. "Find me something I can take to the SIO."

Shrap pulled out her phone. "I have another lead," she said.

"Oh?" His chin lifted. "Does it involve Xhafa?"

"No, it's a guy from the strip club, a customer. The night

Bianca was killed, she left early. She told the girl behind the bar she wasn't feeling well and disappeared around eleven thirty. Apparently, she gave this fellow a private dance, then followed him out."

Trevelyan's eyes narrowed. "How do you know this?"

"I spoke to the bartender." She held up her phone. "This is the guy."

Trevelyan shuffled closer to have a good look. She got a whiff of his aftershave, faint, but still there, even after a long day at the station. Spicy, exotic, manly. Too manly.

"This looks like it was taken from the club security camera."

"It was. Can you find out who he is?"

He hesitated. "I'd need a reason. We do have facial recognition software, but it's used to compare suspects with mugshots."

"You could say it's for an existing case."

His gaze flickered. She could tell he didn't like lying. "It'll only flag if this guy's in the system."

"I know it's a long shot, but if he did kill her, it's not impossible he has previous convictions."

"I could manually check him against men with records of violence against women," he said thoughtfully.

"Won't that take a while?"

"It's better than doing nothing."

"True." She glanced over at him. She'd had a feeling he was one of the good ones. "Thanks, DC Trevelyan."

"It's Gareth," he said, almost reluctantly. Formality seemed ridiculous given their current situation.

She grinned. "Shrap."

"Do you really think this guy's a suspect?" He nodded towards the phone in her hand.

She shrugged. "I'm not sure. I think it's more likely to be

something Xhafa's into. I followed a couple of Albanian youngsters from the club back to a housing estate in Barking. Rough as shit. Local drug dealers, I'm guessing."

"You think Xhafa's distributing drugs?"

"Maybe. I also saw four men in suits go into the club the other day. They got out of a hire car. I'm guessing they were foreigners there to talk business."

His eyes widened. "What did they look like?"

"Italian, maybe? I heard the Albanians are in cahoots with the Italian mafia. It's how they import the cocaine from South America."

"Jesus," he whispered.

"Yeah. Xhafa's into it up to his eyeballs, but what I don't know is whether it had anything to do with Bianca's death."

"How could it not?" he muttered. "Hell of a coincidence, otherwise. Young Polish dancer catches the eye of Albanian drug-dealing boss. A few months later she's dead."

She didn't disagree.

"I'm looking into it," she said vaguely.

One eyebrow shot up. "How?"

She tried to sound nonchalant. "Surveillance mostly. Nobody pays much attention to the homeless. I can pretty much go where I want."

His gaze roamed over her. "You don't look like a homeless person."

Not today.

She gave a wry grin. "I'm in disguise."

"Well, be careful. Any sign of trouble, back off and call 999."

She gave a mock salute. "Yes, sir."

His face reddened. "Okay, do you want to send me that photograph?"

She pulled out her phone again. "Number?"

He gave it to her.

She typed in the digits and texted the image, hearing his phone beep in his rucksack.

Getting to his feet, Trevelyan said, "I'll let you know if I find anything."

"Likewise."

He turned his back on her and climbed the steps to the front door. She waited until his back was turned then hung onto the railing and pulled herself up. She felt like she ought to say something else, but she didn't know what, so she turned and left. He had her number now, and she had his. Yet another reason not to get rid of the burner phone just yet.

26

The first thing Gareth did when he got to work the next morning, after making a strong cup of tea, was run "Shrap" Nelson's name through the Military of Defence database.

He remembered her saying in her initial interview that she'd been in the armed forces, but he didn't realise she'd been in the Royal Military Police. That explained a lot.

He took a sip and leaned back in his chair to read. Sergeant Persephone Nelson – no wonder she went by her nickname – had been in the Special Investigations Branch, the equivalent of the CID.

Sergeant Nelson.

She outranked him. If she was still a serving officer, he'd be calling her ma'am.

Now she was sleeping rough. What had gone so wrong?

He was hit by an insatiable urge to know, but he suspected it wasn't something she'd open up about. In her first interview, she'd been tight-lipped and annoyingly vague. It was surprising she'd given him her real name. She must have known he'd check up on her.

He frowned. What was she playing at?

Was she fostering a relationship in order to use him to help her find her friend's killer so that she could dish out her own form of vigilante justice? She clearly had no faith in the police force, or the investigation as it stood at the moment. Or did she really want to get him to re-open the case?

He read on. Shrap had started her career with the Royal Engineers – an interesting choice for a woman. After five years and two tours, she'd been recruited by the Royal Military Police. Over the course of her career, she'd deployed on operations in Kosovo, Iraq, Cyprus and finally Afghanistan. Was that where things had gone wrong?

It was on the way to a training exercise with local Afghan forces that her convoy had struck an IED and exploded.

He breathed in sharply. She'd been lucky to escape with her life. But it didn't end there. She'd been captured by the Taliban, endured weeks of torture and then dumped on the side of the road in the middle of one of the harshest Afghan winters on record and left to die. And she would have if it hadn't been for two Dutch aid workers who'd called for help. She'd been airlifted to the military base hospital, where she'd spent a further three weeks recovering from her extensive injuries.

He clasped his fingers behind his head and stared at the screen. *Phew.* That was enough to test even the toughest soldier. No wonder she was scarred. God knows what she'd endured during those weeks of torture.

She'd carried on for another year, stationed at Aldershot in the United Kingdom, until she'd finally been assessed and diagnosed with PTSD. She'd been discharged on health grounds shortly after that.

He pursed his lips thoughtfully.

An impressive military career by all accounts. Now she was using her specialised skillset to find out who killed Doug Romberg, her friend and a fellow veteran.

He took out his phone and studied the photograph she'd sent him. The last man to see Bianca Rubik alive.

Bianca had left the club at eleven thirty and followed this man to Waterloo, where she'd been attacked and strangled. The timing fit. The post-mortem had put the time of death at between midnight and one o'clock in the morning, but the timestamp on the CCTV image of Doug hurrying away from the scene was twelve twenty-three, which meant Bianca's attacker had strangled her in that twenty-three-minute window.

Nobody was going to let him run the facial rec on this guy without a damn good reason. So, he'd just have to find one. Trevelyan logged into HOLMES, the police active case database. What current cases did they have on the go?

He found a house burglary where the perpetrator had got away, but not before he'd beaten up the old lady living there, who was now clinging to life in Charing Cross hospital.

That would do.

He took the photograph to DC Stanton, who ran the facial rec software on potential suspects. "Hello, Luke. Are you busy?"

He turned. "Always. DC Trevelyan, isn't it?"

"Gareth, please."

Luke gave a quick smile. "What can I do for you?"

"I've had this come in, a potential suspect on the Lansdowne burglary. Could you run him against the known-offender list please?"

Luke hesitated. "Have you filled in the appropriate form?"

"Just about to." He smiled reassuringly. "Can I send it to you?"

"Sure, email it to me with the case number. I'll put it in the queue."

He hovered inside the doorway. "Do you have a lot to get through?"

"Yeah, a fair bit. Sorry, it's been frantic. I'll get to it as soon as I can. It's not super urgent, is it? If it is, I could put through a rush order, but I'd need a signature from your SIO."

He stiffened. "No, no more so than the others."

Luke nodded. "In that case, I'll be in touch."

"Yeah. Thanks."

He'd just have to be patient. Unfortunately, that wasn't one of his strong suits.

AFTER HE'D EMAILED Luke the photograph and the case number of the robbery, he began looking through mugshots of men who'd assaulted women in the last year, with or without a sexual element.

It was a dismally long list and, after an hour, he gave up. This was fruitless. He had other work to do and couldn't spend the entire afternoon picking through mugshots.

The hours ticked by. He heard nothing from Luke and probably wouldn't for a while. He had no idea where in the queue he was, or how quickly he'd get there. It could be days.

He took a deep breath. What was it Shrap had said about the Albanians? Drug trafficking, Italian mafia connections?

Opening a fresh browser, he googled Albanian drug gangs in the UK and found a page full of articles by major newspapers on the recent increase in drug trafficking into the country. Organised gangs prone to violence were recruiting youngsters through rap and music videos posted on social media. Christ. Drug dealers were advertising now?

He watched one of the YouTube videos, his eyes fixed to the screen. Bloody hell, he could see why the kids were attracted to the industry. These guys drove fast cars, were covered in bling and tossed money around like there was no tomorrow. Rock stars of the underworld.

Who wouldn't want to be awash with cash? Particularly if you had nothing, and no fucks to give – like most of the kids growing up in poverty, living on sprawling housing estates.

He shook his head. How was law enforcement ever supposed to compete with that? In one clip, the gangsters had been burning a police vehicle at the side of the road. Laughing in their faces.

Anger surged through him. Was that how Fiz Xhafa had started out? Was that what his club was used for? To distribute drugs? He'd seen nothing to indicate as much when he'd been there, but then the suspects had been on their best behaviour that night. He knew full well they'd clocked them the moment they'd walked through the door. It was Devi's fault. She couldn't have looked more out of place if she'd tried, but he couldn't really blame her. She'd had to explain to her husband why she was going to a strip club with a male work colleague.

At least he had no one to answer to. He thought about Melanie. About the phone call. Was she missing him? He took a deep breath. He wasn't going to go there. Walking away had been the hardest thing he'd ever done but staying was harder. And he wasn't the type of person who could be 'just friends'.

Trevelyan didn't fall in love easily, so turning off his feelings was next to impossible. He'd put on a good show for a while. Fooled everyone in the department, even fooled *her*. But not himself. Never himself.

He glanced out of the hazy window. It was raining again. The warmth in the office had steamed up the glass. Through it, he saw the top-floor restaurant across the road, the upper deck of a double-decker bus as it drove by and the blurry steeple of a church in the background.

That's how he'd felt about his career of late. Blurry. Nothing was clear. The Bianca Rubik case had been like a shot of adrenalin in his arm, but that had fallen flat. He'd have to come up with something good if he wanted the SIO to reopen the case.

His mind drifted to Shrap, and he wondered how she was getting on with her "surveillance", as she called it. Perhaps she'd find the evidence they needed to kickstart this investigation again, in the right direction this time. He bloody hoped so.

27

Shrap wasn't really a night owl. She preferred the early mornings, but tonight was an exception. She had work to do, and it couldn't wait.

The minicab office was still open. A slender woman of about thirty with talons for nails and long braided hair sat behind the desk, talking on her phone. The glass slider was open, so she could hear every word.

"I swear. He vanished in the middle of the night. Yeah, real scumbag. Now she's on her own."

She approached the window. The girl glanced up, annoyed her call had been interrupted. "Can I help ya?"

"I'm here to see Shakes."

She looked her up and down and raised an eyebrow. "Yeah, right."

Shrap leaned forward so that her face was against the glass. "He's got a delivery for me."

The girl frowned. "Okay. Wait here."

Yeah, she knew the drill.

The girl told her friend to hang on and texted furiously, talons clicking against the screen. How she hit the right keys, Shrap had no idea. She struggled and she didn't even have nails. A moment later, the phone beeped.

"He comin'," she said without looking up.

Shrap nodded anyway and settled back to wait. It was a cool night, but not cold enough to stop the revellers from coming out. Kings Cross station was around the corner and partygoers strolled or stumbled in on their way home. She'd been harassed by a pimp on the way here, and as she waited, she noticed two men smoking outside a nearby pub eyeing her out. Like this? Seriously? They must be desperate.

"Want some company, sweetheart?" called one.

She ignored them and thought about Bianca following the guy from the strip club. What had made her do that? What had the punter said on the phone that had caused her to drop everything and tail him?

A promise of money? But then she'd have gone with him, not followed him.

Someone in danger? Why not call the cops?

She shook her head. It was a mystery.

The corrugated door squealed open and Shakes appeared. He was a lot more punctual this time, now that there was cold, hard cash to be had.

"Alright?" He glanced around with a criminal's paranoia.

"Yeah." Shrap touched her pocket. She had the money.

Shakes nodded for her to come in, so Shrap followed him into the dingy hall. This time she expected it and raised her arms so that Shakes could search her.

The man grunted appreciatively.

"Let's go to my office."

They walked down the corridor. Shrap heard moaning and creaking coming from one of the upstairs bedrooms and kept going. She didn't want to know what was going on up there.

Not her problem.

She ignored her conscience and took out the wad of fifty-pound notes, handing them to the arms dealer.

Shakes flicked through them, grunted again and went to the fridge. He opened it, reached inside and pulled out a firearm. With a glint of a smile, he placed it on the table in front of Shrap.

It was a Russian 8 mm Baikal self-defence pistol. Legally sold in some European countries, it was designed to fire gas pellets rather than bullets, but it could be converted, with the right tools and know-how, to fire 9 mm bullets. The replacement barrel was threaded to fit a silencer. Except she hadn't ordered one of those. She wasn't planning on using the weapon, not unless she had to. It was for intimidation purposes. That was all.

Shrap knew there were thousands of these floating around. Basically, if you were a twenty-year-old drug dealer and you wanted a gun, this is what you'd get.

"Okay?" asked Shakes, his dark eyes on Shrap.

"Yeah." Shrap held out her hand. "Good doing business with you."

She'd keep him sweet until she could get Trevelyan and his department to come back and raid the place. She'd probably have to wait until this investigation was over and some time had passed. It would be a tip-off. Nothing too obvious. And it couldn't come from her. An ex-copper would be the first person they'd think of, and she didn't want to put Frank in danger.

But one way or another, she had to get these illegal weapons off the street.

. . .

THE NIGHT BUS to Shoreditch was deserted save for a tearful woman in her twenties staring out of the window, mascara smeared down her face. Her night hadn't ended well. A breakup? A fight? It was over. She could tell by the slump of her shoulders and the look of utter desolation on her face.

She was young. She'd recover. Time healed all wounds, or so they said. She scoffed. Not all wounds. Some festered, became more and more entrenched in your subconscious until you couldn't shut your eyes without seeing the faces of the people you'd left behind.

She managed to push the nightmare away. She wasn't even asleep, and it was encroaching.

The bus stopped at a red light and a shabby-looking man got on. Another rough sleeper seeking a warm place to spend a few hours. He hadn't got used to the streets yet, but he would. If he survived the winter.

The homeless man took a seat at the back and immediately leaned against the glass and shut his eyes. Exhausted. Constant vigilance would do that to you. Always looking over your shoulder for the next blow.

The streets weren't for everyone. When she'd first left Trevor she'd slept in her car for a few weeks, but then she'd abandoned even that. She couldn't stretch out, she was too tall, her legs too long. That's what she told herself, but the reality was it was too quiet. She didn't want to hear herself think. With her warm sleeping bag and the sheltered porch at the Marriott, she was as comfortable as anywhere. Hell, it was better than some of the places she'd slept in during the last decade.

Most people left her alone. She'd been told she could be hostile, erratic. Well, that much was true. Even she didn't know when she was going to kick off. When the terror would hit. Not an easy person to get to know, Doug had told her.

Doug had done a lot to help her cultivate this image. At first, it was to offer her some degree of protection, but after an unlucky few had seen how well she handled a blade, the lie became true.

In return, Shrap had been there for Doug. Not always, but when it counted. Doug wasn't as lucky as Shrap. He'd become weak and frail, and his drinking made him vulnerable. Shrap liked to think her vigilant presence had seen off more than a few would-be bullies. It became known that if you messed with Doug, Shrap would have words with you. Best to stay clear and harass some other poor sod.

The night bus hissed to a stop. Shrap got off and looked up and down the dark, deserted street. Quiet for a Saturday night, but then this was a residential area. Young working families already asleep or dozing in front of the television. She felt a vague pang of something akin to homesickness, then let it go. That wasn't her life. Not anymore.

She walked towards Xhafa's house, keeping to the shadows of the tall oak trees, avoiding the pools of light cast by the streetlamps and spilling out of undrawn windows. She made no sound and in her dark attire with the hood up, she was hard to spot. The invisible man – or rather, woman.

She felt the hard barrel of the gun pressed against the small of her back. A familiar, yet disconcerting presence. When she'd tried it out at Shakes', the stock had felt good in her hand. She wasn't immune to the surge of confidence holding a weapon gave you. The power of life and death.

A shiver ran down her spine as she thought of what was to come. She checked her watch. It was nearly one a.m. Plenty of time.

. . .

IT TOOK her under two minutes to pick the lock on Xhafa's front door. For all the security at the club, the house had none. She'd known this because she'd watched the other day. Watched them arrive, then leave. No remotes, no alarms, no cameras.

In other words, no business being done here.

Still, in his industry, you'd think he'd be more careful.

The inside of the house was surprisingly neat. The hallway was wide and welcoming. Carpeted floors absorbed the sound, and a fat lamp on the sideboard emitted a dim but reassuring glow. Yesterday's post was on the sideboard, along with a patterned ceramic bowl for keys and such.

Shrap padded along the hall and peeked through the doorway to the right. A large living room stretched into the dining room and finally into the kitchen. Xhafa had done extensive renovations, but the result was spacious and stylish. Sliding doors at the kitchen end led out onto a paved patio. Beyond that, grass stretched back into the darkness.

She roamed around the living room and kitchen, surveying the clean surfaces, the modern appliances and the clear sink. Definitely the work of a cleaner. Xhafa wouldn't have the time or inclination to keep the place in this sort of condition, not unless he was an obsessive neat freak.

Shrap went upstairs. Two bedrooms, one with an adjoining bathroom. There was another bathroom at the end of the landing. The spare room appeared to be unused. The bed had no bedding on it, but an exercise bike stood facing a floor-length mirror.

Shrap frowned. Where did Mikael sleep? He'd entered the house with Xhafa the other night and hadn't come out again. She walked to the window and peered down onto the silent lawn. She could just make out a dark structure nestled at the bottom of the garden. A shed?

Back downstairs, Shrap opened the sliding doors and stepped out onto the patio. Immediately, a security light flashed on. She froze. There was no sound, no rustle from the neighbours, no heads poking over the wall. A slow exhale.

She slunk towards the shed, keeping to the wall. It was bigger than it appeared from the upstairs window. At least twelve feet long and eight wide. Big enough to house the Russian bodyguard. Double doors opened outwards onto the lawn and next to that, three square windows. A large weatherproof padlock secured the doors.

Shrap peeked in through one of the windows and made out a bed, a side table, and at the foot, a small table and two chairs. She couldn't see the far side of the interior but assumed there must be a kitchenette of some sort. At the very least, a place to make coffee.

The shed itself stood on a low wooden deck that backed right up to the rear garden wall. Grabbing hold of the top of the wall, she pulled herself up and peered over. There was a sloping embankment and at the bottom, a murky stream. On the other side was another wall and beyond that, more houses.

Grunting, she jumped back down and went back into the house, careful to wipe her shoes on the mat. It wouldn't do to traipse mud over the carpeting. She relocked the patio door then left through the front and walked back out onto the street.

At the end of the road, she turned left, then jumped over a barbed-wire fence that led down to the stream. Traversing the embankment, she backtracked towards Xhafa's house. Now for the fun bit.

Scaling the wall, she dropped softly down onto the grass. The garden remained in darkness. She was out of range of the security light. Her breath puffed out in front of her as she hunkered down behind the shed. It was a cold night, but she'd suffered colder, and the wooden deck was more forgiving than concrete. It was nearly two o'clock now. A few more hours and Xhafa and Mikael would be home.

Shrap pulled her coat closer around her and settled down to wait.

28

The lights in the house went on. They were home.

A short time later, the garden lit up. Heavy bootsteps stomped across the patio and down onto the grass.

It was time.

Shrap held her breath as Mikael inserted his key into the lock. There was a metallic clunk and a low creak as the shed door opened. Shrap emerged from the shadows.

"Not a word," she hissed, pressing the gun against the Russian's head. The bodyguard froze.

"Who are—?"

"Shut up," she hissed.

In a practiced move, Shrap disarmed the bodyguard, retrieving the gun from inside his jacket. Patting him down, she also took the knife from a sheath around his ankle. No point in taking any chances.

"Inside."

They shuffled forward into the shed. Shrap glanced behind her at the house, the lower half of which was in darkness. Upstairs, Xhafa's bedroom light was on, but the blind was drawn. He had no idea what was going on twenty metres away.

She forced Mikael into a chair and switched on the light. "Remember me?"

A flicker of recognition.

"You're that chick from the club."

"That's right."

He gave a smirk.

Shrap held the gun steady, like she had a hundred times before. The Russian's black eyes inspected it, lingering on the barrel.

"It shoots real bullets, I assure you."

Mikael's gaze narrowed. "What do you want?"

"Information." Her gaze didn't leave his face. One hint of a movement, and she'd pull the trigger. "Information about Bianca Rubik."

"Bianca? Why do you want to know about her? She's dead."

"That's *why* I want to know about her," she said. "Did you kill her?"

There was a surprised pause. "No, I did not."

She studied his face. Was he lying? She couldn't tell.

"Are you sure? Perhaps she overheard something about your boss's business dealings, and he had to get rid of her. Was she threatening to go to the police?"

Colour rose into the ruddy cheeks. "What are you talking about? Bianca was a dancer. She had nothing to do with the business." He stopped abruptly, not wanting to say too much to this stranger holding a gun on him.

"She was close to Xhafa. She could have found out what he was up to and decided to go to the authorities."

"She knew nothing. The boss was very upset when he found out she'd died."

Shrap thought back to the night at the club when he'd been laughing and cavorting with those two thugs from the East London estate. "He didn't look very upset to me."

"You were there?"

"I've been watching you."

A deep scowl. "Who are you? Police?"

Shrap scoffed. "No, definitely not the police. Think of me as a concerned friend."

"You knew Bianca?"

"I knew someone who died because he witnessed her death. An old man. You might remember him?"

"What old man?" No reaction. No glimmer of recognition. "I don't know any old man." Okay, so maybe he was telling the truth.

"You don't know why Bianca died?"

"Some psycho beat her up on the street."

"She left the club early that night. Do you know why?"

"I don't keep tabs on the girls. That's not my job."

"Whose job is it?"

He hesitated.

Shrap nodded to the gun in her hand. "It's loaded, and yes, I do know how to use it."

A sigh. "Peter, the manager. He's in charge of the girls' rota."

"Thank you." Shrap realised how ridiculous that sounded, seeing as the big Russian didn't have a choice. "I'm going to go now. If you know what's good for you, you won't say a word about this to your boss."

"What about my gun and my knife?" asked Mikael.

"If you want them back, you'll stay where you are until I'm gone."

The Russian gave a terse nod. He didn't like the fact someone had got the jump on him, let alone a woman.

Shrap backed out of the shed, scooted around to the back and heaved herself over the wall, dropping softly onto the embankment on the other side. Once she'd found her footing, she threw Mikael's weapons back over the wall and heard a soft thud as they landed on the grass. Then she was off, sliding down the embankment in her haste. She only relaxed when she'd run two blocks and hopped on another night bus heading back towards the city.

SHRAP DIDN'T BOTHER BEDDING down. The sun would be up in an hour. She may as well head down to the South Bank to watch. She was used to being tired. Sleeping rough meant you never got a full night. She dozed when she could to make up for it, but sometimes she relished that zombie-like state of semi-consciousness. It dulled her senses, made everything easier to bear. Sounds weren't as loud, colours weren't as bright, and her nerves didn't fire at their usual high velocity. It took the hyper out of hypervigilance and made her feel almost human again. Almost, but not quite.

The stone angels at the main entrance to Waterloo station gazed magnanimously down as she walked past. I know what you did, they seemed to be saying.

Already the sky was brightening in the east. With it would come the hustle and bustle of the day. Tourists, day trippers, shoppers, all descending on the city. But right now, it was blissfully quiet. Unspoiled. The stones on the promenade turned a soft pink as the sun touched them. The water began to shimmer, and before long, the windows on the buildings around her flushed with a burnished orange glow, embarrassed by their own beauty.

She didn't have much time.

Walking to the railing, she took the gun from her pocket,

wiped it down and threw it as far as she could into the Thames. Within seconds it had been gulped down. Shrap breathed a sigh of relief. That wasn't something she wanted to hang onto. It made it too easy.

Westminster Bridge lit up on cue, making her smile. At least some things were predictable. She settled down on the low wall in front of the hospital, the same place where the two police officers had found her the morning after Bianca Rubik had died. The city came to life, the sun snaking through its veins, lighting up the streets, the waterways, the high rises.

The confrontation with Mikael hadn't gone as planned. Contrary to what she'd thought, she didn't believe the big Russian had killed Bianca. He certainly hadn't remembered Doug. Any murderer who'd callously poured alcohol over an old man and watched him burn would have shown some fragment of recollection.

Who, then?

The two thugs? Maroon Cap and Grey Beanie? But why? They were visitors to the club. Low-level distributors at best. Not part of the wider organisation. Why would they bother with an erotic dancer?

That left the man on the club security camera. The one Bianca had given a lap dance to then followed home. *He* was their only other lead. What had happened with the facial rec? Had Trevelyan found anything? Waves of exhaustion rolled over her and she fought to keep her eyes open. Only time would tell.

29

S he was back in the desert, on patrol. In a town she didn't know the name of. In the middle of nowhere. Local guerrilla gangs had been alerted to their presence and weren't happy about it. Tensions were running high.

A group of robed men on scooters zoomed past, aggressively kicking up dust. It got everywhere. Sweat poured off her, dripping into her eyes. Something was about to kick off, she could feel it.

From across town, she heard the faint but unmistakable rat-a-tat of gunfire. The radio cackled, alerting her team of the trouble. "Contact!" a tinny voice yelled.

The firing got louder. Shrap heard the whistle of stray bullets flying overhead. She ducked, readying her weapon and yelled at the others to fan out. Find cover.

Just in time.

A truck full of guerrilla fighters rode into the square, guns blazing. Shrap discharged her weapon, her shoulder pressed into the arch of a stone wall. The vibrations shook her entire body.

SHE OPENED HER EYES. What the hell...?

Her chest was vibrating.

Sitting up, pulse racing, she glanced around in fright but there was no one there. No dust either. Just the blinding sun in her eyes. She was on Doug's porch.

Exhaling, she slumped back down. It was only her blasted phone.

By the time she'd reached for it, it had rung off.

Bugger.

She took a few steadying breaths, then glanced at the screen. It was Alex's number. Sunday was his day off. Maybe it was a good thing she'd missed it.

She was about to put it back into his pocket when it beeped, and a text message appeared. She clicked on it with a strange mixture of dread and curiosity.

I need to tell you something about Bianca. Meet me at six in Leicester Square? Outside the Odeon.

What was it he needed to tell her? He'd had plenty of opportunities to speak to her about Bianca before now. Or was this some kind of ploy? A set-up. Mikael, maybe?

No, Mikael wouldn't know Alex was involved. She'd spent an hour and a half in the club at most. Not enough time to make a friend.

She had an overwhelming urge to snuggle back down, close her eyes and shut out the world. The sun's rays were deliciously warm, now that she knew she wasn't in the blazing Afghan desert, and for once her rib didn't ache.

Meeting him would mean cleaning herself up again. Changing back into her new clothes, washing her hair, putting on make-up. It suddenly felt like a mammoth undertaking.

But if he really did have information on Bianca...

She propped herself up on an elbow, fingers poised over

the screen. Her gaze dropped to the discarded newspaper, curled up and turning brown. Doug's paper.

Making up her mind, she replied: *See you there.*

LEICESTER SQUARE WAS BUSY. The crowds swirled around, making her dizzy. Colours flashed before her eyes, music from buskers and singers merged in her brain and grated on her already fraught nerves. The laughter and chatter felt unnaturally loud, but that was just her.

Everywhere, people were enjoying themselves. Tourists laughed at a sketch artist drawing caricatures on an easel, while a focused young man scrambled around on the ground creating intricate chalk flowers, much to the amazement of passers-by.

Shrap edged towards the grassy area in the middle, an oasis of calm. Sweat prickled her forehead and under her arms. She was breathing heavily. Where was Alex?

She gazed around, but focusing on faces made her nauseous. Stumbling to a bench, she sat down and put her head in her hands.

Breathe.

In. Out. In. Out.

"Shaz? Are you okay?"

She looked up. Alex.

"I'm fine." A forced smile. "It's just a headache. Actually, it's a bit noisy around here. Do you mind if we walk?"

"Sure."

He shivered and tucked the front of his brightly coloured scarf into his leather jacket. "Not a day to be out, anyway."

It was bitingly cold.

They ambled towards Charing Cross Road and St

Martin-in-the-Fields. Once out of the hubbub, her head cleared and she could think again.

"I'm sorry to text out of the blue," he began his voice rushed and breathy. "But I think you're going to want to hear this."

Shrap perked up. "Is this new information?"

"Yes, there are two things. Remember when you asked why Bianca left the club early on the night she died?"

"Yes."

"Well, apparently she told Jasmine she had an idea, and if things worked out, she wouldn't be coming back."

Jasmine. The sultry dancer from the club.

"She actually said that? That she wouldn't be coming back?"

Alex nodded.

Shrap scratched her head. It must have had something to do with what Bianca had overheard.

They reached the Strand, crossed it and walked down a broad alleyway towards Victoria Embankment. Terraced buildings stretched upwards on both sides, white against the grey sky, doors painted a glossy black like they were yawning. At the end of the alleyway, the silver Thames sparkled enticingly. The alley smelled faintly of urine, but it was quiet and they could talk.

"You said there was something else?" she prompted.

He slowed the pace, gnawed on his lower lip, then said, "Bianca was having an affair with a married man."

Shrap came to an abrupt halt. "Who?"

"This guy from the club. He was different. Upmarket. You could see he had money. Anyway, he took a liking to her." He rolled his eyes. "Not that that was unusual. Most men did."

Shrap put her hand on her hips. "Alex, this is important information. Why didn't you say anything before now?"

His shrugged, waving his hands in the air. "I didn't know. I suspected there might have been something going on between them, but I wasn't sure. Not until I spoke to Jasmine—"

"What did Jasmine say?"

"We were talking about Bianca. Reminiscing, you know. I mentioned how upset Fiz was when we learned what had happened, and she said the banker would be more upset since they were an item."

"The banker?"

"Yeah, he worked in the city. I'm not sure if he actually was a banker, but that's what we called him." He scoffed.

"Was he often at the club?"

"Fairly often. Afterwards, he'd wait around the corner for her, in his Audi."

"Did Fiz know?"

"No way. He'd have killed her." Alex grimaced. "Figure of speech."

Shrap paused as she assimilated this. Bianca's flatmate hadn't said a word. They had another suspect. The banker.

"I thought she wasn't into men?" Realising how that sounded, she corrected herself. "I mean, I thought she didn't date."

"This guy was different."

"Oh? Why's that?" But she thought she could guess the answer. She was right.

"He paid for her tuition. Jasmine said she used to call him her sugar daddy."

A sugar daddy who may have killed her.

"Alex, I need you to tell me everything you can remember about this man. His age, description, everything."

He grinned. "I can do one better than that. I can give you his name."

30

"**G**regory Pincher."

Shrap stared at him. "How do you know that?"

"He paid his bar tab with a credit card." He looked pleased with himself. "I went in early and looked through the till slips until I found it."

"Thank you," she breathed, committing the name to memory. Alex stomped his feet to keep warm. They started walking again.

"Why are you helping me?" Shrap asked.

"I want to see Bianca's killer brought to justice, and…" He hesitated. "She was a good person. I feel like I owe it to her to help you find out who did this."

Shrap got that. It was the same with Doug. "Well, I'm grateful for the information. I know you took a risk getting it."

"You will let me know, won't you?" he said. "What happens with Bianca's killer."

"I promise." She tapped her pocket. "I've got your number."

Alex surprised her with a brief hug. She didn't have time to respond before he drew back. "It was good knowing you, Shaz."

"You're going?"

"Yeah, it's my one day off. I've got things to do."

She nodded. "Thanks again."

Gregory Pincher.

She repeated the name in her head so she wouldn't forget it.

"You're welcome. Take care, Glitter Girl."

She smiled. "You too, Alex."

SHRAP USED the browser on her phone to google Gregory Pincher. He wasn't a banker, but a partner at Deloitte, the global consulting firm. According to his LinkedIn profile, he'd started off as a chartered accountant and worked his way up to Director of Financial Operations. It had taken a further four years to make partner. In total, he'd been with the company for close on fifteen years.

The same amount of time she'd been in the armed forces.

Pincher's home address was harder to find. She searched but there was only so much she could do on her cheap burner phone. In the end, she decided to pay Jed a visit. She picked up a bottle of red, which she knew the techie was partial to, and walked across town to his flat.

"No," said Jed, before he'd even fully opened the door. "I am *not* breaking into any more clubs, or anywhere else for that matter."

Shrap supressed a grin. "That's not why I'm here, mate."

"Oh." Jed glanced at her suspiciously. "Why are you here, then?"

"I need an address. It shouldn't take you more than a few minutes." Jed eyed the brown paper package in her hand. "What's that?"

"A present." She took out the bottle and held it up. "It's also to say sorry for last time, and thanks for your help. I couldn't have done it without you."

Jed tilted his head and read the label. "Okay, you can come in."

Shrap followed Jed into the flat. The soft hum of the computer servers relaxed her, as did the warmth. It was a welcome contrast to the bitterly cold wind that had sprung up outside.

"What's the name?" asked Jed, sliding into his computer chair. It was so big that it engulfed him. With his slender form and pointy ears, he reminded Shrap of a pixie sitting on an oversized leaf.

"Gregory Pincher." She placed the bottle of wine on his desk.

Jed typed the name into his computer and within seconds had pulled up various sources of information. He scrolled through the first few then uttered a soft "ah-ha".

"You got something?"

"Mr Pincher's done very well for himself." He read out an address in one of London's most expensive neighbourhoods.

Shrap patted him on the back. "Thanks, you're a star."

THE PINCHERS LIVED in a Grade II listed Georgian splendour near Hampstead Heath. The house was typical of the era, perfectly symmetrical with an elaborate entrance and sash windows. The avenue was pretty too. Autumn trees flung their leaves across the pavement, spurred on by the icy breeze. Shrap's eyes watered as she studied it.

A Porsche Cayenne stood in the driveway alongside an electric Audi GT plugged into a purpose-built charging station. That was the car Alex had mentioned.

It was nearly midday. Kids were at school and their parents at work. While she watched, a woman walked past with a yoga mat under her arm. Another strolled by pushing a baby in a pram. Both avoided eye contact with her.

She did a lap of the residential block, admiring the mix of Georgian, Edwardian and Victorian properties alongside quaint cottage-style houses. It was quiet, too quiet. The silence would drive her mad. She needed noise to drown out the voices in her head.

When she got back to the front of the house, a blonde woman was coming out with two chocolate Labradors tugging at their leashes. She wore leggings and a bright pink fleece, with a scarf tied loosely around her neck. As soon as she opened the back of the SUV, the dogs jumped in, tails wagging. Time for walkies.

The SUV backed out of the short driveway and accelerated down the road in the direction of the heath. It was close enough to walk, really, but perhaps the woman didn't want the hassle, or she was short of time.

A security camera on the outside of the house under one of the cornices caught her eye. She hadn't noticed it before because she'd been looking at the house from a different angle. She shifted position to get out of its line of sight.

Did the wife know about her husband's affair with the dancer? She had to assume not, since they were still together, although that didn't mean anything, really. Maybe she knew and had turned a blind eye, or perhaps he'd confessed and she'd forgiven him.

Nah, she was betting the wife knew absolutely nothing about it.

She wanted to talk to Pincher, but she had to do it alone. In the old days, she'd haul Pincher in for questioning. Sit opposite him at a wobbly table in an interview room and get him talking. Now she didn't have that luxury. Pincher wasn't obliged to talk to her. She had no authority. She was a nobody.

Still, it was worth a shot.

Shrap spotted a bus rambling along and jumped on at the nearest stop. Everything in this part of London seemed to move at a slower pace. Even the birds seemed to hover in the sky, going nowhere.

The bus took her into the West End, where life got up to speed. Pedestrians marched along the pavements, cars tooted their horns and the smell of fast food permeated the air. Shrap suddenly realised she was starving. She got a burger from McDonald's and sat down on a bench to eat it.

Deloitte's London headquarters was situated in Holborn. If she made her way there, she might catch Pincher as he left the office. Given the hundreds of people Deloitte employed, spotting Pincher wouldn't be easy, but she had to try. She knew the man hadn't taken his car to work, which meant he'd catch a cab or an Uber home. A pick-up outside the front of the building.

Being a Monday, she doubted the financier would have social commitments after work, so she was pretty sure she had a good chance at spotting him. She knew what Pincher looked like from the photographs on the corporate website, as well as the red-faced, chubbier version on his LinkedIn profile. The trick would be intercepting him before he got into the car. Or maybe she didn't have to...

. . .

IT WAS GONE six before Pincher made an appearance. Shrap was getting worried she'd missed him when the fifty-something in a smart, Saville Row suit and shiny shoes appeared outside the building. Pincher checked his phone, then glanced up and down the street.

A navy-blue Prius pulled to a stop beside him.

Perfect.

As Pincher climbed in on the building side, Shrap got in on the other side. Both the driver and the financier turned to gawk at her.

"I'm afraid this car is taken," Pincher said in the dry tone of one used to being in charge.

"I'm Shrap Nelson," Shrap said. "I'm investigating Bianca Rubik's death. I thought we could have a little chat in private."

Pincher paled and stared at Shrap. "Are you with the police?"

She was getting tired of that question. "Do I look like the police?"

"No." His gaze roamed over her, followed by confusion. "Who are you, then?"

"A friend of Bianca's, but we can go to the police station, if you'd prefer? Or we can have a little chat on your way home."

"Alright, boss?" asked the Uber driver over his shoulder.

Pincher composed himself, then nodded. "It's okay. Drive on."

The driver took off up the street.

Shrap breathed a silent sigh of relief. Her plan had worked.

The man frowned. "What do you want?"

"Were you having an affair with Bianca Rubik?"

"What's that got to do with anything?"

"Well, seeing as she was strangled in a backstreet by a mysterious stranger, it has everything to do with it."

He swallowed. "I didn't have anything to do with her death."

"But you were having an affair?"

"Yes, I was helping her with her tuition fees and—"

"And she was sleeping with you in return?"

"It was a mutually agreeable arrangement."

"I see."

"Look, she came on to me, okay? At the strip club. I was there with some friends and she enticed me to a private dance. She was very beautiful. One thing led to another and we started seeing each other. It was all above board."

"Except you're married," Shrap said, watching him.

He glanced down at his wedding ring. "Yes, Annie doesn't know. She'll go ballistic if she finds out. Please don't say anything to her."

"Which is why we're meeting here, Mr Pincher, and not at your home."

He whimpered, pathetically grateful. A man with everything to lose.

Shrap wasn't about to destroy his life, not unless he was the killer.

"Mr Pincher, can you account for your whereabouts on the night of the third of November?"

"Is that when she was murdered?"

"Yes."

He thought back, gnawing on his lower lip. "I don't remember. I'll have to check my calendar."

"You do that."

Pincher dug in his pocket for his mobile phone. Hands

shaking, he brought up the calendar app. "I was at a corporate function in Marylebone that evening."

"What time did you get home?"

"Shortly after ten."

"Was your wife with you?"

"No, she didn't come out with us, but she was home when I got back. You're not going to ask her to confirm it, are you?"

"I'm not, but the police might want to."

His shoulders sank and his complexion took on a greenish hue. "God, no. She'll leave me. I'll lose the kids. Everything."

To be fair, he should have thought of that before he was unfaithful; however, Shrap wasn't one to judge. God knows she'd done plenty of things she wasn't proud of.

"You might be able to keep your affair out of it," she said, "if you have a word with the detective first."

Pincher was nodding, his hands clenched together in his lap. "Yes, yes, I'll do that. When do you think...?"

"I don't know. My investigation is separate to theirs, but I'm sure they'll get to you eventually." When she told Trevelyan what she knew.

Shrap glanced at the trembling financier. No way did this guy murder Bianca. He was more afraid of his wife finding out about the affair. A guilty man would have bigger things to worry about. Still, he could be lying. During her time in the military police, she'd seen many a guilty person put on a convincing display for the authorities, some of which she'd even believed herself.

She'd leave it to Trevelyan to double-check the man's alibi. She didn't have the authority to go contacting the senior partners in the firm, nor did she want to break the news about the affair to Pincher's wife.

"You can stop here," she told the driver, who pulled over outside a newsagent.

She didn't say goodbye to Pincher, who was staring ahead like his world was about to implode. Maybe it was. Shrap almost felt sorry for the guy.

A blast of frigid wind hit her full in the face and she dipped her head, stuffing her hands into her coat pockets. Winter was definitely on the way.

Walking down Tottenham Court Road towards Leicester Square, she considered catching a bus, but wanted to clear her head. Her suspect list was looking disappointingly thin. Now she'd ruled out the Parliament-smoking Mikael and Bianca's married lover, she was back to the Bianca's mysterious customer at the club.

Shrap turned right into the Strand and was hit by a gust of wind so strong she staggered backwards a few steps. Hell, this was some gale. The awning above the Marriott would make a racket tonight, it would be better to sleep on Doug's porch, as she'd come to think of the basement flat in Waterloo. As long as she crept in there after the rest of the block had gone to sleep, no one would notice her.

Her phone pinged and she sheltered in the doorway of a coffee shop while she read the text. It was from Trevelyan. Her pulse surged.

"Can we meet?"

31

Trevelyan hurried along The Cut towards the Anchor and Hope. Bloody hell, the wind was cold. It whipped at his hair, tugging it in all directions. He snuggled into his winter jacket and quickened his step.

Not that he was worried about his appearance. Not for her. Although, there was something about the ex-military policewoman's piercing blue gaze that he found unnerving, like she saw too much, but said too little.

He pushed open the door to the pub and looked around, letting his eyes adjust to the dimness. It was virtually empty save for an old man at one end of the bar nursing a Guinness. Somewhere in the back he heard the clash of snooker balls.

A woman walked out of the gloom.

Shrap.

She gestured towards a table where they wouldn't be overheard by the barman or the old man, neither of whom had glanced up when he'd walked in.

"Hello," he said, as they sat down.

She nodded in return.

The table was sticky, so he leaned back, trying not to touch it. Shrap crossed her legs under the table. She was studying him, gauging his reaction, so he gave her what he hoped was a disarming smile and said, "Do you want a drink?"

"Sure, if you're buying. A beer would be great."

He got up again, went to the bar and ordered two pints. It would help take the edge off. He didn't know why she unsettled him. It was ridiculous, really, considering he was a London Metropolitan Police officer and she was... Well, he wasn't quite sure what she was.

He paid for the drinks and returned to the table. As he sat down, Shrap said, "Did you find out who the man in the photograph was?"

"Yep, facial rec found a match. He's a jewel thief called Leonard Blake. He spent the better part of the last eight years inside HMP Wandsworth for armed robbery."

Her eyebrows shot up.

"Yes, he ripped off a Kensington jewellery store with his accomplice, Giles Wakefield. They stole a hundred thousand pounds' worth of merchandise. The police arrested them at Blake's home, but the loot was never recovered."

"You mean there's a stash of jewellery still out there?"

"Yeah. Both Blake and Wakefield refused to do a deal and so the location of the jewellery was never discovered."

"Bloody hell." She reached for her pint.

"What do you make of it?" he asked.

She took a thoughtful sip. "Bianca Rubik overheard a phone conversation between Blake and someone else. A conversation that spurred her into action. After the lap dance, she grabbed her handbag and followed him out into the street. That was the last sighting of her."

"You think this has something to do with the stolen

jewels?" His mind was working overtime. Why else would she suddenly up and leave?

"Maybe."

Gareth clicked his fingers. "What if Bianca overheard Blake telling Wakefield or someone else that he had the jewels? She figured she'd follow him and steal them for herself."

"From what I've heard, she wasn't like that," she said, frowning. "I'm not sure she'd resort to stealing."

"No? Don't forget she had a kid she never saw, and she worked at a strip club taking her clothes off for strangers. A hundred grand is a lot of money. She wanted to be a solicitor. Wouldn't you jump at a chance to shortcut that process?"

"Hmm... I might."

"Of course you would. She had adequate motivation. With the money from the jewellery heist, she could start again. She could pay for her studies and bring her child over from Poland. It's a win–win."

"It does make sense." Shrap smoothed down her hair which was as windswept as his own. He noticed she was wearing make-up. Just a smattering, but it illuminated her eyes and gave her cheeks a rosy blush.

"Can you think of another reason why she'd suddenly leave like that?"

"No." She tapped her fingers on the side of the glass. "You might be onto something. Do you have an address for this guy?"

"Yes." He grimaced. "But I can't just go and pick him up." Because the case was closed.

"We could question him at his house."

"We?"

"He doesn't need to know I'm no longer a cop."

"No way." Gareth shook his head. "What if he reports me? The SIO would have a shit-fit if he knew I was still working a closed case."

"He won't." Shrap let out an unladylike snort. "What burglar is going to voluntarily contact the police? Especially if the jewels are still out there. He'd just be drawing attention to himself."

She had a point. Realistically, what were the chances? They *could* pay him a visit. His mind wandered back to the crime scene photographs of Bianca Rubik lying on the pavement, her sightless eyes staring at the heavens, her mouth half open in a cry for help. Help that had never come.

He shuddered. That woman deserved justice.

"Okay, how do you want to do it?"

They went in his 'hot hatchback', a Ford Fiesta ST3 that he'd bought after his transfer to Southwark. It had been a reward for getting out of there, away from *her*. He'd envisioned weekend jaunts to the countryside, a spot of golf, maybe a couple of pub lunches – he was partial to a battered cod and chips – except he hadn't done any of those things. It hadn't sounded that appealing on his own.

He glanced at the woman beside him. She sat stiffly, arms pinned to her sides as if she was uncomfortable being inside the car with him. He wanted to ask her questions, find out more about her, but small talk didn't seem appropriate, somehow.

"I think the best way to play it is to pretend we know nothing about the stolen jewels," she said, her brow creased. "If we focus on the murder, he might be more willing to talk to us."

"Unless he killed her," he replied.

She shrugged. "Yes, in which case he'll clam up faster than you can say Southwark CID."

He indicated right and turned into Camden High Street. Leonard Blake lived close to Kentish Town, near the railway line, according to the satnav. The street was busy with the afterwork crowd. Even with the windows closed, they could hear music pumping out from the bars and cafés. The shops were still open, and all manner of clothes, shoes and handbags were arranged on tables on the pavement.

"Also, start slowly. If he lies about where he was on that Saturday night, we'll know. You can use it to rattle him."

"I know how to conduct an interview," he replied, with an edge.

"Sorry." She turned to look out of the window. "Old habits and all that."

"I understand."

They drove the rest of the way in silence. When they got there, he pulled into a designated parking bay across the road. Blake lived in an ugly brown building that must have been built in the seventies. Thick brick balconies overlooked the road, devoid of pot plants or any other sign of habitation. No one wanted to sit out there and overlook the street.

"Flat 9," he said, getting out of the car.

Shrap followed.

He was about to press the downstairs buzzer when she reached out and grabbed his hand.

"What?"

"Wait."

A young woman dressed for a night on the town opened the security door.

Shrap caught it before it closed.

The woman didn't acknowledge them, she just kept walking.

The wind whipped around the lower stairwell, whistling

like a banshee. "First floor, I think," Gareth shouted to be heard over the screeching.

Shrap took the stairs two at a time. He had to hurry to keep up. It had been smart not alerting Blake they were there. If the jewel thief knew they were the police, he might not have let them in. This way he'd have no choice but to talk to them.

Gareth was relieved to get out of the wind at the top of the stairs. They turned left and walked along an exposed corridor to flat 9. He glanced at Shrap, who nodded.

He knocked three times. Firmly. A no-nonsense knock.

Shuffling and footsteps, then a male voice said, "Who is it?"

"The police, Mr Blake. We'd like to ask you some questions."

A pause.

"Okay, give me a minute to put some clothes on."

Shrap shook her head. "He's going to make a run for it."

"How do you know?" Gareth asked.

"He was wearing shoes. I could hear them on the wooden floor."

"Shit. What should we do?" He couldn't break the door down. It wasn't that kind of visit.

"You get the car. I'll follow on foot." And she took off down the stairs at a run. Gareth followed as best he could, nearly losing his footing on several occasions.

"Bloody hell," he muttered, pushing open the door at the bottom of the stairwell. For a seemingly fragile vagrant, Shrap had disappeared incredibly fast.

He looked down the street and saw the tall, willowy Shrap running after a shorter, stockier man. He'd got out of there quickly – must have climbed out of the window and jumped from the balcony. Already, they were turning the corner into the next street.

Pulling his keys out of her pocket, he jumped into the car and took off in the other direction. Perhaps he could cut them off around the block. He turned the corner and swerved to avoid a couple of pedestrians. Damnit, where was the blue light when you needed it?

Another corner – and there they were! Shrap was gaining on the jewel thief, although if he made it into the fenced off industrial area, they were screwed.

He put his foot down and screeched to a halt in front of Blake. The ex-con changed direction and darted towards the fence. Shrap sprinted behind him, a look of sheer determination on her face.

The jewel thief jumped at the fence and swung over like a monkey. Shrap went for it, hurling her slim frame at the fence and pulling herself up. Then her face crumpled, and she let go, falling back to the ground with a frustrated moan.

"What's wrong?" Gareth asked, running up.

"My ribs," she gritted, clutching her side with her other hand. She had gone a shade paler, although that could be the effect of charging up the street after the suspect. She didn't move for a moment, just sat gritting her teeth as Blake disappeared around a factory building.

"Fuck," she muttered.

"Why'd he run?" Gareth stared into the distance where the figure had vanished. "If he didn't have something to hide? I think he's our guy."

Shrap gripped the fence and pulled herself to her feet. "Could be. Could be that he heard the word police and panicked."

"Should we go back to his flat and wait for him?"

"No point. He won't go back there now." Shrap stared in

the direction in which he'd vanished. "You could put out a BOLO on him and get Uniform to pick him up."

"On what grounds?" He paced up and down. "I'm not supposed to be on this case, remember?"

"He ran," said Shrap.

"Yes, but like you pointed out, he could be overly sensitive considering he's just been released from prison and there's a cache of jewels out there somewhere."

"His parole officer might be able to help," suggested Shrap.

A slow nod. "Maybe I'll pay him a visit. It'll have to be off the books, though."

Shrap looked tired after the sprint around the block or maybe it was the pain that gave her face that pinched look. "What happened to your ribs?"

She hesitated. "Got into a fight."

"Seriously?"

"It happens."

He could tell he wasn't going to get anything more out of her. Wearily, they climbed into the car. "Where can I drop you?" he asked.

"Anywhere near Waterloo will be fine."

A woman without a home. No known address, it had said on the witness sheet. It was on the tip of his tongue to ask her about Afghanistan, about what had happened there. Why she was living on the street.

Discharged on health grounds. PTSD.

She was a loner, granted, and he never knew what she was thinking, but she seemed competent. She'd clearly been able to hold down a job. Sergeant while with SIB. She was smart, she was fit and able, a tad undernourished, perhaps, and she could stand to put on a few pounds, but she wasn't in ill health, apart from her rib.

But he knew better than most that not all pain was physical.

Something must have happened to trigger her homelessness. A breakdown? A fallout with her partner? Had she been kicked out of the family home? He didn't remember reading anywhere that she'd been married. Was she violent? A danger to society?

Got into a fight.

Only to the bad guys.

He glanced at her stoic expression and decided now wasn't the time. Whatever reason she had for sleeping rough, it could wait. It was none of his business anyway.

32

As soon as Shrap walked into the day centre, she knew something was wrong. It was the way in which everyone was talking in hushed tones, how people who never read the newspaper now poured over it. How Budge and the volunteers were sombre and serious, rather than their usual upbeat, smiley selves.

"What's happened?" she asked Budge.

"Another murder," he muttered. "Right here on The Cut."

A jolt went through her. "When?"

"Last night."

"What?" She hadn't heard a thing and she'd only been around the corner on Doug's porch. Granted, it was two roads away, but sirens in the dead of night were loud and curled around the buildings. You'd think she'd have heard something.

"A young girl – Petra, her name was. They found her body early this morning in a pub car park behind some bins." He shook his head. "Awful way to go."

"How was she killed?"

"Strangled." Budge moved away. "Tragic. She was so young."

Shrap sat down next to an elderly man who was folding up the paper, his rheumy eyes gazing into the middle distance, his hands wrapped around his mug of tea.

"May I?" Shrap reached for the paper. The old man grunted.

Front page news.

SECOND SEX WORKER MURDERED

She gritted her teeth. Bloody journalists. Didn't they do their homework? Or did sex worker sound better than erotic dancer in a headline?

There was a photograph of a smiling young girl – supplied by her devastated family, no doubt. She started. She recognised her from the group of women she'd spoken to when she'd been looking for Bianca. The young redhead.

Jesus.

Her breath quickened. Petra Burton-Leigh. Seventeen years old. Hailed from Sevenoaks in Kent.

She read on. The article was short, having been written in a hurry, probably moments before the paper went to print. It didn't mention anything about the young woman's death other than she was strangled and her body found in the street behind the Old Vic theatre by an assistant. There'd be more in the later editions, once the reporters had had time to tap their sources and assimilate the information.

One murder had lost traction pretty fast, but two hinted at something far more sinister. Same MO. Same vicinity. What did it mean?

She got herself some toast and coffee and went back to her chair. Had Bianca's death been a serial killing? An opportunist who had a thing for sex workers? Who wanted to teach them a lesson? Dressed as she had been, Bianca may have been mistaken for a prostitute. Heavy make-up, shiny shoes, provocative attire. She sighed. It wouldn't be the first time some sick bastard had targeted them for their profession.

This threw out her whole theory. If it wasn't someone close to Bianca, then she'd been barking up the wrong tree this whole time.

Had Doug been killed because he'd witnessed the murder, or for some other unconnected reason? No, it had to be linked. Too much of a coincidence.

She shook her head. What would Trevelyan make of it? It fell in his jurisdiction. Would Southwark Police connect the two crimes or treat them as isolated cases?

What did the post-mortem say?

She crunched her toast in annoyance. Damn, she missed having access to that kind of information. Her brain was firing off questions, and she had no way of getting the answers.

"You okay, Shrap?" Budge stopped by the table.

"Yes, I'm fine. I knew her, that's all." She nodded to the newspaper article.

"Same," Budge said sadly. "Used to come in for a cuppa before closing sometimes. Didn't get on with her stepdad, that's why she left home. Poor love hadn't even finished school."

Another young life cut down before it had even got started. And the worst part was, she had no idea where to turn or what to do next. Suddenly, the jewel thief didn't seem such a likely suspect anymore. Would he have killed two women? Had he got a taste for it after he'd strangled Bianca?

No. Something told her she was off base with that

theory. If the two murders were related, it couldn't have been Blake. He'd disappeared into the factory grounds last night miles away from Central London. It had taken Trevelyan half an hour to drive them home. A man on foot wouldn't have had enough time to get back, stalk his next victim, strangle her, dump her body and disappear into the ether before she was discovered by the landlord just after two a.m.

What had happened after Bianca had followed Blake out of the club that night? If only she could speak to the guy. Question him properly. There could be a simple explanation: she tried to keep up with him but lost him once they got to Waterloo. Or maybe they'd had an altercation and he'd left her standing on the pavement. Or maybe he'd spotted her tailing him, strangled her and left her for dead.

In which case the two murders weren't linked.

She downed her coffee and took out her phone. It had one bar left. She stood outside the day centre and called Trevelyan's mobile. It rang several times before the detective answered.

"DC Trevelyan."

"It's Shrap. I just heard."

"I can't talk now. I'll call you back in five." He hung up.

Fair enough.

She went back inside and plugged in her phone. There were power points along the wall, a kickback to when this used to be an office block. The charity had taken it over about ten years ago and converted it into a haven for the homeless. The place was a godsend. They offered free breakfasts, showers, a change of clothes when yours got too threadbare, toiletries and countless teas and coffees. All run by Budge and a host of volunteers.

It wasn't only the material things, it was the friendly

smiles, the warm welcomes, the access to a medical professional, a benefits advisor and a job centre councillor if you
wanted to find work. Shrap didn't need any of those things.
For her, it was the routine. Knowing there was a safe place to
go to for a hot drink and to ease the ache in her belly, or her
heart, after a restless night's sleep grappling with the memories and the faces of the dead who haunted her.

She dreaded to think where she'd be if it wasn't for
Budge and his gang of friendly volunteers. They even had a
garden of sorts out the back. At one stage Budge had been
talking about dividing it up into smaller lots and allowing
the "guests", as he called them, to go out and have a dig
around. A form of therapy. But it had never really got off the
ground. Now the weather had turned, it was unlikely to
until the spring.

Shrap took a pencil from one of the tables dedicated to
the job centre and sat down to do the sudoku. Maybe it
would take her mind off the investigation. It didn't. She was
halfway through when her phone rang. She glanced at the
screen.

Trevelyan.

"Hey." She answered straight away.

"Sorry about that." He sounded tense. "I was in a briefing. This dead girl. Christ, Shrap. What if it's the same guy?"

"Is it the same MO?" The paper said it was, but she'd
learned not to trust journalists.

"She was strangled just after midnight. Same timeframe
as Bianca Rubik. Big hands. A man's hands, according to the
preliminary pathologist's report. We're waiting on the post-
mortem."

"Any sign of sexual assault?" she asked.

"No." A pause. "Shrap, it couldn't have been Blake. We
left him in Camden."

"I know, but are the deaths connected?"

"Hell of a coincidence, don't you think? Two girls murdered within two weeks in the same area. Both strangled. Okay, Bianca had ligature marks on her neck and this girl has clear finger marks, so not exactly the same MO. Still, maybe the killer didn't have anything to hand."

"Could be." She thought for a moment. "Any DNA at the crime scene?"

"Not that we know of. Forensics took swabs, obviously, but the lab results haven't come back yet. Another day or two. There was nothing obvious. We're trawling through CCTV footage as we speak."

This time there'd be no Doug hurrying away from the scene. No one to pin it on.

"Will you keep me posted?" She knew she was asking a lot.

"It's difficult. I could get suspended if my boss knew I was talking to you."

She heard the stress in his voice. "I'm sorry, Shrap. I have to go."

The line went dead.

She sat staring out of the window, the unfinished puzzle in front of her. Chances were forensics were still working the crime scene. Getting up, she went to the communal bathroom, where she showered and brushed her teeth, then grabbed her phone – now at three bars – and walked up The Cut toward the Coach and Horses.

The car park was behind the pub, not visible from the road. The side entrance was cordoned off and a white forensic tent had been erected over where the body had been found. Petra would be long gone now, stashed in a morgue awaiting her turn under the knife. She shuddered. It was awful thinking of her like that.

Only a few weeks ago she'd been full of life, smiling flir-tatiously, hanging out with the more experienced ladies of the night. Had they lost track of her? Had she gone off with a punter and never come back? Did they see anything?

She massaged her arm, frustrated. Now it was healing, it was itchy. She needed more information if she was going to make sense of this.

"Sorry, this area is off-limits," a uniformed police officer told her.

She backed away. Couldn't see inside the tent anyway, but she didn't have to. She'd been to enough crime scenes in her time and knew the process. Forensic technicians were scouring the area for any evidence that might indicate who the perpetrator was. A stray hair, a cigarette butt, a boot print in a muddy puddle. Perhaps a tuft of hair or a fibre. Anything they found would be bagged and tagged, entered onto an evidence spreadsheet and sent to the lab for processing.

The report would then be sent to DC Trevelyan and his team for analysis and to follow up on any leads it may provide.

She thought of Fishnets and her gang. There was a slim chance one of them had seen who Petra had gone off with, if indeed she had gone off with someone. It was still too early for them to be out, and given what had happened last night, they might not make an appearance tonight. Still, she had to try.

She decided to spend the rest of the morning in the library, seeing if any of the other newspapers had anything to add to what she already knew. Then she'd go and launder her clothes; they were beginning to smell. Inevitable, when you're lying on dirty porches or in doorways every night.

It was one of the things she didn't like about living on

the street. Cleanliness had been something of a virtue in the army, and even though they'd gone for days without showering when on ops, back at the base they were stringent about personal hygiene and the condition of their uniform and weapon. Still, it was a small price to pay for being invisible.

It got dark around five forty-five these days. Once the sun had sunk below the high-rises, she'd come back and see if she could find Fishnets and her gang. They wouldn't talk to the police, but they might talk to her.

33

The moon was out when Shrap finished at the laundromat. She'd spent the last few hours, after closing, helping Milly repair one of the industrial-sized dryers. The middle-aged Ukrainian only had two, but they were an essential part of her revenue. In addition to walk-in customers, Milly serviced several local B&Bs who dropped off their linen to be washed and ironed. Without that second machine, her to-be-laundered pile was stacking up.

As usual, Milly had let her change in the back, and even let her use the tiny kitchenette to make a sandwich. "You need to eat, luvvie. You are far too thin."

It had felt good working with her hands again. Before she'd transferred to the military police, she'd been one of only five women who'd signed up for the Royal Engineers and trained in everything from demolition and mine warfare to building bridges and fixing field equipment, including heavy machinery. When she'd left, there were nearly thirty women in the sappers.

Who would have thought she'd be using her skills to

change oven lightbulbs and fix dryers? Still, at least she had something to offer, and what she was discovering was many of these small-business owners didn't have the funds to get things fixed themselves. Their existence was so fragile that they had to rely on people like her to do the job for them. Something she was only too happy to do.

"I'm going to show you where I leave the spare key," Milly told Shrap when she left that evening. They'd gone out the back, the front having been locked up and the shutter pulled down. "Just in case you need to get in, you know, if it gets too cold."

She told Milly not to worry, but she insisted. "It's here, underneath the third brick from the door. It's loose, see? I keep it there in case I forget mine at home. Some mornings my brain don't work too well." She gave an embarrassed smile.

"Thank you, Milly, but I'll be fine. Really."

"It's no bother." She wagged a wrinkled finger at her. "I don't want you freezing to death. Who'd help me fix my machines then?"

She chuckled. "Okay, deal."

There was a fence at the back with barbed wire coiled along the top. This was more for the benefit of the newsagent next door than the laundromat since the gate leading to Milly's shop had a broken latch and didn't shut properly.

"You should get that fixed," she told her.

The Ukrainian woman shrugged. "Nobody's going to break into my little place with the newsagent one side and the fish and chip shop on the other. Besides, I don't keep any money on the premises."

"I'll sort it for you next time." They walked into the alleyway behind the row of shops.

"You're a good girl, Shrap," Milly said, before she bid her goodnight and waddled off down the road.

Backpack full of fresh clothes, she loitered around the intersection where she'd seen Fishnets and the other ladies last time. It was bitterly cold, so she marched up and down to keep warm. Where were they? Had they decided it was too dangerous to ply their trade tonight?

She kept watching and waiting. The moon shone bright on the damp pavements, then disappeared again. Too much effort. Eventually, she saw the brunette with the heavily kohled eyes. Last time she could barely see them, this time they were filled with fear, darting left and right, scrutinising every vehicle that stopped on the double-yellow in front of her.

"Hello," she said, walking up.

The brunette stared at her for an instant, then recognition dawned. "Oh, hiya. What are you doing out and about on a night like this?"

"I heard about Petra," she said.

The sex worker's face fell. "Yeah. Poor lass. We're all a bit jumpy, to tell you the truth."

"I can imagine. Are you sure it's safe for you out here?"

"Well, it's like I told Marie, I gotta make the rent. It's due next week and my landlord ain't giving me any more chances." She glanced around her. "I figured that strangler ain't likely to come out again the very next night, is he? Too obvious. I've seen police patrolling the area, they're on the lookout."

Shrap hoped she was right.

"When was the last time you saw Petra?"

The brunette narrowed her eyes. "You sound like the police."

"No, but remember the other murdered girl?"

"Yeah."

"She was strangled in the same way Petra was."

Her eyes widened. "That's who you were looking for?"

"That's right. Bianca." She lowered her voice. "I want to find out what happened to them."

"Wouldn't we all?" She shot Shrap a sideways glance. "What's it to you, anyway?"

"It's a long story, but my friend was accused of murdering Bianca, when I know he didn't. I'm trying to prove him innocent." She didn't mention he was dead.

"Your friend?"

"Yeah." She hesitated. "He's a good man. He saved my life a few years back."

The brunette gazed at her, curious but detached. In her industry it didn't pay to know too much. Or to let on that you knew.

"I last saw her standing right where you are now," she said.

"What time was that?"

"Around eleven. I hooked a guy in a Ferrari – wasn't about to turn him down, was I? That's the last I saw her." Her voice faltered. "Marie was here, though. She might have seen where she went."

"Where's Marie now?"

"She'll be back soon. The Toyota Tazz didn't look like he had the money to go a full round, if you know what I mean." She gave a wry grin.

That meant a quick blowjob around the corner. She shut her eyes. What these women did to make ends meet.

Sure enough, not ten minutes later, Marie was back. She wore exactly the same outfit as before. A short skirt over fishnet stockings, red high heels, a blouse showing an indecent amount of cleavage, and rich, curly brown hair cascading over her shoulders. She was probably in her late thirties or early forties and the look in her eyes said she'd had just about enough of this lark.

"Hey darlin'." She sauntered up. "Did you find your Polish friend?"

The brunette bit her lip.

"What?" Marie glanced between the two of them.

"That Polish girl was the first one that was murdered," she said. "She's trying to find out who done it."

Marie raised an eyebrow. Naturally suspicious. She didn't blame her.

"Shrap," she said. "My name's Shrap."

She confirmed what the brunette had said and explained why she was trying to find out who the strangler was. She didn't have a problem coming clean with these women. They wouldn't talk to the police.

"What do you want from us, Shrap?" Marie wasn't going to make this easy for her.

"Did you see who picked Petra up?" she asked bluntly.

"Yeah, but how do you know that's the guy who done her in?"

"I don't, but it's a good place to start."

Marie shrugged. "Well, I can't tell you the number plate or nothing, 'cos I wasn't really paying attention, but I can tell you it was a big black SUV."

"An SUV? What make?"

"I dunno. They all look the same to me."

"Did you see who was driving?"

"Nah, had tinted windows."

Shit.

"What time was this?" she asked.

"Eleven fifteen, eleven twenty, somewhere round there."

That was pretty early. The victim's body had been found

just before two a.m. Almost three hours later. But then, she didn't know how long she'd been lying there. He could have killed her and dumped the body before midnight, but the chances were someone would have found her sooner, if that was the case. The pub car park closed at midnight, but the staff would be taking refuse out to the bins after closing.

"And you didn't see her after that? None of you?"

"No, I didn't. Ronnie didn't either. She went home early. Some guy did a number on her."

"Me neither," added the brunette.

"Is Ronnie alright?" She tried to remember which one she was.

"She will be. Bastard liked it rough. Some of them do, you know."

She cringed but didn't say anything. They didn't need her pity, or her judgement. Just like she didn't need theirs.

"Okay, thanks." She glanced at Marie. "There's nothing else you remember about this SUV, is there? Anything that would help me identify the driver?"

She thought for a moment. "He was playing some sort of rap music. That's all I can tell you."

"Rap music?"

"Yeah, it was loud. The whole car was throbbing with it."

Shrap frowned. That was something, at least. A younger guy. Not many men over the age of forty would listen to rap, at least not at that volume.

"Thanks Marie, you've been very useful. If you think of anything else, let me know."

"How? You have a number?"

"Yeah. Actually, I do." She pulled out her phone.

"Text me," Marie said. "Then I've got it."

She read out her number and Shrap dutifully sent her a blank text.

"Gotcha." Marie's lips parted in a fuchsia smile.

Shrap thanked them again and walked off down the street. That night she dreamed of a black SUV with Petra's pale face at the window screaming for help. But there was nothing she could do.

areth Trevelyan was not having a good morning. The news of the second murder had shocked the station. DCI Burrows had been called to the crime scene at two a.m., along with DS Heely and DS Brenner, and none of them had slept a wink.

Gareth had been called in at the crack of dawn, along with the rest of the team, to find out who the dead girl was, where she lived and who her next of kin were.

Now he was hovering outside the SIO's door, debating whether or not to go in.

"Trevelyan, get in here!"

Too late.

Taking a deep breath, he pushed open the door and went inside. Burrows was going to go ballistic when he heard what he had to say, but in light of the second murder, he couldn't keep it to himself anymore.

"You wanted to see me?"

"Yes, guv. There's something I need to tell you."

"Well, spit it out then. I don't have all day." He had big sweat patches under his arms and his hair was stuck to his head. The strain was beginning to show. If the two deaths turned out to be connected, it put the result of the first murder in doubt. Burrows wasn't the type of man to admit he'd made a mistake.

And Gareth was about to rub it in his face.

"Sir, there were a few leads from the Bianca Rubik case that I followed up on independently." At the SIO's death stare, he hastily explained, "I wanted to tie up the loose ends and since the case was closed, I didn't report on it. Except now, with this second murder, I think they might be relevant."

Burrows' barrel chest heaved up and down as Gareth waited for the explosion.

"Jesus Christ, Trevelyan! You're here to concentrate on active cases, not closed ones."

"I know, sir, but if you'll hear me out—"

"I specifically told you to draw a line under that investigation."

"I know, sir. But—"

"It's a waste of department resources. We don't have the budget to go chasing down loose ends. Every case has loose ends, for Christ's sake."

"I found another suspect," he managed to get out.

Burrows paused, his face redder than Gareth had ever seen it.

"What suspect?"

"There's a man we should bring in for questioning. His name is Leonard Blake, and he's got form."

The chest stopped heaving. "Previous?"

"Yes, guv. He's an ex-con, a jewel thief. Knocked off a couple of jewellery stores and got eight years. He was released last month."

Burrows stared at him. "Why should we be looking at

him? What's he got to do with these girls?"

"He was at the strip club where Bianca Rubik worked. She gave him a private lap dance."

"Is he a sicko or something?"

"I don't know, but she left shortly after him. The bartender thought she wanted to talk to him." Okay, that wasn't strictly true, but he couldn't mention Shrap or the CCTV image she'd shown him.

Burrows stared at him. "The night she was killed?"

"Yes, sir. Blake could be the last person to have seen her alive."

"For fuck's sake." Burrows swiped at his greasy hair. "Does Blake have any connection with this second girl?"

"I don't know yet, sir. That's why we need to bring him in for questioning."

Burrows paced up and down, sweat patches widening. A long moment passed. Eventually, he said, "Okay, do it."

Trevelyan grinned. "Really?"

"Yeah, really. Get Uniform to bring him in and let's see what the bugger has to say."

"Yes, guv!"

"Petra Burton-Leigh is in the system for soliciting." Devi jabbed her screen. "We brought her in last year but let her go with a caution. Her mother came to pick her up. She was sixteen at the time."

"Christ," murmured Gareth. "She's practically a child."

"Contact the mother," bellowed Burrows, who'd come out of his office. "Heely and Brenner, go and talk to the family. Find out why she was on the streets and if she'd been in contact with them lately."

"Yes, guv." They both got up and reached for their coats.

"Petra gave an address in Southwark," said Trevelyan, who'd immediately pulled up the solicitation report. "It was last year, but it might be worth checking out."

Burrows grunted. "Take DS Chakrabarti with you."

Gareth raised an eyebrow at Devi, who gave a curt nod.

"Looks like you might have been right after all," Devi acknowledged, once they were in the car.

"We don't know if the two cases are linked yet," he muttered.

"True, but if they are, Burrows is going to be in the shit."

That made him smile. Just a little.

"I think this is the place." Gareth parked the car outside a brown-brick high-rise resting in the shadow of the Shard and flanked by more modern buildings. He glanced up to where it stabbed the overcast sky.

"I wouldn't like to live up there," Devi murmured. "Not after Grenfell."

"I don't suppose they have much of a choice." He got out of the car.

The lift was broken so they walked up sixteen flights of stairs to the eighth floor. "That's my exercise for the day," Devi panted at the top. Gareth could feel his thighs burning.

"Let's hope someone's home," he said.

They rang the doorbell, grimy with use. A full minute ticked by.

"Looks like a dead end," muttered Devi.

He rang again. Eventually, a sleepy voice said, "Yeah?"

"Hello, this is DC Trevelyan and DS Chakrabarti from Southwark Police Station. May we come in? We'd like to ask you some questions about Petra Burton-Leigh."

There was a pause, then a soft sigh and the door opened. A petite blonde woman with a massive shiner on her cheek regarded them suspiciously. Her eyes were red rimmed from crying, and she clutched a tissue in her one hand and a hair-brush in the other.

"I take it you knew Petra?" Gareth said, taking in her grief-stricken appearance.

She sniffed, then gave a small nod.

"I'm sorry for your loss," he said.

The woman tried to smile but failed. Instead, she let out a half-moan, half-sob and turned away from the door.

Devi stepped forward and put an arm around her. "Come on. Let's sit down."

Gareth followed them in.

"How about some tea?" Gareth suggested, nodding at Devi.

She walked into the open-plan kitchen and looked around. Spotting the kettle, she filled it up and systematically opened all the cupboards until she found the mugs.

In the meantime, Gareth sat Petra's friend down on the well-worn couch. She wore a pink dressing gown and her feet were bare. "What's your name?"

"Veronica," she said. "But everybody calls me Ronnie."

"Okay, Ronnie. DS Chakrabarti will make us a nice cup of tea and we'll have a little chat. Does that sound okay?" He took the hairbrush out of the woman's hand and laid it on a small coffee table.

"I keep trying to get ready," Ronnie gulped, staring at it. "But then I think about poor Petra, and I start crying all over again."

"Did you know her well?" Gareth asked. That bruise on her cheekbone looked bad. It was recent too, judging by the deep purple colour.

"She lived here. We were flatmates."

Excellent. The address on the system was still relevant.

"Were you in the same line of work?" he asked, gently.

"Yeah. We looked out for each other, you know? Except last night..." She buried her face in the used tissue.

"Except last night...?" Gareth prompted.

"Last night, I wasn't there. I-I wasn't feeling well, so I went home early. Usually, I'm out with her." She shivered despite the warmth in the flat. The central heating was on high.

"Do you know what happened?" Gareth asked, his hopes sinking. If this woman wasn't out with her, she wouldn't be able to offer much in the way of information.

"No. Not really. When Petra didn't come home, I called her mobile, but it was switched off. That's very unlike her. We keep in touch, for security."

"Can you give us her mobile number?" Gareth asked. "We might be able to trace her last known position."

Ronnie dug in the pockets of her dressing gown and drew out her phone along with a bunch of other used tissues. She pulled up her contact list and scrolled down to Petra.

"Here it is." She handed the device over. Gareth took a photo of the screen with his own mobile phone, then handed it back. "Thank you."

Devi came back with the tea. "Here, get this down you." She set two cups down on the coffee table and took hers over to an armchair on the other side of the narrow living room.

"I should have been there for her," Ronnie mumbled, ignoring the steaming cup in front of her. "Marie and the other girls are great, but they don't know her like I do. She was so young. She shouldn't even have been on the streets." She shook her head as a new flush of tears ran down her face.

"Why was she working as a..." Gareth struggled to find

the appropriate word. Sex worker sounded so demeaning in light of what had happened, but none of the alternatives were any better.

"A prostitute?" She sniffed. "Her bastard stepfather, that's why. Her mother hooked up with this rich guy, but he was more interested in Petra than his wife, if you know what I mean."

"Did he sexually assault her?" Devi asked.

Ronnie snorted. "What do you think? Anyway, she tried to tell her mother but there was a big row. Her mother wouldn't believe her. So, Petra ran away. She said if she was going to have sex with old men she may as well get paid for it."

Devi tensed. "Why didn't she report him? He could have been arrested for sexual assault on a minor. She was a child, for goodness' sake."

Gareth glanced at her. It wasn't like her to lose her cool.

"Do you know who her mother is? Some hoity-toity posh bitch who runs a bunch of charities. There's no way they would have listened to Petra. Her mother called her a liar and said she was making up stories to get attention."

"Unbelievable." Gareth shook his head. That mother had a lot to answer for. She had her daughter's blood on her hands. And as for her husband...

Devi exhaled, trying to get her emotions in check.

"When last did you hear from Petra?" Gareth steered the interview back to the night in question.

"At about nine thirty. She texted saying she was fine, but it was flipping cold and she wasn't going to stay out late. That's why I got worried when she wasn't home by midnight. That's when I began calling her."

"We'll check her phone records," Gareth said to Devi.

She nodded. "Also, let's look into the stepfather. He's got a motive."

Ronnie didn't hear, she was too busy blowing her nose.

"Ronnie, was Petra acting strangely at all in the last few days? Was she worried about anything?"

"No, I don't think so. In fact, she was happy because one of her customers had paid her really well the night before, so she had some spare cash. She was putting it towards dance lessons. That was her real passion. She wanted to be a dancer."

Another sob wracked her slender frame. Gareth's heart broke for her. It was such a tragic loss, and for what? A paedophile stepfather who couldn't keep his hands to himself.

Devi was clearly furious too. She sat stiffly, mouth in a thin line.

If nothing else, he was going to rake that man over the coals – and the mother too. She ought to have known better. She ought to have trusted her daughter.

"You don't know who this customer was?" Gareth asked.

"No, although she said he drove a fancy car. A black SUV."

"She didn't say anything else about him?"

Ronnie thought for a moment, the tissue now a scrunched-up ball in her hand. "He was foreign, I think. Had an accent, although she said it was quite sexy. And he was young too, and good-looking." She snorted. "That doesn't happen very often. Usually, they're middle-aged and out of shape. Some of them can't even get it up."

Too much information.

"Okay, and is there anything else you can remember that might help us identify this man?"

"What you want to find him for? He was a good guy. He ain't the one who done her in."

"We'd just like to talk to him," Gareth said with a vague smile. He didn't want to leave anything to chance. He may have liked what he'd seen and come back for more. He may have been testing the waters the first time round. He may have nothing at all to do with her death. But they wouldn't know until they'd spoken to him.

"No, nothing I can think of," she said.

"Where did he pick her up?" asked Devi.

"The Cut, where we normally hang out. That's our stretch."

Gareth made a mental note. The Cut was peppered with CCTV cameras. With a bit of luck, the SUV would be caught on one of them and they could get a plate.

35

"We need to talk." Shrap stepped out of the shadows on Borough High Street, making Trevelyan jump.

"Bloody hell, Shrap. Do you have to keep sneaking up on me like that?"

"Sorry."

He shook his head. "I can't discuss this new case with you, you know that. I'm in enough shit as it is for going after Leonard Blake."

"You told your boss about that?"

"Yeah, but I didn't mention you. I said the lead had come from the bartender at the club. I've kept you out of it."

"Thank you." At least she didn't have to explain how she'd got the video footage.

"I wasn't doing it for you. I was covering my own arse."

"Fair enough. Hey, do you want to grab a coffee? I've got some information on this second girl, Petra."

"You know who she is?" Trevelyan looked surprised. She couldn't help feeling a little smug.

"Yeah."

"How?"

"Coffee? I could do with a cup."

He sighed. "Okay, let's go in here."

There was a small café on the high street that was still open. A hang-dog barista took their order and they sat down at a table by the window.

Outside, it was cold and dark. Pedestrians hunkered into their scarves and coats as they scurried home. The bars were getting boisterous as the after-work crowd got stuck into their second or third drink of the night. The illuminated clock on the church tower said quarter to ten.

The barista brought over their drinks. "We close at ten," he reminded them, stifling a yawn.

"How do you know the victim?" Trevelyan asked. He had five o'clock shadow and rings under his eyes. She remembered those first twenty-four hours after a body was found, how gruelling they could be. All systems go. Follow up on every lead before it had a chance to go cold.

"She was a sex worker. I spoke to her friends on the street."

"Fellow prostitutes?"

"Yeah, they're frightened. Two girls in as many weeks. You can imagine."

"What did they say? Any leads?"

"Maybe." She drummed her middle finger against her cup. "But first, what did your boss say about Blake?"

"He told me to bring him in. We're going to question him under caution."

"That's good." Shrap nodded.

"Except you know he can't have killed Petra. He was nowhere near Waterloo that night."

"And he doesn't own a car," added Shrap.

Trevelyan's eyes narrowed. "What's this about a car?"

She leaned forward, lowering her voice. "Marie, one of The Cut regulars, told me that she last saw Petra getting into a black SUV the night she disappeared. She didn't get the plate or see the driver, but she did say..." She stopped. Trevelyan had gone dead still. "What's wrong?"

"Did you say a black SUV?"

"Yeah."

"Shit." He gave his head a little shake. "Petra's flatmate told me this rich, foreign-looking guy picked Petra up in a black SUV a couple of nights ago. Mid-twenties, early thirties."

"Same guy?"

"Could be." He stared at Shrap. "What if he was on the prowl, searching for his next target? He sees Petra, picks her up but for whatever reason didn't go through with it that night."

"Maybe he was sampling the goods first," said Shrap.

"God, that's awful." He scowled. "Did this Marie say anything else?"

"She mentioned loud rap music coming from inside the car."

"Rap music?" Trevelyan frowned. "That backs up what her flatmate said about his age. She also mentioned he could have been foreign. Eastern European, maybe."

Shrap stopped drumming. "Albanian?"

"You mean like Xhafa and his connections?"

"Possibly. Bianca was a dancer there. Perhaps that's how he picked his first target. At the club. Then the second, while prowling The Cut after dark."

"I need to speak to the flatmate again," Trevelyan muttered. "Perhaps Petra mentioned something about where they went? It might give us some indication of which area he lives in."

Or hunts in, thought Shrap.

"Our team's ploughing through CCTV footage of The Cut from a couple of nights ago. We're hoping to find the black SUV."

"Now you can look at last night's footage too," Shrap added.

He gave a quick nod. "I think we might be onto something here."

She felt it too. The quickening of the pulse, the rush of blood to the head. "Still, it's worth questioning Blake if you can find him. Remember, these two homicides might not be related."

"I know, although at this point, I'm more interested to hear if he saw anything on the night of Bianca Rubik's death. He may have witnessed what happened."

They finished their coffees. The barista was already stacking the chairs on top of the tables – their cue to leave.

"There's one other thing," Shrap said, as they stepped outside and were hit by a blast of frigid air.

"What's that?" He blinked against the cold.

"Bianca Rubik was having an affair with a married man."

"What?" His mouth fell open. "How did you find that out?"

"The bartender. I met up with him last Sunday."

"Oh, I see." His eyes flickered over her face. She knew what he was thinking.

"It's not like that," she said. "Alex called me. He said he had to tell me something about Bianca."

"Did you find out who the man was?"

"Yes, and I got his address."

Trevelyan's eyes lit up. "Good work. Except, how come you only thought to tell me this now?"

She shrugged. "Leonard Blake seemed more important at the time, but there's something else you should know."

He arched an eyebrow. "I don't know if I can handle any more surprises."

"I checked out his house. His wife drives a black SUV."

36

Dark blue, as it turned out. Not black.

Gareth gazed at a DVLA photograph of Gregory Pincher's wife's Porsche Cayenne. Technically speaking it was *his* Porsche Cayenne, since it was his name on the hire purchase agreement. Still, dark blue could be mistaken for black at night.

He'd run the number plate through the ANPR database but got no hits for either of the nights in question. If that had been the car, it had studiously avoided any of the cameras.

Thankfully, the CCTV team were having better luck. They'd picked up forty-three possible black SUVs driving up or down The Cut between the hours of ten and midnight the night before, and plenty more from several nights ago when the timings were less clear.

Ronnie couldn't remember exactly what time Petra had disappeared with her fancy man although it was after eight, because they'd got a takeaway coffee around eight from the fish and chip shop and sat at the bus stop to drink it.

Petra hadn't said anything about where they'd gone, but

Ronnie didn't think it had been back to the bloke's house. "She woulda said. Usually, it's a quickie in the back of the van, you know?"

Gareth didn't, and he didn't want to.

Around lunchtime he got news that two coppers in Camden had picked up Leonard Blake. They were bringing him in for questioning.

He hadn't mentioned anything about Gregory Pincher, because he wasn't sure how to explain that lead without bringing Shrap into it, and that was the last thing he wanted to do. If Burrows found out he was colluding with somebody outside the force – a homeless civilian, no less – he'd have his badge.

"I want to question him," he said to Burrows once Blake had been shown to an interview room.

The SIO had given him a stiff nod before marching off. He still wasn't forgiven for investigating when the case was closed. Or maybe it was because he'd proved him wrong. Either way, Gareth wasn't in his good books.

"Will you sit in with me?" he asked Devi.

"Who's this guy?" his colleague asked on the way to the interview room.

He gave her a quick update. "He's an ex-con who was at the strip club the night Bianca Rubik was killed. We – I mean, I – think she followed him home."

"*She* followed *him*?" Devi asked, confused.

"Yes, according to my source, she left right after him. We don't know why."

"But you think he might have had something to do with her death?"

"It's possible. He might also be a witness."

Devi nodded, although he could tell she was still confused. This guy had appeared out of nowhere, based on a lead only Gareth had followed up, and nobody knew who he was or how he was connected to the case.

Gareth was getting funny looks from the rest of the team. This wasn't a great way to ingratiate himself. Going off on a tangent with some vigilante homeless ex-veteran wasn't going to win him any friends.

"I'm sorry I didn't tell you about Blake before," he said to Devi. "I was worried Burrows would have a shit-fit if he found out."

Devi gave him a sideways glance. "He probably would have. He's not happy you went behind his back, and even less so that you turned out to be right."

He shot her a small smile. "The only thing I was right about was that the old guy, Doug Romberg, didn't kill Bianca Rubik. Other than that, I'm as in the dark as everyone else."

They got to the interview room door.

Devi raised her eyebrows. "Let's see what he has to say, shall we?"

"Present are DC Gareth Trevelyan, DS Devi Chakrabarti, Leonard Blake and Susan Redfern, Blake's legal representative," announced Devi for the purposes of the recording.

Leonard Blake was a wiry man of average height with a pock-marked face and roving eyes. He shuffled in his seat and kept glancing at the door, as if he wished he could bolt through it.

"Leonard Blake," began Devi. "You are not under arrest and you do not have to consent to being interviewed. You are free to leave at any time unless you are arrested and are entitled to legal representation throughout. Refusing to attend this voluntary interview may result in you being arrested. Is that clear?"

His fisheyes darted from Devi to Gareth and back again.

"Is that clear?" repeated Devi. "Could you answer for the benefit of the recording?"

"Yes," muttered Blake. He reminded Gareth of a sulky teenager.

"Right, let's get started, then," said Gareth. The solicitor looked surprised, as did Blake. They'd both expected Devi to lead the interview.

"Mr Blake, where were you on the evening of the third of November?"

He frowned. "I don't know."

"It was a Saturday night, if that helps," Gareth said.

All he got in reply was a blank stare.

"Shall I refresh your memory?" He glanced down at his notes. "You were at a gentleman's club called Whispers in the West End of London on that evening. Isn't that correct?"

Still nothing.

"Mr Blake declines to answer," said Devi.

"You were seen by multiple witnesses," continued Gareth. "The barmaid, the manager of the club, the dancers..."

"Okay, Jesus." He threw up his hands. "I was there. So what?"

"Do you recognise this woman?" He slid a glossy photograph of Bianca Rubik across the table. It was one her parents had emailed through. Clear blue eyes, a happy smile, hair caught by the wind. She looked beautiful.

He winced. "Yeah, I remember her."

"Could you explain where you remember her from?"

"From the club, like you said."

Gareth studied him. He sat hunched forward, his hands clasped together on the table. "Is that all?"

"Yeah, she gave me a lap dance. Pretty girl."

"And you didn't see her after you left the club that night?"

"No, why would I?"

"Because she left at the same time you did, Mr Blake. In fact, she followed you out onto the street."

His eyes flashed toward the door again. *Gotcha*, Gareth thought.

"I don't remember that."

"Don't you? We have evidence that she followed you down the street. It was caught on CCTV. Why do you think she did that, Mr Blake?"

"Maybe she took a liking to me. Who the fuck knows?"

"Are you sure you don't remember seeing her after you left the club?"

"No. I told you already."

"My client has answered that question, DC Trevelyan," cut in the solicitor.

Gareth moved on.

"I'm not sure if you know this, Mr Blake, but the woman who followed you, Bianca Rubik, was killed later that night. Her body was found near Waterloo station in the early hours."

"What?"

He seemed genuinely shocked. Then he slammed his hands down on the table, making Gareth and the solicitor jump. "Oh, no. No, no, no. I know what this is. It's a stitch-up. You're not going to pin this on me. I had nothing to do with this girl's death."

"Well, then you'd better stop lying to us and tell us what

happened that night," said Gareth. "All we want is the truth."

"No, it's not," he scoffed. "All you lot want is a patsy to pin it on. I'm the designated arsehole, am I? Is it because I have a criminal record? I was there the night she got killed and so now you think it was me."

"This is your chance to tell us your side of the story," Gareth pointed out. "Put the record straight."

He rocked back and forth, his gaze swimming around the room. "You fuckers," he muttered.

"What did you see, Mr Blake? Did you see what happened to Bianca?"

He stopped rocking. "Okay, I did see her, right? She's hard to miss. At first I didn't think she was following me, I just thought we were going the same way. But then when I crossed the road, so did she. When I crossed the river, so did she."

"Where were you going?" asked Gareth.

"I was going to meet a mate at a bar on the South Bank."

"Carry on."

"Well, I turned around and waited for her to catch up, but she didn't. It was like she suddenly got scared or something. By this stage I wanted to know what she was up to, so I ran after her." He shrugged. "She took off up the road. I couldn't keep up. That's when the car stopped."

"What car?" snapped Gareth.

"The car, the black SUV. It pulled over and the driver offered her a lift. She jumped in. The car took off and that's the last I saw of her. I swear."

37

"It can't be a coincidence," Shrap said.

She'd met Trevelyan in a sandwich shop up the road from the police station. It was risky, but at three in the afternoon the lunch crowd had long gone. They got takeaway coffees and stood inside the door, talking in low voices. To anyone watching, they were two strangers waiting for their baguettes.

"Could it be Gregory Pincher's?" the detective asked, lines etched into his forehead.

"It could be, although he said he was at a work function until ten."

"When did you speak to him?"

"The other day. I hijacked his Uber." Shrap couldn't resist a grin. "I threatened to tell his wife about his affair. He had no choice but to talk to me."

His eyes widened. "You're good."

"Thanks. I used to be."

"Why don't you get back into it?" he asked. "The force would be lucky to have an investigator of your rank and experience."

She glanced away. "Nah, I'm better off where I am for now."

He turned his attention back to the case. "Ten o'clock is still early enough to have picked up Bianca Rubik after she left the club."

"He said he went straight home." Shrap liked that he hadn't pushed her on the issue of getting a job. If he knew her rank, he'd read her file, which meant he knew about the PTSD, yet he hadn't brought it up. She appreciated that.

"Was his wife with him?" he asked.

"No, according to Pincher she was at home when he got back. He could be lying, though. We won't know until you question her."

"Hmm... It might be better if we go and see them, rather than bring them in for formal questioning. He's just a person of interest at this stage. I didn't pick up his vehicle on any cameras in the area."

She grinned at his use of 'we'.

He corrected himself. "Me, I mean. Obviously, I can't take you with me."

"Obviously," she agreed.

"There's only one problem." He ran a hand through his hair, flustered. "He's your lead, not mine. How am I going to explain how I got onto him?"

"A confidential informant?" she suggested.

"Who, you?"

"No, not me. Alex, the bartender at the club. He's the one who told me about Pincher."

Trevelyan thought about this. "I suppose I could say he gave me the lead, except I used him as a source for Leonard Blake. I hope no one suggests bringing him in for questioning."

Shrap hoped not too.

"If that happens, let me know. I'll speak to him first."

But Trevelyan was already thinking ahead. "I'll go and see the Pinchers this evening. Gregory should be back by then."

A man in a police uniform walked into the shop and nodded at Trevelyan. Without another word, Shrap slipped out of the door and took off down a side street. She'd have to wait until tonight to find out whether Pincher's alibi checked out.

SHRAP WAS JUST BEDDING down when she heard a furore at the end of the street. Patting her pocket to make sure she had her knife, she went to investigate. A teenage kid in a dark beanie was being beaten up by two older guys who looked to be in their twenties. The kid was curled up on the ground and they were kicking him in the ribs, giving him quite a pounding.

"Hey!" Shrap raced up.

They stopped and turned.

"Piss off," growled the skinny guy wearing a backwards cap. "Unless you trynna get cheffed up?"

Shrap glared at him. "I'm afraid I can't do that."

She stood with her feet slightly apart, right hand close to her pocket, like a cowboy about to draw. Her eyes were locked on the scrawny shitbag.

The other one, stockier, with his boxers showing above his low-hanging jeans, turned to face her. "You fuckin' wot?"

"If needs be." She stood her ground.

The two men chortled and glanced at each other. Backwards Cap shrugged. "Bet."

Boxers' hand snuck into his pocket. Shrap caught a glint

as he flicked open a switchblade. "You're gonna wish you kept your fuckin' mouth shut."

Two could play that game.

"I doubt that."

She'd already summed them up. High on crack or some other substance, young, inexperienced, with no military training or fighting experience.

They were just big kids themselves, really. Except the teenager on the ground was rolling around groaning. Assault was assault, no matter how old you were.

The guy with the knife lunged. Shrap caught his wrist and twisted it back until he howled in agony. The knife clattered to the ground. Shrap kneed him in the solar plexus. Just hard enough to wind him. Letting go, she watched as the guy doubled up in pain.

She picked up the discarded knife. The other guy – if he'd known what was good for him – should have taken the hint and run away at that point, but he didn't. Instead, he launched himself at Shrap.

She ducked and tossed the guy over her shoulder using his own momentum. He landed hard, grazing his hands and elbows.

"Fuck!" He scrambled to his feet, blood up.

Before he had time to take another run, Shrap had covered the ground between them and palmed the guy in the nose. Blood squirted everywhere. Before he had a chance to recover, she grabbed him from behind and held her knife to his throat.

"Now take your friend and get the hell out of here," she hissed in his ear. "Before I call the cops."

Backwards Cap grabbed his mate, who was still gasping on the ground, and together they limped off down the street.

Shrap turned her attention to the teenager. "You okay?"

The kid nodded, although he had a nasty cut on his cheek and was still holding his ribs. Shrap knew what that felt like.

"Do you want me to call an ambulance?" she asked.

The kid shook his head.

"Your mum? A mate?"

"Nah, I'm okay."

"You don't look okay."

The kid tried to get to his feet, but grimaced and fell back down.

Shrap helped him up.

He stared at her, wide-eyed under the streetlamp. "That was sick, the way you beat up those two waste men. Where'd you learn how to fight?"

"The army." She nodded after the two thugs. "Who were they? Why are they after you?"

The kid shrugged, adjusting his beanie. There was blood smeared on his oversized T-shirt. "Just a couple of wankers. I tagged their turf. Been doing it for weeks. Got away with it too." Shrap saw a satchel lying in the road behind him.

"Except for tonight."

"Yeah." He winced. "They were waitin' for me. Must have clocked it was me last time."

"I guess you'll have to find somewhere new to tag now."

The kid laughed, then groaned.

"What's your name?" asked Shrap.

"Jadon. You?"

"Shrap."

"That's a bare weird name."

She shrugged. "It's my nickname."

He looked at what she was wearing. "You sleepin' rough?"

"Yeah, what's it to you?"

"Nuffink." He grinned. "Glad you were there. Thanks for stepping in, you absolutely owned those guys."

Shrap chuckled. "You're welcome. Stay out of trouble, Jadon."

The kid gave her a mock salute and picked up his satchel, which rattled with spray paint cans. Tossing it over one shoulder, he hobbled off down the road.

"DAMN IT," Shrap muttered when she got back to her bed.

She'd missed a call from Trevelyan.

"Sorry," she said, after she'd rung him back.

"Not a problem. I was just calling to give you an update." She heard a creak and imagined him sitting down on his couch or bed.

"Go ahead."

"Well, at first Pincher was fairly hostile. He didn't want to let us in. I used your trick and said I could explain why I was there to his wife, or I could keep it general. He was pretty accommodating after that."

Shrap chuckled. "What did they say?"

"Well, I explained that a vehicle matching theirs was seen in the vicinity of a homicide and asked for their whereabouts the night of Bianca's murder. Like you said, Gregory was at a work function in the city and Annie, the wife, was at home. She confirmed her husband got back shortly after ten and they went straight to bed."

"Did you believe her?"

"I think so. There's no reason not to. I suppose she could be covering for him, but she seemed sincere. Concerned, almost. She said she hoped the murderer would be apprehended soon."

"You could take the vehicle in for analysis."

"I could do, but I'm not sure it warrants it yet. I asked them where they were last night, and this time he was home while she was at her weekly book club. She gave me the names of her friends. I'm going to check them out tomorrow."

"Gregory could have popped out unnoticed."

"He could have done, except she had the Porsche Cayenne, so he would have had to take the Audi."

"It was definitely a black SUV that Marie saw," Shrap said with a sigh. "Couldn't have been him, then. Bugger."

"It was worth a shot," he said.

"Sorry it didn't pan out."

"At least we tried. I'm off to bed now, I'm knackered."

He sounded it. "Okay, sleep well."

She didn't know why she'd said that. It seemed too personal, intimate even.

He hesitated. "Thanks."

The line went dead.

38

Gareth dialled the last number on the list. All four other ladies had confirmed Annie Pincher had been at the book club meeting on the night of Petra's murder. He didn't even know why he was bothering with the last one, except it would look odd on his report if he left one name out.

Lizzie Thorogood.

"Hello, this is DC Trevelyan from Southwark CID. Is that Mrs Thorogood?"

A guarded "Yes."

"I'm calling in regard to a book club meeting you attended last week with Annie Pincher and a few other ladies.

"Yes, they said you'd be calling. How can I help you?"

"I just need you to confirm that Annie Pincher was indeed there for the duration of the meeting?"

"Yes, she was."

He groaned inwardly, not that he'd expected any different. All five accounts were the same. Annie Pincher had arrived at eight o'clock and left shortly before eleven.

They'd all had a glass of wine – only one, mind you, because most were driving – and discussed the book of the month, a particularly racy literary novel called *Moonlight and Sawdust*, whatever that meant.

"Thank you," Gareth said, then a thought struck him. "Do you remember which car she was driving?"

"Actually. I do. We left at the same time. She was in her husband's Audi. When I commented on it, she said the Porsche was having a service."

Gareth went cold.

"The Audi. You're sure?"

"Absolutely."

"Thank you, Mrs Thorogood."

He hung up and stared at her screen. The Pinchers had lied. Gregory could have taken the Porsche and picked up Petra.

He scratched his head. But why would his wife lie to protect him? Surely, she can't be aware of his nocturnal activities. That he frequented strip clubs, had affairs with the exotic dancers and picked up prostitutes. There was no way a wife would condone that type of behaviour, particularly one of Annie's stature. Even calling her book club friends had mortified her. So why the lie? Unless, of course, the SUV was in for a service. Then again, why not just say that in the police interview?

He went to Devi's desk and told her about the phone call.

"Bring them in," Devi said straight away. "You've got no choice. They lied to a police officer. I'd also suggest bringing the SUV in for forensics to check over."

"Right. Will do."

He made the necessary arrangements.

"It's time to get serious," he muttered as he put down the phone.

"I've got something!" yelled DS Brenner, making him jump. His usually pale face was speckled with colour.

All heads turned towards him.

"Forensics found foreign DNA underneath Petra Burton-Leigh's fingernails." He grinned at them. "She must have scratched her attacker. I'm running it through the database now."

That was good news! If they could find a match, it might lead them to their killer. Even if the DNA wasn't in the database, it would come in handy when questioning suspects. A simple DNA test would tell them if they had the right person. A murmur of excitement swept over the squad room. They'd been working long hours and needed this morale boost.

That afternoon there was a department meeting led by Superintendent Ridgeway. He could tell by the look on Burrows' face that something was up. They all filed into the briefing room and waited for the Super to arrive. He was a formidable man in his early fifties with a short buzz cut and very straight shoulders. He wouldn't look out of place in a military uniform.

"Ladies and gents, your Waterloo killer has attracted a lot of attention in the press. Two sex workers killed in the same manner in under two weeks."

Gareth put up his hand. "Er, Bianca Rubik wasn't a sex worker, sir. She was a dancer and a law student."

The Super's eyes flickered in his direction. "My mistake." He stood up even straighter and gazed out at the department. "In any event, we're under pressure from the Police Commissioner to solve this case or it will be handed over to one of London's Major Investigation Teams."

There was a collective gasp of horror. No one wanted the most interesting case in years to be handed over to the local murder squad.

"Putney MIT have an excellent reputation with repeat offenders," he continued. "They've successfully apprehended several serial murderers in the last five years. You might have read about them in the papers. They're the go-to guys for this type of thing."

So far, they only had two murders. It took three with the same MO for it to be deemed a serial killer case, except he didn't say that. Now wasn't the time.

"How long do we have?" asked DCI Burrows.

"A week at the most," Ridgeway replied. "After that, we'll have no choice but to transfer the case over to Putney."

Murmurs of objection rumbled through the room.

The Super held up his hand. "To be fair, we've had ample time. We missed the connection with the first murder and closed the case prematurely, in my opinion." His gaze swept over Burrows, who stared stonily at his feet. "The DNA evidence is promising, and I believe you have a suspect in tow. I'll look forward to seeing your results."

Nobody said a thing.

Without another word to Burrows, or anyone else, the Super swept from the room.

"What a load of crap," said Devi, once they'd got back to their desks. "Anything high-profile and the bloody murder squad gets it."

"Hopefully one of the suspects in custody will crack and confess." Heely glanced at Gareth.

"We can hope," he murmured.

"Out of the two of them, he'll crack first." Devi had been

at the unofficial interview at the Pincher's the evening
before with Gareth. She was a good judge of character and
had summed up their personalities straight away. "She
wears the pants in that relationship," she'd told Gareth on
the way back.

"He's not going to crack if he's the killer," Heely cut in.

"The wife's tough," Gareth agreed. "I don't think she'll
break."

"Perhaps she doesn't know her husband is strangling
women," suggested Brenner, who'd joined in their
conversation.

"How could she not know?" exclaimed Heely. "She's his
wife. She must be covering for him."

"Let's go ask her, shall we?" Gareth glanced at Devi. "She
might not be so quick to cover for him once she realises the
sentence for aiding and abetting."

Devi snorted. "I'm right behind you."

"Good luck," called Heely. Brenner gave them a
thumbs up.

"Thanks." He flashed them each a tight smile. Baby
steps.

"WHY DID you tell DS Chakrabarti and me that you went to
the book club in the Porsche Cayenne when you took the
Audi?" Gareth asked, once they'd got the official introduc-
tions out the way and had commenced with the interview.

Mr and Mrs Pincher had been kept in separate holding
cells prior to questioning. He'd been picked up at work,
which he was furious about, while she'd been collected
from her home in Hampstead Heath. They'd had no contact
since early that morning. No time to get their stories
straight.

"I forgot," she said.

"You forgot? But you told Lizzie Thorogood that your car was in for a service."

"I mean I forgot when you were questioning me last night. I always take my car, so I didn't even think when I said it."

She was lying, Gareth was sure of it.

"We checked with your nearest Porsche dealer and your vehicle hasn't had a service since 2018."

"We don't use them." The answer came easily. Well-rehearsed, or the truth. "They're too expensive. We use a local garage down the road."

Gareth glanced at Devi. "We'll need their details, please."

"Of course." She looked them up on her phone and passed it over. Devi wrote them down.

"Thank you. Now, I'm afraid I'm going to have to ask you some personal questions, Mrs Pincher."

She gave a stoic nod.

"Did you know your husband frequented a gentlemen's club in Covent Garden called Whispers?"

A faint blush appeared in her cheeks. "He didn't *frequent* it. He went once with a group of mates on a stag do."

"Do you remember when this was?"

"I don't. Sometime last summer, I think."

Devi made another note. They'd pick that up with Gregory when they interviewed him.

Now for the crunch.

"Were you aware that your husband was having an affair with a dancer from Whispers Gentlemen's Club called Bianca Rubik?"

A hush fell over the room and Gareth was sure it got a few degrees chillier.

"He mentioned he'd met someone there," she said in a strangled voice, "but he said she gave him a lap dance, that's all."

"I'm afraid that's not all, Mrs Pincher. Your husband had been seeing Miss Rubik regularly since that night. He was also paying her university tuition."

"Impossible," she spat. "I would know if he was having an affair. I would notice money coming out of our account."

"We believe he used a private account," Gareth said. They hadn't managed to get a warrant for Gregory Pincher's bank records yet, but they'd confirmed the payments with the online university through which Bianca had been studying. The termly fees had all been debited from an account in Pincher's name.

Her gaze hardened. "Which account?"

"I can't give you that information, but I can tell you we've confirmed it with the relevant institution."

"Bastard." It was a coarse whisper.

"Are you saying you had no idea about the affair?"

"No, of course I didn't." She was trembling with rage, or perhaps something else. Gareth could see her shoulders shaking.

"Would you like a glass of water, Mrs Pincher?" he asked. As much as he disliked the woman, she'd had a tremendous shock.

"No, thank you. Let's just get this over with."

"I'll get to the point," Gareth said. "The reason why you and your husband are here is because this woman he was having an affair with, Bianca Rubik, was found murdered on the third of November. She was last seen getting into a black SUV on the Strand at around a quarter past eleven."

Annie Pincher stared at him across the table. The trembling stopped. Time seemed to stand still. Eventually, she whispered, "You think my husband had something to do with it?"

"That's what we're trying to find out," Gareth said evenly. "Your husband claims he was at a work function that night. When we spoke before, you said he'd got home shortly after ten. Does that still stand?"

"Yes."

"Are you sure he didn't go out again after that?"

"No, of course not. We went straight to bed. I'd waited up, watched some stupid thing on television, and then we went up together. He had a headache, if I recall, and took a painkiller. He didn't move all night."

Gareth scrutinised her for signs she was lying but couldn't find any. After the shock of her husband's affair, she was noticeably subdued, but there was nothing in her tone or demeanour to suggest she was making things up.

"Okay, thank you, Mrs Pincher. That will be all."

"I can go?"

"Yes, I'll just come with you and sign your release form and you're free to go."

"What about my husband?"

"We've still got to interview him."

Devi left the room to go and check up on the car service details that Annie had given them. If the Porsche Cayenne had indeed been off the road the night Petra had been murdered, then that would rule him out.

If it didn't, then things could take a very different turn.

39

They'd arranged to meet at the coffee shop in Borough High Street as it was open until ten.

Friday night. The place was bustling. Too busy for her liking, but it was too late to change venues. Trevelyan was sitting at a table near the back, two coffee cups on the table in front of him.

"I got you an Americano," he said, when she approached. "I hope that's okay."

A man jostled her, and she glanced around, her mouth suddenly dry. The after-work crowd. Scruffy rucksacks and tired expressions. The pre–going out crowd, excitable and buoyant. Everywhere, people were on their iPhones. "It's fine, thanks."

She was about to suggest they take their coffees outside, but a tide of people surged in, bringing the cold with them, so Shrap sat down and focused on the detective. "Your text was intriguing."

"Yeah, it's been quite a day. We arrested the Pinchers."

"Really?" He looked tired and dishevelled. His shirt was

crumpled, and his hair stuck up all over the place. She quite liked it like that. "On what grounds?"

"They lied about their car. Mrs Pincher told me she'd driven it to book club the night of Petra Burton-Leigh's murder, when in fact she'd taken her husband's car."

"Why did she lie?" Shrap asked.

"She claims she forgot she'd taken his car that night. The SUV was booked in for a service. My colleague spoke to the garage owner, who confirmed it. There's no way Gregory Pincher could have been Petra's fancy man."

"Shit." Shrap leaned back in her chair.

"I know. She was furious when I told her about his affair, though. I don't envy Gregory Pincher this evening. I doubt their marriage will withstand this."

"Couldn't be helped," said Shrap. "It's not your fault he was unfaithful. I'm only amazed he's been able to keep it from his wife for so long."

"She didn't have a clue." Trevelyan stared into his coffee. "Imagine that."

"He was obviously very careful." There was something in his gaze that she couldn't place. A bittersweet memory, perhaps? "Have you ever been married?" The words were out of her mouth before she could retract them.

"Er, no." He flushed, just a little. "I'm not sure I'm the marrying type. How about you?"

"Nearly. Once. It didn't work out. He's married to someone else now."

"I'm sorry."

Yeah, so was she. She'd lost everything because of this blasted PTSD. Her career. Her man. Her home. Her life.

Now she had a new one. It wasn't much, but it was all she could manage right now.

Hey, at least she was alive. She had Doug to thank for that.

"What about the SUV?" She couldn't give up just yet. Gregory Pincher was their most likely suspect. Their only suspect. "Did you take it in for processing anyway?"

"Forensics are going over it. We won't get the report until tomorrow at the earliest."

"If either Bianca or Petra were ever in that car, there ought to be some sign of them."

"I wouldn't hold your breath. Gregory was at home with his wife the night of Bianca's murder, and after what Mrs Pincher discovered this afternoon, she wouldn't vouch for him unless it was true. The night Petra was killed, the car was at the garage. Oh, we also did a DNA test. It wasn't Gregory's DNA under Petra's fingernails."

That was that, then. Gregory Pincher was in the clear.

"Crap, I really thought it was him." Her shoulders sagged.

"We'll carry on ploughing through the CCTV footage in the vicinity of the two murders." Trevelyan tried to sound upbeat. "Maybe we'll get lucky."

Maybe.

"Although, if we don't come up with something soon, the case is being transferred to the murder squad."

"What?"

"Putney MIT want the case. We've got a week."

That was even worse. Then she'd have no way of knowing what they were working on or what progress they'd made.

"That's bad," she said, thinking out loud.

"Tell me about it."

Another wave of customers swept in. The café was

getting overcrowded. Shrap began to feel the familiar prickles of panic as the claustrophobia set in.

"I need some air," she said abruptly, taking her coffee outside.

"Okay." Trevelyan put on his jacket and joined her. "Everything alright?"

"I don't like crowds much. Not used to it." It was amazing how easily the excuses ran off her tongue.

"I had an uncle who served," he said quietly. "Uncle Phil. He was a great guy. Then one day they told me he'd passed away. I was a teenager at the time, so I didn't understand what had happened. It was only later that my father told me he'd shot himself."

Shrap stared at him for a long moment, then glanced away. "It happens a lot."

"There is help out there, you know."

She couldn't bring herself to look at him. "I know."

A car drove past, rap music blaring. Something pinged in her brain. She snapped her fingers.

"What?" Trevelyan asked.

"Marie said the SUV that picked up Petra had rap music playing inside. She heard it through the open window."

"So?"

"I know someone who listens to that sort of rap music. Two guys, actually."

"You do?"

"Yeah, and they both knew Bianca."

———————

40

"We can't go in there," Trevelyan said. They were sitting outside Whispers in his car. "They'll recognise me. And you…"

"I'm not in my disguise." She gave a self-deprecating smile.

"Exactly. So why are we here?"

"These two guys, they're friends of Xhafa's. Minor drug dealers. They were here the night Xhafa met with the Italians."

"What about them?"

"They arrived in a BMW convertible, metallic blue, gangster rap blaring out of the speakers."

"And you think it was one of them who killed those girls?"

"I don't know. It might be." She shrugged. "I'm grasping at straws here. They're violent thugs, armed and unpredictable. Mix that with some cocaine and alcohol…"

"That's not enough proof."

"No, but it wouldn't hurt to check them out."

"Do you know their names?"

"No, but I have their number plate."

He raised an eyebrow.

"Old habits." And she and Frank had followed them to the housing estate on the east side of London in the early hours. The number was burned into her brain.

"It's a blue BMW, you say?"

"Yeah."

"Not a black SUV?"

"No."

He shook his head. "I don't—"

"They have buckets of cash," Shrap interjected. "It's not impossible that there's a black SUV hidden on the estate, or somewhere else." She narrowed her eyes. She couldn't recall seeing one, but then she hadn't been looking for it.

"You went there, didn't you?"

She cringed, feeling a ghost pain in her rib from the beating. "I might have done."

"Why? What is it about these two that you're not telling me?"

"Nothing. At the time I thought Bianca – and Doug – may have been killed because of something Xhafa was into. That's why I followed the Albanians. But I've since realised they're small fry."

"And yet here we are."

"Yes, here we are."

There was a pause.

"Do you think they'll come back?" he asked.

"They're here quite a bit, according to Alex."

"The bartender?"

"Yeah." She kept her eyes on the club.

"We can't just wait for them to show up." He glanced at the digital clock on the dashboard. "It's nearly nine thirty. Don't you think they'd be here already?"

"Not particularly. This place only gets going late."

As it was, customers were strolling in, some on a whim, others by design. Some smartly dressed, others in jeans and puffer jackets. Trevelyan shifted uncomfortably.

"We could be here all night."

"Why don't you drop me here?" Shrap suggested. "I'll call you if they come back."

"Then what? I can't arrest them because your gut says they're involved. We have no proof."

"No, but we could follow them. See where they go."

"You know where they live."

"Okay, you're right. There's no point in you staying. I've given you the reg number and the location of the estate. You can find out who they are and run them through the system."

"What about you?" He glanced across at her. "Are you going to be alright?"

"I'll be fine."

It was starting to rain. Dark clouds in a dark sky.

"It's not very nice out there," he said.

"It never is this time of year."

He didn't say anything as she got out. The cold wrapped itself around her and the drizzle pricked at her skin. Not nice at all.

She moved away from the car and raised a hand in farewell. He gave a terse nod and drove off, leaving her standing in the rain.

She turned around and walked towards the shop doorway where she'd watched from before, wishing she had her backpack, which was stored in the locker at Waterloo station. At least her coat was warm, and if she hunkered down enough, she could get out of the rain.

She'd give it a couple of hours and then head back to her

neck of the woods. She wasn't even sure why she was here. Trevelyan had been right, there was nothing they could do apart from observe. Still, it was better than doing nothing.

An hour passed and there was no sign of the blue BMW or the two thugs. She began to doze off, lulled by the pitter-patter on the hard ground. To keep awake, she stood up and walked around the block. There was Xhafa's Mercedes, gleaming under the security light near the staff entrance. She rounded the corner and came to an abrupt halt. Facing her was Mikael, the big Russian, and he wasn't happy.

"You!" he snarled, reaching for her.

Shrap didn't have time to get away before the first punch landed. The Russian was taking no prisoners, he certainly didn't seem to care she was a woman, and she fell to her knees as his monstrous fists pummelled her. She crawled into the foetal position to try and protect her head.

Fuck! How had this happened?

Rolling away, she scrambled to her feet, hand reaching for the knife. Not again. She was tired of being beaten shit-less by ruthless Eastern European men. She swung back, the blade catching the bodyguard on his chin. The Russian touched his face, surprised to find his hand wet with blood. Growling, he lurched forwards, slamming a meaty fist into Shrap's stomach, winding her.

She gasped for air. Christ, it hurt to breathe. Another blow landed on the back of her neck, sending her tumbling to the ground. She landed in a puddle, dropping the knife.

Blood rushed to her head.

She scrambled forwards and launched herself into the Russian's legs, sending him stumbling backwards. He tripped over the curb and landed on his butt. Shrap jumped on top of him, a red mist descending. She punched Mikael in the face several times, not caring what she was doing to her fists, or to the man lying beneath her.

The burly Russian pushed her aside and she fell onto her back. Shit, the guy was strong. A kick landed on her rib, still tender from her last beating. She screamed in agony. Another kick and she instinctively curled up into a ball. It was then she felt the switchblade in her jeans pocket, the one she'd confiscated from the two young guys in the street. Reaching for it, she flipped it open and almost crying with pain, pushed herself up onto her hands and knees.

The Russian was gearing up for another debilitating kick. In one smooth motion, Shrap brought the knife down and stabbed Mikael in the foot. The blade went clean through. There was a small metallic clink as it made contact with the tarmac underneath.

The Russian howled and backed off. He hissed something in Russian and bent down to pull the knife out.

Shrap didn't hang around to see what he'd do next. She took off like a bolt of lightning, down the road, around the corner and into the darkness. Mikael didn't follow.

41

Gareth had just got home when his phone buzzed. Frowning, he looked at the number. Shrap?

He answered it straight away, but all he heard was sobbing.

"Shrap? What's wrong? Has something happened?"

He heard a howl, like an animal in pain.

"Shrap!" He shouted into the phone but got no reply. Had she called him by accident? Did she need his help?

"Oh, God. God, no." Another moan and then more sobbing. There was a swishing sound, like she was stumbling through bushes or tall grass.

Fucking hell. Something had happened.

Trevelyan reversed out of his driveway and stepped hard on the accelerator.

THE CLUB WAS in full swing. Music thumped from within the red velvet mouth and the doorman smiled as he admitted more paying customers.

Shrap was nowhere to be seen.

Trevelyan drove around the block, but there didn't appear to be anyone around. Where had she got to?

He tried calling her again, but it went straight to voice-mail. Either her battery had died, or she'd switched off her phone.

Think! Where would she have gone?

She didn't live here, not in these parts. Her turf was around Waterloo station. Would she have tried to make her way back there?

He got out his phone and pulled up Google Maps. If she was on foot, which way would she go? There was a park of sorts that she could cut through. Perhaps she'd done that? He'd heard rustling on the line, like she was stomping through undergrowth.

He drove down the road to the park entrance and cut the engine. It was still raining, harder now. Big droplets splattered on the windscreen.

Gareth got out of the car and peered into the darkness. "Damn you, Shrap," he whispered into the gloom. He couldn't leave her out here. She was in trouble, he knew it. She hadn't sounded well.

Using his phone's torch app as a light, he entered the park. It was eerily dark, and the rain disoriented him. He followed the diagonal footpath that sliced through the green lawns, cutting them in two.

"Shrap!"

The only answer was the ground hissing as the rain hit it.

He moved on, deeper into the park. She might not even be here. She might be on her way home right now and he was wasting his time. Yet something made him push on.

"Shrap!"

Then he heard a soft moan coming from the bushes to

his left. He shone his torch in that direction. A human form, lying on their side, among the flower bed.

"Shrap? Is that you?"

His heart pounded in his ears. What if it wasn't? What if it was some other homeless person who didn't take too kindly to the interruption?

He had to check, so he moved closer, shining the light on the person's back. He recognised the woollen coat.

"Shrap! Oh, my God. Are you okay?"

She didn't turn around. He put a hand on her shoulder. It was rigid. It was then he noticed her eyes were shut tight and she was trembling, holding herself and moaning softly.

"Shrap, it's me, Gareth. Are you hurt?"

He tried to roll her over, but she didn't budge. She emitted a low guttural groan and continued to shiver like she was in the grips of a fever.

"Not again," she murmured. "Not again."

He sat down beside her and put his hand on her shoulder. "Shh... it's okay. You're safe now." He had no idea if he was saying the right thing.

She seemed to quieten. After a while, the trembling stopped. Shrap didn't show weakness, so seeing her like this was both shocking and a little frightening.

"You're okay," he whispered. "Nobody's going to hurt you. It's just you and me here in the garden."

Her muscles relaxed beneath his fingers and her breathing steadied. The moaning stopped. She still hadn't turned over, but she was calming down.

"Are you hurt?" he whispered into the darkness, no idea if she could hear him.

She grunted, then tried to move and winced.

"What happened?" He leaned over her to look at her face.

Shit, was that blood?

Her one eye was swollen closed and blood caked her face, or at least the side of it he could see.

"I'll call an ambulance."

"No," she whimpered, grabbing his wrist. "No ambulance."

"Well, I can't leave you here like this." Even as he spoke the words, the rain came down harder. The flower bed was fast becoming a muddy moat.

Trevelyan hesitated, then made a decision. "Come on, I'll take you back to mine."

He managed to lift her to her feet. She swayed dangerously, leaning on him for support. He didn't mind, she wasn't heavy.

Slowly, they made their way back to the car.

She didn't say a word on the way home, just sat with her eyes shut and her head angled away from him. He glanced at her hands, grazed and bloodied. What the hell had happened? He'd only been gone for twenty minutes.

His questions could wait. The most important thing was to get her cleaned up so he could see the extent of the damage.

He pulled into his driveway and cut the lights. The last thing he wanted was his nosy neighbours looking to see who he was bringing home. They'd think she was drunk or something, the way she was swaying and leaning against him. Not a good impression, especially for a police officer.

He helped her out of the car and let her lean on him until they got to the door. Unlocking it, he led her inside and deposited her in an armchair in the living room. His place was rather bare, he hadn't had time to decorate it yet.

When he'd moved here, he'd decided a new start was necessary, and had thrown out anything that reminded him of Melanie. That included CDs, the rug they'd made love on, the one photograph he'd had of them together on holiday in Indonesia and anything else remotely nostalgic.

Turning the heating up, he grabbed his medical kit and some painkillers and went back into the lounge. She looked like she'd fallen asleep.

God, she was filthy. Dirt from the flower bed had seeped into her clothes and her boots were caked with it. Even her hair was stuck to her head with mud, or was it blood?

Going back to the kitchen, he filled a bowl with hot water, then got a sponge and a gym towel from the store cupboard in the hall. He had to get that blood off before he could see how badly injured she was. She needed a bath, but he didn't think she could wash herself, and he wasn't about to do it for her. That was crossing the line.

Kneeling beside her, he dipped the cloth into the hot water and gently wiped her face. She twitched, but then relaxed when she heard his voice. "It's only me. I'm going to clean you up, okay?"

She opened her good eye, then grimaced and closed it again.

"Shh... don't move. It's okay. Everything is okay now."

He had no idea if it was, but his words seemed to sooth her. At least she was compos mentis, and not locked in that terrifying catatonic state.

The water turned red. He threw it out and refilled the bowl, then continued to wipe her down. When the worst was off, he used the flannel to cleanse around her eyes. She winced when he touched the sore one.

"That's quite a shiner you've got there," he said.

She grunted. "The Russian caught me by surprise."

"What Russian?" When he'd left her, she'd been alone on the pavement.

"Big Mike."

Who the hell was Big Mike?

"Is that who you punched?" He wiped the blood off her knuckles and cringed as he saw the grazes. That would require some antiseptic ointment.

She had elegantly shaped hands, except they were covered with old scars, almost like silver spiderwebs. Battle scars. He shivered. What must she have been through?

"Can I take off your coat?" he asked. It was filthy, and blood and mud had run up her sleeves.

"Shit," she moaned as he tried to remove it. "My rib. I think it's broken."

"Let me have a look. Let's just get this off you."

He gently pulled the coat off her arm, then peeled it around her back and off the other arm, trying not to nudge her. She fell back with a grunt.

"Can I check your ribs?"

She gave a little nod.

Gingerly, he lifted her hooded top and winced when he saw the bruising.

"That bad?" she murmured. His eyes flew to her face, and he saw her one good eye was watching him.

"It's not great," he admitted. Great maroon streaks flared across her torso, turning a deep purple on her left side.

She tried to smile but couldn't. "It hurts to breathe."

"I'm no expert, but it looks like it could be broken. We might have to call an ambulance after all. You could have punctured a lung or something."

She didn't respond.

"I need to put an icepack on it. Can we get this off? It's wet and covered in mud."

She didn't complain as he threaded her arms out of the sleeves and lifted the soiled hoodie over her head.

"Sorry," he muttered, when she gave a shuddering wheeze.

The tattoo snaking over her wrist and up her arm was both mesmerising and menacing. It spoke of another life, another time. He realised he really didn't know her at all.

There was a bandage on her arm. Tightly wrapped, with spots of blood prickling through. She'd recently had medical treatment.

Using the sponge, he wiped off the worst of the dirt and grime. His hands weren't as steady as he'd like them to be. The rest could wait until she was stronger.

"I'm sorry you saw me like that," she whispered. "It's not... it's not me. It's because of..." She faded off.

"I know," he said. "You don't have to explain."

She fell silent.

"I'm going to disinfect these cuts." He reached for the Savlon. "This might sting a bit."

She nodded but let him smooth the antiseptic lotion over her knuckles, the palms of her hands, and the cut on her head where Mikael's boot had broken the skin.

That's what had caused all the blood, but then head wounds tended to bleed more than any other place on the body. He remembered when he was a boy, he'd bumped his head on the corrugated-iron roof of the shed and within minutes, he'd been dripping with blood. It had given his mum quite a fright when he'd run in crying.

"Okay, that'll do."

Shrap was nodding off, her head to the side.

He took the bowl to the kitchen and cleaned it out, washing his hands in the process. Then he poured himself a shot of whiskey and downed it.

What a night.

But he'd found her, and she was okay. Sort of. She'd be

in a world of pain tomorrow, but for now, he'd done what he could.

When he went back to the lounge to check on her, her chest was rising and falling in an even rhythm. She was asleep. That was probably the best thing for her.

Taking a blanket off the couch, he spread it over her knees. She might get cold in the night, especially with just her T-shirt on. Her soiled clothes lay discarded on the floor. There was no way those were redeemable. Still, she didn't have anything else to wear, so he picked them up and after removing her wallet from the pocket, put them in the washing machine. Unfortunately, he'd thrown out every last shirt that Melanie had left at his place before he'd moved. Not that he expected she'd wear another woman's clothes.

Starving, he made a sandwich, ate it, then went upstairs to bed. He left the door open in case she needed him in the night, then climbed under the covers. Within seconds, he was asleep.

42

"You're up." Trevelyan said.

They stood facing each other in his kitchen. The smell of toast and bacon wafted over to her, making her stomach rumble.

He'd been awake for some time. She'd heard him pottering around, boiling the kettle, singing softly out of tune. She'd caught him by surprise, walking in unannounced. Barefoot and in her jeans and T-shirt.

"Thank you for last night," she said. "I'm sorry you had to come and get me."

He waved away her apology with a flick of his hand. "How are you feeling?"

"I'll be okay," she said. She couldn't see through one eye, and she felt like she'd been in a war zone.

"I definitely think you should get that looked at." His gaze fell to her ribs.

She'd get Tessa, the doctor at the day centre, to check her out on Monday. She wasn't there over the weekend.

"I'll get out of your hair," she said. "As soon as I find the rest of my clothes."

"I washed them," he said quickly, awkwardly. "They're in the dryer."

He opened the machine and handed them to her. "Feel free to take a shower before you go."

"That's okay. You've done more than enough..."

"Honestly, it's no bother."

She hesitated. A shower would be great. She felt like she was caked in mud, despite her vague recollection of him cleaning her up. Jesus.

He sent her upstairs to the bathroom with a fresh towel. It was all tiles and chrome and mirrors, but no personal affects. It smelled like him.

She took her time, watching the dirt sluice off her and run down the plughole. It must have been bad. She couldn't remember most of it.

Mikael. The fight. Darting into the park to hide. Then the terror set in... Men screaming... the smell of burning flesh... Doug's hand grabbing hold of her and pulling her away from the hot breath of the train.

She turned her face up towards the shower nozzle. Fuck, that hurt. The pain captured her full attention, drawing her back to the present. She exhaled, spraying water out of her mouth and waited for it to pass.

When she finally came back downstairs wearing her tatted jeans and freshly washed shirt, he handed her a cup of coffee and told her to sit down.

"I'm okay, really. I don't want to impose."

"Well, I've made breakfast, so you may as well eat."

Gingerly, she sat down. It smelled good and she was hungry. Still, he'd already done too much. Seen too much. She needed to get out of here, back to obscurity, so she could lick her wounds in private.

"Who is Big Mike?" he asked, putting a plate of eggs,

bacon and toast in front of her.

"Big Mike is Xhafa's personal bodyguard," she said.

His eyebrows lifted. "Why did he beat you up?" He gasped. "Was he the one who—"

"No, it wasn't him. There was a point where I thought it might be, though, so I questioned him. This was him getting his own back."

"I see." His eyes narrowed. "Perhaps you'd better stay away from the club in future."

A dry laugh. "I will."

AS SOON AS she could get away, she did. It hurt to walk, but not as much as her wounded pride. Christ, what must he think of her? She shook her head as she walked towards the tube station. He'd offered to give her a lift, but she'd refused. She couldn't accept any more of his charity, not if she was to look him in the eye again.

Even that was doubtful.

She clenched her fists. Fuck Mikael. Fuck the army. Fuck everything.

She got on the tube, using the card she kept in her wallet. Luckily, that had remained in her coat pocket along with her phone that showed a missed call to Trevelyan at 10.17 last night. That's how he'd known she was in trouble.

She didn't remember calling him, everything was a blur.

The first thing she did when she got to Waterloo was retrieve her rucksack from the locker. Using the public toilets, she changed into a fresh shirt and threw away her soiled top. As it was, people were eyeing her out because of the bloodstains on it, or maybe it was because of her black eye. Either way, she looked like a battered wife.

She stopped at the discount store but even their prices

were too high. She had to be careful not to spend more than her army pension allowed. She'd already cleaned out most of it when she'd bought the gun.

In a second-hand store, she found a replacement coat several sizes too big, but it was good quality, warm and half the price of the other jackets she'd seen. While she was there, she got a woollen scarf for less than a quid to go with it. Sorted.

By now her rib was throbbing and she had a blinder of a headache, so she retreated to the quiet of the library to read the weekend papers – as well as she could with one eye. The librarian balked when he saw her but didn't say anything.

All the dailies carried articles on the dead women. She was pleased to see some savvy journalist had dug into Bianca Rubik's background and she was now toted as being a promising dancer and law student, rather than a sex worker or stripper.

According to the same article, Petra had also had aspirations as a dancer, except she'd had no formal training. A source close to the victim had said she was saving up for dance lessons. She wondered who the source was? Her flatmate?

Her phone was dead.

Getting up, she asked the library assistant if she could plug it in somewhere. He pointed to a power point next to the computers. She hobbled over, clutching her side, and lowered herself onto one of the chairs. Then she fired off a text message to Gareth. She didn't want to bother him again, but this was important.

Did Petra's flatmate say anything about dance lessons?

Twenty minutes went by, and she was about to move back to the comfy chair with the newspaper when her phone buzzed.

Yes. Petra wanted to be a dancer. It was her passion.

She thought about this for a moment. Could that be a link between them? Had Petra ever worked at Whispers, or any other strip club?

A few minutes later, her phone buzzed again. It was Gareth. He'd sent her a question mark.

She replied: *Could be a link? Can you check if Petra ever danced at the club?*

She got a thumbs-up in reply.

She did go back to the armchair then. The hard-backed ones were too uncomfortable for her damaged ribs. Ten minutes later, her phone buzzed again. It didn't stop. Gareth was ringing her. She got an irate look from a browser nearby, but she ignored them and hobbled over to her phone.

"Yes?"

"I just spoke to Peter, the manager at the club. Petra Burton-Leigh auditioned there two weeks ago."

43

Shrap froze as his words sunk in.

"That's the link," she said in a throaty whisper. "That's how he's targeting them."

"But they didn't hire her," Gareth said. "She wasn't good enough."

Shrap's brain ticked over. "I saw the two Albanians at Whispers one afternoon. They had a meeting with Xhafa before the club opened. They could quite easily have witnessed an audition."

"I'm not sure you're on the right track with the Albanians," he said hesitantly. "They don't own a black SUV."

"How do you know?"

A pause. "I'm at work."

"You went into work on a Saturday?"

"Yeah." Slightly defensive. "I wanted to check out the reg number you gave me."

She couldn't help smiling. He was as bad as she'd been when she was investigating. Couldn't leave a case alone, not if there were still leads to follow up.

"And?"

"It's registered to an Amir Uzuni. Born in Berat, Albania. He's thirty-two years old."

"Is there a photograph?"

"Yeah, I'll send it through."

She felt the phone vibrate against her ear. Glancing at the picture, her pulse ticked up a couple of notches. Grey Beanie.

"That's him," she said. "That's one of the two guys at the club. The SUV could belong to the other one."

"I only have the one name," he said. "His address matches the location you gave me in East London."

"Damn, so we have no idea who the other guy is."

"Would your friend Alex know?"

She hesitated. She could ask him, but she didn't want to get him into trouble. Not after the risk he'd already taken.

"I don't know, I suppose he might be able to find out. We don't want to let them know we're on to them, though."

"We don't even know if it is one of them yet."

That was true. Perhaps she was being overzealous. Seeing what she wanted to see.

Foreign. Rap music. Rich.

Then again, maybe not.

"Okay, I'll ask him, but if it is one of those two, then all the dancers, including Alex, are at risk. None of the women in that place are safe."

"I know," Trevelyan said quietly. "That's why we've got to catch this guy."

SHE MET Alex the next day outside the Southbank Centre. A frigid wind blew off the Thames, sending pedestrians scurrying for shelter in the bars and cafés.

"Jesus, what happened to you?" He stared at her black eye.

"Got into a fight."

"Wow, and here I was thinking you were such a nice girl."

She managed a wry grin. "Sorry to disappoint you."

"Was that because of your investigation into Bianca's death?" He was quick to join the dots.

"Yeah, sort of. I interrogated the wrong guy."

He shook his head. "Now you want me to dig up more dirt for you, is that right?"

She nodded sheepishly. He'd seen right through her. "I'm sorry to have to ask, Alex, but I need to know the names of those two Albanian chaps that frequent the club. Friends of your boss."

He frowned. "What do you want to know about them for?" His eyes widened. "Do you think one of them killed Bianca?"

"I'm not sure," she said honestly. "That's what we're trying to find out."

"*We're*?"

"I'm working with the police now."

"Ah." He looked her over. "Still a good girl, then."

She smiled. "Do you know their names?"

"I know they call the one guy Uzi, but I don't know their real names."

"Uzi? That's catchy."

He smirked. "Well, they're not very nice guys. They don't treat the girls too well, either."

"How do you mean?" She recalled the hard slap on the bottom.

"Some of the girls have given them private dances.

They're disrespectful, that's all. Sometimes a bit rough. But they're friends of Fiz's so nobody says anything."

It was as she thought.

"Is there any way you could find out their names without anyone noticing?" She bit her lip. "I know I'm asking a lot, and I don't want you to get into trouble, but it could be important."

He hesitated. "I'll see what I can do. No promises though."

She squeezed his hand. "Thanks, Alex."

He glanced down at her grazed knuckles. "I'd hate to see what the other guy looks like." Then he gasped. "Shit. Mick came in with a black eye and a swollen nose last night. Said he'd had an altercation with a troublemaker outside the club. That wouldn't happen to be you, would it?"

"Nah." She shook her head. "I know better than to take on someone like Mikael."

He pursed his lips. "He is a brute. I pity the man –" he coughed – "or woman who gets into a fight with him."

Yeah, she was feeling pretty sorry for herself too.

They said goodbye shortly after that.

"Be careful, Alex," she called, as he turned away.

Instead of replying, he raised his hand in a wave and kept walking.

THE WEATHER WENT from bad to worse, and by the time she got back to The Cut, she was being pounded by a slushy mix of sleet and rain. She quickened her pace, but it hurt to breathe. Doug's porch was not an inviting option tonight. Neither was the back entrance of the Marriott.

She needed to rest. Her vision was blurry in her bad eye and the pounding in her head was worse. She could go to the hostel, but there was always some sort of drama there and she wasn't up to another fight tonight. Then she remembered Milly telling her to use the back room at the laundromat if she was desperate.

Her current condition probably qualified.

She found the key where she'd left it, under the third brick from the door, and went inside. The pounding of the sleet against the windows pockmarked the stillness and she was glad it wasn't dead quiet. As the warmth began to thaw her out, she sent a silent thanks to Milly.

She bedded down on the pull-out couch in the back room and was about to drift off when her phone rang.

Trevelyan.

"We got the results from the forensic search on Annie Pincher's vehicle," he said before she could even say hello, as if it were an extension of their last conversation.

"Are you still at work?" she asked. Outside, the sky had turned from slate grey to black, and it was still pelting down. Hard spears of rain rather than slush rattled the thin windows, but it was equally dismal.

"Yeah, I'm leaving soon. The weather was so dire I thought it best to stay put."

He was making excuses for working through the weekend.

"What did the forensics say?" she asked.

"Nada. Absolutely nothing. The car was spotless. Not a hair, fibre or any other kind of DNA."

She clenched her jaw. "Well, we'd ruled Gregory Pincher out anyway, so it's to be expected."

"I guess so. Sorry to disturb you, I just thought you'd like to know."

"Yeah, thanks."

A pause.

"How are you feeling?"

"Tender." Her entire torso was one big bruise. The Russian had done a number on her. It didn't help that her rib had probably been fractured before and this had compounded the injury.

"Hopefully this will be a lesson not to tangle with big Russian mobsters."

She snorted. "Duly noted."

They hung up shortly after that. Another dead end.

The DNA only served to underline the fact that Gregory Pincher was innocent. Of murder, that is. For his other indiscretions, Shrap had no doubt his wife would make him pay.

———

44

His day started with a briefing. Senior Investigating Officer Burrows was informing them that the Putney Major Investigation Team were swooping in to steal the case out from under their noses in a few days' time.

Should he mention the link to the strip club?

If Burrows thought they had a lead, he'd descend on the place and question everyone, and the two Albanians would get wind of it and disappear. That was the last thing he wanted.

Besides, all he had was a washed-up prostitute's testimony that Petra had been picked up by a foreigner in a black SUV playing rap music. Hardly a reliable witness.

The DCI would laugh at him.

He exhaled loudly, causing Devi to glance across.

No. He'd give it a few more days and see what they could find. The team were hard at work analysing the CCTV footage from The Cut on the night Petra died, as well as in the vicinity of the Old Vic, where Bianca had been murdered. They might be able to isolate a vehicle or at least give them a new lead.

Shrap had told him Alex was going to try to find out the other Albanian's name. So far, he had Amir Uzuni, aka Uzi. He shivered despite the central heating in the squad room. Violence was second nature to these guys. They traded in it, used it for intimidation and to get what they wanted. He hoped Alex was being careful.

Their big break came later that day. Murphy, one of the CCTV operators, exploded into the squad room. "Sir, we think we've got something," he told Devi, who immediately leaped out of her chair. Gareth followed.

The CCTV room was small and claustrophobic, filled with screens, whirring hard drives and too many bodies. Murph pointed to a screen where the operator had paused a grainy image of a dark SUV cruising up The Cut. Gareth recognised the pub he'd been to with Shrap that one time, the Coach and Horses.

"We caught this vehicle on camera a few nights ago," he said. "It was one of several SUVs that popped up. That's not significant in itself. However –" he paused for effect – "we picked it up again the night the second victim was killed."

"Petra," whispered Gareth.

"Yes. At 11.27 it passed the CCTV camera outside the Coach and Horses. The windows are tinted so the image is dark, but when we blew it up, we got this..."

The operator flicked a switch and the man's face came into view. It was still hard to make out his features, but he had a square jaw, a thick neck, tattooed hands on the steering wheel and he was wearing a grey beanie.

"Can you send me that?" Gareth asked.

Devi turned to him. "Why? You know him?"

"I want to cross-check it with a DVLA photograph I looked at on the weekend."

The operator nodded.

He went back to his desk.

"What DVLA picture?" Devi shot him a look that said, *What are you up to?*

"It's a lead the bartender at the strip club gave me," he said, not looking at her. "Two Albanian guys, regulars at the club. He said they were dodgy, so I ran the one guy's plates."

"And?"

"Apart from a six-month driving ban for speeding a few years back, he's clean. No criminal record in this country."

"What about in Albania?"

"I haven't checked, but he was a kid when he arrived here, so I doubt there's anything serious."

"Yeah, probably not worth it."

"He does look like the guy in the CCTV image, though."

He pulled up the photograph from Amir Uzuni's driving licence. Devi peered at the screen. Then she frowned. "It could be him. It's hard to tell."

"Same square jaw, same thick neck. Pity we can't see his hands."

"Yeah, those tats were pretty specific."

They both gazed at the picture on her screen. "Is it or isn't it?" he muttered.

"It could be," she said finally. "But it won't stand up in court. Especially not with the hat on."

"No, probably not." He fell back into his chair. "There is the dancing connection though. He would have known both victims."

Devi's head jerked towards him. "What?"

Shit. He'd forgotten he hadn't mentioned it to anyone at

work. Discussing it with Shrap had made him feel like it was common knowledge.

"Oh, it's something I was following up. I didn't want to mention it before I had concrete evidence."

"Gareth?" She said his name slowly, like you would a naughty child.

"Well, Bianca was a dancer at the club, right?"

She nodded.

"And Petra wanted to be a dancer."

"How d'you know that?"

"Don't you remember? Her flatmate told us. She was going to spend the money the rich guy gave her on dancing lessons."

"Jesus, you've got a good memory."

"I wrote up the report. Anyway, I wondered if there was a connection with the club." Shrap had wondered. "So I called the manager, Peter, and he told me Petra had been there for an audition."

Devi was staring at him, her mouth agape.

"They didn't hire her," Gareth said. "She wasn't good enough. But she'd been there, which meant any of the staff or the management could have seen her."

"This is huge," she whispered. "You've found the connection between the victims. We've been looking for that ever since Petra was killed. We have to inform Burrows."

"Do we have to?" His eyes pleaded. "He'll go in guns blazing and the killer will see us coming a mile away. That's why I didn't say anything. I wanted to find out who it was before we scared him off."

"You think he works there?" Devi ran a hand through her long, black hair. "Then, what's this about the Albanian?"

"Amir Uzuni – or Uzi as he's called – is a friend of Xhafa's. He's always hanging around the club. He could quite easily have seen Petra's audition. He may even have spoken to her."

"Wow." Her eyes flew back to the screen. "This guy could be our killer."

"We need proof before we go to Burrows," he insisted. "If we bring him in now, his solicitor will make mincemeat out of us."

Devi fell silent, thinking about what he'd said. "Okay, you might have a point," she conceded. "That CCTV image won't hold up. It could be anyone."

"If only we could get his DNA," he said. "It might match that under Petra's fingernails."

Devi snapped her fingers together. "If we brought him in, he might consent to a DNA swab."

"Really?" He raised an eyebrow. "You think his solicitor is going to let him do that?"

"Yeah, probably not. Not when we've got nothing on him." Devi sighed.

"We might be able to get his DNA another way." Gareth thought aloud.

"How?" Devi stared at him. "And if we do, is it even admissible?"

"No, probably not, but it would tell us once and for all whether he's our guy. At least then we'd know."

His colleague was shaking her head. "I don't know, Gareth. It's risky. What did you have in mind?"

He held up his phone. "I have to make a quick phone call, then I'll let you know."

It took a while before Shrap picked up.

"Hello?" Her voice sounded tinny, like she was in an enclosed space.

"Can you talk?"

"Yeah, go ahead."

He told her about the SUV they'd picked up on camera. "It drove past the Coach and Horses at exactly 11.27 the night Petra was killed. We picked it up a few days earlier, as well. Same vehicle. Same area."

There was a pause.

"Didn't Petra's flatmate say he'd picked her up once before?" she asked.

"Yes, if it's the same guy."

"Then it would make sense for him to be in the area on both those occasions." Her words quickened.

"Exactly. We blew up the image and you can vaguely make out the driver. The windows are tinted, but it could be your Albanian friend from the club."

"Who? Xhafa?"

"No, one of his gangster buddies. Blue BMW, remember? I looked up the licence number on the DVLA database."

"Seriously? It looked like him?"

"I said *could be*. It's hard to say."

"Could you send me the picture?"

He bit his lip. He'd get into such shit if anyone found out. But then he'd been colluding with her this whole time. In for a penny and all that.

"Okay, sending it through now."

He accessed the photograph from his email and attached it to a WhatsApp message. Her phone buzzed when she received it.

"Got it."

There was a tense silence as she opened the text.

"That's him," she exclaimed softly.

"How do you know? The image is grainy at best. His face is in shadow and—"

"The beanie," she cut in. "He was wearing that exact same hat when I saw him at the club."

There was quiet as her words sunk in. Gareth took a shaky breath. "Really? You're sure?"

"One hundred per cent."

"Holy crap. He's our guy. He killed both those women."

"It looks like it." Shrap sounded strange, like she couldn't quite believe it either.

"Except we have nothing on him," he fumed.

"Bring him in for questioning," Shrap said. "Do a DNA test. Didn't you say you had the killer's DNA on file?"

"Yes, but on what grounds? We can't arrest him because he looks dodgy. That photograph isn't definitive. Unless you want to come in as a witness?"

She snorted. "Good one."

"I didn't think so."

He took a steadying breath. "I was wondering if Alex could perhaps get his DNA for us. A glass, maybe? When he's next at the club. I know it's not strictly legit, but—"

"He doesn't have to," she interjected. "I already have his DNA."

"You do? How?"

"We got into a fight. I've got his blood on my shirt."

"But I thought it was the big Russian…"

"Not that fight. Another fight."

"For God's sake, Shrap."

"Do you want it or not?"

"Yes, of course. But how am I going to explain that one to the powers that be?"

She hesitated. "I'll have to come in, won't I?"

"If we use your shirt, yes."

There was a heavy pause. "Okay, I'll get the shirt and

bring it in this afternoon. I'll say I got into a fight with the suspect."

"How did I find you?" God, this was getting complicated. If they weren't careful about this, he could see a suspension in his future. He might even lose his job.

"You didn't. I found you. I came in to lay a complaint for assault. It was a coincidence. You took the shirt off me and talked me out of it."

Would that work? He wasn't sure. "When did this assault take place?" he asked.

"Three weeks ago."

"It's a bit late to lay an assault charge," he said, his heart sinking. No one was going to buy this.

"Which is why you talked me out of it," she said.

"And you walk in at the exact time that we need this guy's DNA? It's a bit too convenient, don't you think?"

"Do you have a better idea?"

He thought for a moment. "Maybe. What if you said you were investigating the case in an independent capacity and you got into a fight with the guy? It's all true. You used to be in the military police. A person in that position might take matters into her own hands."

She didn't respond.

He continued, "You suspected him but couldn't do anything about it on your own, so you came in to speak to me. You've already sent me one anonymous note, which my DCI knows about, so it wouldn't be a stretch if you came in in person."

Shrap was silent. Gareth waited, holding his breath.

Eventually, she said, "Okay. I can do that. For Doug."

45

A t three o'clock, a neatly dressed Shrap walked into Southwark Police Station, bloody shirt in hand. She wore freshly laundered jeans, her best shirt and her new black coat. A far cry from the grubby vagrant who'd been brought in for questioning three weeks ago. The only thing that gave her away was the black eye. She couldn't disguise that.

She gave her name to the duty sergeant and was told to wait. Five minutes later, Gareth and a woman she didn't know came down to meet her.

"Ms Nelson, this is DS Chakrabarti. DS Chakrabarti, this is Shrap Nelson." The two women shook hands, but Shrap didn't miss the suspicious look the young detective gave her.

"DS Chakrabarti is part of the team working the case," Gareth told her.

"Won't you come with us?" Chakrabarti led the way through a set of revolving doors.

"She doesn't trust me," Shrap whispered to Gareth before they got to the lift.

"Relax, it's going to be fine." He shot her a reassuring

smile, which didn't make her feel any less anxious. This was the last place she wanted to be, but if it meant catching Doug's killer, then so be it.

She got into the elevator with Chakrabarti and Trevelyan. No one spoke. They went up two floors and emerged into a small lobby. Through the glass she could see a busy squad room. The doors opened and the sounds flew at her. Telephones, printers, voices.

She froze.

"You okay?" Gareth asked.

"Yeah."

It was like going back in time. This could be her office. Her telephone. Her printer.

In Afghanistan. Iraq. Cyprus. Different places, the same sounds.

Trevelyan's voice brought her back. "When you're ready, we're over here."

She followed him through the open-plan office and into a room at the end. Soundproof, thank God. She looked around. There were no cameras or recording equipment, but then this wasn't a formal interview.

Trevelyan's colleague gestured for her to sit. Shrap studied her. It was the same woman who'd gone to the strip club, but this time she was in her element. Smartly dressed. Young but ambitious. Married. A straight arrow. How much did she know?

"Ms Nelson," she began. "Would you mind telling us what your connection is with Mr Uzuni?" So DS Chakrabarti was the one asking the questions.

"I am a personal friend of Doug Romberg, one of the victims," she said. "I was investigating Mr Uzuni in connection with his death."

"What made you think that he had something to do with your friend's death?"

"Doug Romberg witnessed the death of Bianca Rubik, a dancer at Whispers Gentlemen's Club. I believe that's why he was killed. I went to the club to find out more about the victim, and I met Mr Uzuni. He knew Bianca, so I put him under surveillance to see if it would lead anywhere."

"Put him under surveillance?" DS Chakrabarti asked.

"I watched him."

She nodded. "And did it lead anywhere?"

"Not at that stage," said Shrap. "I followed him to a housing estate in East London. He assaulted me so I hit him in the nose. It was self-defence."

"And why are you here, Ms Nelson?"

"I'd like to lay a charge against Mr Uzuni. I've brought in the shirt I was wearing at the time to prove that he assaulted me." She put the bag containing the bloody shirt on the table.

Trevelyan looked flustered. She was going off-book, but it was better this way. He'd soon realise that.

"When did this assault take place, Ms Nelson?" Chakrabarti asked.

"Three weeks ago."

"Three weeks ago. Why are you laying a charge now, if you don't mind me asking?"

"I've been having blurred vision and I think it's got something to do with the concussion he gave me."

The Sergeant glanced at Shrap's black eye. It was open now, but still bruised and swollen. "Are you sure it hasn't got something to do with that shiner there?"

"What this? No, this was recent. I've been having blurred vision for weeks, ever since the assault."

Trevelyan said nothing.

"Okay, Ms Nelson. If you're sure you want to lay a charge, we can do that. I should warn you, however, that three weeks after the event is quite a long period of time. Without evidence of your injuries, I'm not sure it'll do much good."

"What about the shirt?"

"That just proves he bled. It doesn't prove Mr Uzuni assaulted you."

She frowned. This was all part of the game. She could get the doctor at the clinic to vouch for her, no problem. She'd explain the extent of her injuries, including the concussion and fractured rib, but that wasn't why she was here.

She chewed on her lower lip. "I see what you mean."

Trevelyan's lips turned up in the faintest of smiles.

"Would you like to rethink the charge, Ms Nelson?" she said.

She pretended to think for a moment, then her shoulders sagged. "Yeah, okay. I'll leave it." She glanced at the two detectives. "I'm sorry to have wasted your time."

"Not at all," said Chakrabarti. "I'm only sorry we couldn't be of more help."

Shrap got up to leave.

"Your shirt," Trevelyan said, reaching for the bag.

She shrugged. "You can dump it."

"As you wish, madam."

It was as simple as that.

SHRAP SMILED as she lay down on Doug's porch. The newspaper was still there. Old and brown. The last thing Doug had read.

"We're getting there, mate," she muttered, as she unscrewed a small bottle of wine. She didn't often indulge, but her rib was killing her, and she didn't want to go back to the laundromat again. Once was enough. She'd cleaned the place down and left it as she'd found it so Milly wouldn't know she'd been there. The wine would help her relax.

She raised the bottle to the sky. "We're getting there."

46

The sunrise was getting noticeably later. It was still beautiful, but the warmth had gone. The oranges weren't as vibrant, the yellows not as vivid. Instead, cold shadows stretched along the Embankment, fighting against the light. Sometimes, like today, they won.

Shrap shivered and turned away from the river. It gargled behind her, splashing up against the base of Waterloo Bridge. She felt the moisture on the back of her neck, carried by the wind. It was time to go.

Today was the day. Today they'd know whether Amir Uzuni was their killer.

She couldn't concentrate on anything. Not the newspaper, not the chatter in the day centre, not even what the doctor had said when she'd checked her over and redone her bandage. She picked up "not as bad as yesterday" and "do you need any more painkillers?"

To which she'd replied that she didn't.

Painkillers dulled her senses, which offered temporary respite, but they were also addictive. She didn't take anything stronger than a paracetamol. She couldn't afford a drug habit. Besides, even though she was afraid of the voices in her head, she was equally afraid that one day they'd stop. And she'd start to forget.

She was walking down Borough High Street when she got the call. Trevelyan's voice, hoarse with excitement.

"It's a match. We got him, Shrap. We got him."

She exhaled. *Thank you, God.*

The release of tension made her giddy. She put a hand on a shop wall for support.

"Shrap? Are you there? Did you hear me? We bloody got him."

"That's awesome. Are you going to bring him in?"

"We've got the firearms unit heading to the estate as we speak. We'll have him in custody in a matter of hours, thanks to you."

"And you," she said.

She heard him smile. "We make a good team."

She wasn't sure about that.

"Let me know how it goes."

He said he would, and they hung up.

Shrap glanced up at the Shard shimmering in the midday sun. It cut into the sky like a knife, severing the air around it with lethal precision.

Right now, firearms officers were descending on Uzuni's East London flat. Would he go quietly, or would he fight? If he had warning, he'd try to run. No doubt about that.

Next would come the interview, led in all likelihood by DS Chakrabarti. Trevelyan would sit in. He'd want to be part of the action.

They'd ask him why his DNA was under a dead woman's fingernails. How was he going to get out of that one? They'd show him the photograph of the SUV and ask if that was him. The photo itself proved nothing. It was purely circumstantial. But with the DNA evidence, it would serve to put him away for a long time.

Unfortunately, unless he confessed, there was nothing linking him to Bianca's murder, and therefore nothing to link him to Doug's. Uzuni could go down for killing Petra Burton-Leigh, but nobody else.

IT WAS ten o'clock before Trevelyan texted her again.

Can we meet?

She frowned. After their last conversation, that wasn't good.

Where?

My place? One hour.

It made sense. Their café had closed, and she didn't fancy meeting in a rowdy pub. He didn't either, by the sounds of things.

She sent him a thumbs-up.

Bermondsey was a twenty-minute walk away. She could use the exercise. Her body was stiff from the bruising. It would be good to get the blood circulating again.

"Thanks for coming." He opened the door.

"I was concerned when I got your text. I thought perhaps something had gone wrong." She walked into the house. It was warm and smelled faintly of coffee.

"Well, it didn't go according to plan, put it that way."

She followed him into the kitchen. "What happened?"

"Would you like something to drink?"

She shook her head. "I'm good. Thanks."

"You don't mind if I do?" Without waiting for an answer, he poured himself a scotch.

"That bad?"

He managed a weak smile. "You could say that."

A bad feeling gnawed at her gut.

Trevelyan sank into the breakfast nook and put his glass down on the table. "The raid was a success. We got Uzuni, along with his cohort, a man called Thomas Balaj. They put up a bit of a fight, shot an officer in the leg, but were subdued in under ten minutes."

"Sorry to hear about the officer," she said.

"He'll be okay. The bullet missed the femoral artery, thank God."

Else Uzuni would have another murder charge to add to his growing list of offences.

"Then he lawyered up. They both did. It turns out the vehicle we caught on camera was registered to Balaj. He had no idea Uzuni was using it to pick up women."

Or so he said.

Trevelyan took another sip. He looked exhausted. Messy, wind-swept hair, too much stubble, dark shadows denting his eyes. His hand shook as he held the glass.

"When last did you eat?" she asked.

"Can't remember." A quick flick of the wrist. "There were more important things to do."

"Got any snacks?" she asked, getting up.

"Top cupboard to the left." He stifled a yawn.

She opened it and pulled out a pack of crackers. "Cheese?"

"Fridge."

She got out the butter, cheese and half a cucumber and put it on the table. Then glancing around, she spotted some cutlery in the washing up wrack and took out a knife, a fork and a plate.

"You've got to eat." She put the plate down in front of him.

"Thanks." He gave her a tired smile and picked up the knife.

"Now, tell me what happened."

He cut a slice of cheese and put it on a cracker. "We took a DNA sample when we got him into custody, as per standard procedure. At that point he didn't know what he was being arrested for. The sample went straight to the lab."

The DNA from the shirt wouldn't be admissible in court, but the official one would.

"At first he denied everything, but when confronted with the evidence, he wavered."

"He didn't confess?" Shrap stared at him disbelieving.

"No, it's never that easy." He hacked at the cucumber. "He admitted to using his friend's car to pick up Petra Burton-Leigh. He admitted having sex with her. Twice. Once a few days ago and once the night she was murdered, but he denied strangling her."

Shrap was silent. Bloody typical. They shouldn't have expected anything less, really.

"There is a time lag of about two and a half hours between when he picked her up and when her body was discovered by the pub landlord, so he's relying on that to cast reasonable doubt."

"Fucker," ground out Shrap.

"Yes, well we spoke to the CPS and they've said we've got enough to charge him. Now it's up to a jury to decide."

"The DNA under her fingernails must be enough to convict him."

"Not necessarily. He claims they had vigorous sex and she scraped his back with her nails. He even had the scars to prove it."

"Shit." He'd thought of everything.

"We're testing the vehicle for her blood, but since he's already admitted she was in the car..." He petered off.

Shrap found she was clenching her fists.

"What about Bianca Rubik?"

"He recognised her from the club but said he didn't know her. Apart from the odd lap dance, they'd never even spoken. Unfortunately, there's nothing to prove otherwise."

"There are cameras in the club," Shrap said.

"I know. We had the footage sent over. Uzuni claims he was at the club on the night of Bianca Rubik's murder."

"What?"

How had she missed that?

"We studied the footage. It's true. That was why I wanted to meet with you. We spotted Bianca leaving the club around eleven o'clock, but at that time, Uzuni and his pal, Balaj, were enjoying cocktails with Xhafa at a table on the other side of the room." He picked up the glass. "There's no way he killed Bianca Rubik."

"Holy fucking Christ." Shrap leaped to her feet. "You're telling me we've been wrong this whole time? That the two women were killed by two different perps?"

He downed the rest in one go. When he was finished, he set the glass down on the table and met her gaze. "That's what I'm telling you."

47

Shrap wandered the streets in shock. How had they got it so wrong? Two women, both strangled, both left for dead in the same vicinity, their bodies found less than a mile apart.

Both had a connection with Whispers. Both had died within two weeks of each other.

Surely that wasn't a coincidence.

Yet what was the alternative? Two separate killers? Or could Uzuni be telling the truth and he hadn't killed Petra? Was the real killer still out there?

Her head throbbed. Above her the clouds cast ominous shadows across the ground. She could smell rain. The air was pungent with it.

She'd failed. She'd taken a chance and she'd lost.

It was over.

They were no closer to catching the killer now than they had been when all this began. It had been a stupid idea to get involved in the first place. Why had she ever thought she could solve this case? She wasn't a detective anymore. Pretending to be one didn't make it so.

Although, just for a moment, she'd actually believed it was possible. That she could find Doug's killer and clear her friend's name.

She scoffed.

She'd even convinced Trevelyan, a serving police officer, to trust her. She'd put his career on the line, and for what? The man they'd caught would probably get off, and they were no closer to finding the killer, or killers. The whole thing was a disaster.

The sky rumbled, as if in agreement. A big, fat raindrop landed on her forehead. It was going to bucket down. She didn't care.

Eventually, soaked to the bone, she collapsed on Doug's porch. She'd stopped at the off-licence and bought herself a bottle of Bells. For the rest of the night, she didn't want to think about the investigation. She didn't want to think, period.

"Sorry, mate," she said, as she raised the bottle to her lips. "I tried."

JESUS, her head hurt.

She opened her eyes and blinked. The sun was up and for the first time in ages, she'd missed the sunrise.

Fuck it. New beginnings were overrated.

Her hand knocked the bottle of Bells beside her. It was a quarter full. That was something. She must have passed out before she'd had a chance to finish it. Doug would be disappointed.

She sat up and groaned. The mornings were the worst, before her body had had a chance to warm up. She sucked in a breath and waited for the pain in her ribs to subside.

She debated getting up, but what was the point? The

case had given her something to do, but now that was over. The day stretched ahead without form or purpose.

What had she done before? How had she spent her time?

Her existence seemed to be divided into two parts: before Doug's death, and after.

Get up, Private! her old Sergeant's voice yelled at her.

Groaning, she got to her knees. The only days in the last seventeen years that she hadn't got out of bed were the ones she'd spent in the military hospital in Kabul.

Routine. She needed a routine.

The day centre was open. She'd go there, shower and change, and have something to eat. At least it would get her up.

She packed her backpack and set off down the road. It was a busy weekday morning and commuters rushed past desperate to get to the office. A wave of nausea hit her, and she leaned against a wall until it passed.

Christ, she was a mess.

She started walking again, conscious that people were giving her a wide berth. She didn't blame them. Even she didn't want to be near her.

A car pulled over a few feet away and a woman got out. She was clutching a Chihuahua. Shrap watched as she transferred it to the other arm and then brushed the hairs off her expensive woollen coat.

She frowned, something stirring in her addled brain. Damn this hangover. It almost felt as bad as her concussion. What was it about that woman's coat?

Shrugging, she walked on towards the centre.

"Bloody 'ell," said Budge as she walked in. "You look like shit."

"Thanks."

"I can smell the booze on ya. You go on a bender last night or something?"

"Something," she muttered, and kept walking to the showers. He tutted behind her.

The hot water soothed her aching body. It washed away the dirt and the sweat, but it couldn't get rid of the heaviness that had settled over her.

At least now she didn't have to pretend anymore. She could just be herself. She could wear her scruffy clothes and fade into the background. No loud clubs, no surveillance, no meeting other people. That was what she wanted, right?

That's why she'd relocated to the street in the first place.

Trevelyan's face popped into her mind, but she pushed it away.

We make a good team.

She scoffed and turned off the taps. Stepping out, she wrapped a towel around her waist and stood in front of the mirror. It had steamed up and all she could see was a hazy, undefined image of herself. Swiping at it, she ran a comb through her hair and brushed her teeth, but that was the extent of it.

She had just finished her toast and tea when the phone rang. How had it not died already? She glanced at the screen. Alex.

Shit, she'd forgotten she'd asked him to have a nose around.

"Alex?"

She heard panting. "Holy shit, Shrap. I thought they were going to kill me."

"What are you talking about? What's happened?"

He gasped several times, like he was hyperventilating. "Peter found me looking at the reservation book. He took me into this back room. Fiz came in, with Mikael." Another gasp. "I've never been so scared in my life."

Her heart pounded. "Alex, where are you?"

"I'm outside the club. They've just let me go. I thought they were going to kill me." His voice cracked.

"I'll be right there. Wait for me at the bus stop at the end of the road. You got that? Wait there."

"Okay."

She left her backpack in Budge's office and, saying she had to go, ran out of the centre. A bus would take too long, as would walking, so she hailed a black cab. It was an exorbitant expense and one she couldn't afford, but she had to find Alex.

She called Trevelyan on the way, her phone wavering on one bar.

Please don't die now.

"Shrap?"

"It's Alex," she huffed. "He's been interrogated by Xhafa and his men. I'm on my way to the club now."

"Is he alright?"

"I think so. They caught him snooping. Put the fear of God in him." She gulped. "It's my fault, Trevelyan. Shit, I should never have asked him to poke around."

"I'll meet you there," he said. "Leaving now. We'll bring him back here and get a statement."

Fifteen minutes later, the cab dropped her off at the bus stop, where a shivering Alex was waiting, puffing hard on a cigarette.

"Alex, are you okay?" The bartender's face was covered in blotches, like he'd been slapped repeatedly. There was dried blood on his lower lip and his clothes were filthy. He'd lost his leather jacket and the hand holding the cigarette was trembling.

She sat down beside him.

"Alex, I'm so sorry."

He stared straight ahead, the cigarette burning down.

"Did they hurt you?"

He shook his head. "Not really. They slapped me around a bit, but that's all." He took a shuddering breath. "They kept asking me what I'd said to the police about Uzi and his friend. I told them I hadn't spoken to the police, but they didn't believe me."

"Uzi was arrested yesterday," she told him. "For Petra Burton-Leigh's murder."

"Who's that?"

She'd forgotten he didn't know anything about the second victim.

"Bianca wasn't the only one."

His eyes widened. "Was it Uzi? Did he kill Bianca?"

"No, not Bianca." It hurt to admit it, but his alibi was indisputable. "We think he killed Petra. She was a dancer who auditioned at the club a few weeks back."

"Yeah, we've had a few girls try out lately," Alex said. "None of them made it. Fiz has got high standards. He only recruits the best."

Shrap glanced towards the club. "You're better off out of there. Those guys are bad news. Xhafa's mixed up with the Italian mob, Uzi and Balaj are drug-dealing scum. They're very dangerous men."

"I've been sacked anyway." He took another furious drag. "They told me to get out and never come back."

"It's just as well. There are plenty of other bar jobs around."

"Not many that pay as well." He blew a fume of smoke into the air.

They were still sitting there when an unmarked car pulled up beside them. Trevelyan got out.

"Alex, this is DC Trevelyan with Southwark Police. I've been working with him on the case."

Alex threw his cigarette on to the ground and studied the detective.

"It's good to meet you, Alex." Trevelyan held out his hand. Alex shook it. "Do you feel up to giving us a statement?"

"I'm not pressing charges." There was real fear in his voice.

"You don't have to," Trevelyan said. "Just tell us what happened."

He gave a tiny nod.

"Come on, then."

Trevelyan opened the back door and gestured for them to get in. Shrap hesitated for a second, then climbed in beside Alex.

Trevelyan got in the front and started the car. Soon they were zipping through the morning traffic towards Southwark. They parked underground and took the elevator up to the second floor. Trevelyan led them through the squad room to the private interview chamber on the other side. This time there was a recording device set up, cameras mounted to ceiling, the works.

"You don't mind if we record this interview?" Trevelyan asked Alex. "We want to be clear about what happened."

"They're not going to know I'm here, are they?"

"They'll never know," Shrap assured him.

DS Chakrabarti came in holding a tablet. Trevelyan introduced them and then asked if anyone wanted tea or coffee. Alex, who needed to warm up, nodded eagerly. A

short time later, Trevelyan was back with two coffees, one
for Shrap and one for Alex.

"Thanks."

He sat down. "Right, shall we get started?"

They went through the preliminaries: name, address,
occupation. Then Trevelyan said, "Alex, will you tell us what
happened?

Alex wrapped his hands around the mug. "Shaz asked
me to see if I could find out the names of these two
Albanian men who came to the club, so last night, when I
got to work, I checked the reservation book."

Shrap bit her lip. She felt bad about that.

"Actually, that was my idea," Trevelyan said. "Just so
we're clear. I asked Shrap to ask you to look into it for us.
She didn't want to, she thought it was too dangerous, but we
knew you'd be best placed to get that information. I'm sorry
we brought you into this."

Alex glanced at Trevelyan, then Shrap.

"Please continue, Alex," DS Chakrabarti said.

"Peter, the manager, caught me. He asked what I was
doing, so I said I had some friends coming in and wanted to
reserve a table for them."

"That was quick thinking," said Shrap.

He gave her a weak smile. "It didn't work. He didn't
believe me. He said the boss wanted to have a word and
grabbed me by the arm and locked me in this room at the
back. I didn't even know it was there." He shivered and
gripped the coffee cup tighter.

"What happened next?" Trevelyan asked.

"Fiz, that's Mr Xhafa, came in and asked me if I'd spoken
to the police. I said no and that I didn't know what he was
talking about. What would I go to the police for? He stared
at me for a long time, then asked what I knew about his

business. I said it was a Gentlemen's Club and that's all I knew. That's when he left the room."

"He left?"

"Yeah, he went into the office next door with Mikael, that's his bodyguard."

DS Chakrabarti raised an eyebrow. "What does he need a bodyguard for?"

"Exactly," said Shrap.

"Fiz was furious. He said Uzi and Thomas had fucked everything up. I could hear because he'd left the door open. Peter was still in the room with me."

"What else did they say?" Trevelyan was leaning forward now, across the table.

"He asked why Uzi had to get himself arrested now, of all times. With days to go before the shipment arrived."

"Shipment?" DS Chakrabarti's head shot up. "What shipment?"

"Drugs." Shrap and Trevelyan spoke at the same time.

At the sergeant's inquiring look, Shrap said, "Xhafa's on a National Crime Agency watchlist. He's allegedly got ties to an Albanian organised crime syndicate in the UK. They're bringing in cocaine from South America, via ports in Europe controlled by the Italian mafia."

"How on earth do you know that?" Trevelyan asked. "I had to get specific permission to access those files."

"I've got a contact at military intelligence." Had a contact. She wouldn't be speaking to Trevor again.

Trevelyan stared at her.

DS Chakrabarti cleared her throat. "Can we just be clear? This shipment Xhafa mentioned, that would be a drugs shipment coming into the UK?"

"Most likely, yes." Shrap met his gaze.

"Did they say when?" she asked Alex.

He shook his head. "I don't think so, but from the way they were talking, I'd say it was imminent. Fiz was really upset. He said now they'd need someone else to go down to Tilbury because the police would be watching."

"Crap, we'd better get the NCA in here," said DS Chakrabarti. "They're going to have to send people down to the docks."

"Good idea," Trevelyan agreed. This was outside their remit. She turned back to Alex. "Alex, you've been really helpful. Is there anything else you can tell us about the shipment?"

The bartender thought for a moment. "I don't think so. After that, they locked me in the room for a while. Then Mikael came in and asked me the same questions again, except he wasn't as gentle." He winced and touched his thick lip.

"We'll get a medic to take a look at that in a minute," Trevelyan said.

"They must have believed you if they let you go?" said Shrap.

"I didn't know anything." His voice was high-pitched. The trauma was still raw. "I didn't know about the drugs, you didn't tell me about that. I didn't know Uzi had murdered that girl, and I hadn't talked to the police. The only person I've talked to is you."

"You did great." Trevelyan smiled. "Thanks to you, we might actually be able to intercept this shipment and arrest part of the syndicate."

That's all they'd be able to do. The main syndicate would just regroup and select someone else to manage the imports. Unless they took down the entire syndicate, it would only be a temporary solution. But it would get this lot of drugs off the street. That might save some lives. And if they were lucky, they'd be able to arrest Xhafa and his crew.

"Let's get that lip seen to," Trevelyan said, getting up.

"I'll get on the phone to the NCA and fill them in," Devi said. She turned to Alex. "They may want to ask you some more questions, but we'll play them the recording first. We won't keep you here any longer."

"Thanks." He turned to Shrap. "You definitely owe me a drink after this one."

"Deal."

Trevelyan looked at Shrap. "Do you want a lift anywhere? I can get a car?"

Shrap shook her head. "No, thanks. I'm good. I've got to get going."

"Okay, I'll just take Alex downstairs, then I'll see you out."

She sat down to wait.

As Alex and Trevelyan left the room, she heard Alex say, "Why is she wearing those old clothes? She looks like a tramp."

Trevelyan's reply was lost in the hubbub of the squad room.

48

Shrap stood as Trevelyan came back into the room. "He's with the medic now. Seems okay."

"Thanks, Gareth," she said, awkwardly.

They walked together to the door, past the computers, the printers, the detectives on their phones. Shrap tried to ignore the yearning inside of her. Just being here made her long for something she could no longer have. No longer had.

"You sure you don't want a ride somewhere?" Trevelyan said.

"Nah, I'm fine. Honestly."

They'd reached the door. "Okay, if you're sure."

She hesitated, unsure what to say. Goodbyes were never her strong suit.

Trevelyan saved her. "Thanks for your help." He ran a hand through his hair. "I'm sorry about Alex, but he gave us some good intel. Nothing that helps with the case, mind you."

"Yeah. Pity that." She stared at an auburn strand that he'd dislodged. It lay against his blazer, copper in the overhead light. Then it struck her. She knew what had bothered her about the dog hair on the woman's jacket.

"The Pinchers' SUV," she blurted out.

"Yes?"

"You said forensics didn't find any hair or blood or anything in it."

"No, it was squeaky clean."

"It couldn't have been. That's the car she uses to take the dogs to the heath. It should have been covered in hair."

Trevelyan frowned and shook his head. "I specifically remember the technician telling me the car was spotless, like it had recently been cleaned."

Shrap snapped her fingers. "That's because it had. They didn't just get it serviced, they got it deep cleaned too."

He paused. "Shit."

Shrap faced him in the lobby. "We ruled them out before because we thought the murders were connected, but if it was two separate killers, then Gregory could have picked up Bianca after she left the club that night."

Trevelyan was shaking his head. "Annie said her husband got home with a headache and took a painkiller, which knocked him out. She swore he didn't move all night."

"*He* might not have." Shrap held his gaze.

"But that doesn't mean she didn't," Trevelyan finished. "Plus, she had motive. Bianca was having an affair with her husband. She must have known. A woman always knows."

There was that look again. Sadness, but with a touch of resentfulness. Like he knew.

"If she did, then it was all planned out in advance," said Shrap. "She waited until her husband was asleep. Took the Porsche and went to the club. Perhaps she was planning on waiting for Bianca to come out, but then she left early, after Leonard Blake."

Trevelyan picked up the theory. "She followed her towards the Strand, then when Blake realised he was being followed and confronted Bianca, Annie swooped in to save the day."

"She probably stopped to ask Bianca if she needed a lift. Bianca wouldn't have known who she was. Her main thought would have been to get away from Blake, and she'd trust another woman."

Trevelyan let out a slow hiss. "Do you think it's possible?"

"I think it's worth questioning her about it. She's pretty highly strung. If you push her about the affair, really rub it in, I think she might crack."

Trevelyan nodded, his eyes gleaming.

"Ask her about Doug. If she killed Bianca, she must have gone back the next day for Doug." She stiffened. "She bloody stood there and watched him burn."

"I will." Trevelyan put a hand on her arm. "I promise. We'll get justice for your friend."

49

DCI Burrows was in such a good mood that he agreed Shrap could come in and watch the recorded interview with Annie Pincher. It wasn't live, but Gareth felt that they owed Shrap that much. If it hadn't been for her, they'd never have looked at anyone other than Doug Romberg for Bianca's murder.

"Good Morning, Sergeant Nelson," DCI Burrows gushed. He was a sucker for a title.

Gareth hid his grin.

"Please, call me Shrap." She shot him an accusing look.

She was "in disguise" again, as she called it, although he was beginning to suspect she was getting rather used to dressing normally. How she managed it, he had no idea. She looked good, her face clear and devoid of make-up, clean clothes. Even the coat was clean.

You'd never believe she was the same filthy vagrant he'd first met.

Even back then, he'd detected the spark of intelligence in her eyes. There were some things you couldn't hide, no matter how much you wanted to.

They sat down in Burrows' office. He pulled up the pre-recorded interview on his desktop computer and left them to it. "I'm sorry I can't stay. I'm meeting a Detective Chief Inspector Rob Miller from the Putney murder squad." He beamed. "I'm going to have great pleasure telling him their services are no longer required."

The interview began.

Annie Pincher, drawn and tense, sat opposite Devi and himself. The view was side on.

Gareth had been allowed to conduct the interview since he knew the details of the Pinchers' involvement better than Devi. Next to the suspect was her attorney, a middle-aged man with a shock of white hair.

"Mrs Pincher, could you confirm where you were on the night of the third of November."

"I was at home, with my husband."

"In a previous statement, you said your husband had a work function that night."

"Yes, but he got back sometime after ten."

"You also said he had a headache when he got home."

"What's that got to do with anything?" Her eyes narrowed.

"Could you answer the question, please?"

Out of the corner of his eye, Gareth saw Shrap nod in response to his questions.

"Yes, he had a headache. I gave him a painkiller and he went straight to bed."

"Did you go to bed at the same time?"

"Yes, I did."

He saw Shrap's eyelids flicker. She knew she was lying.

"When we spoke to your husband, he confirmed he took the painkiller, and it knocked him out. He said he slept through until morning."

"That's right."

"Then he wouldn't have noticed if you left the house."

Annie Pincher froze. She blinked several times in rapid succession. "I did not leave the house."

"Could you explain why your Porsche Cayenne was picked up on an ANPR camera on Haverstock Hill Road near Belsize Park at a quarter to twelve that same night?"

She didn't reply.

Gareth slid a photograph across the table towards her. "This is your vehicle, isn't it?"

Annie Pincher glanced down, visibly pale.

"I-I don't know."

"It's your licence plate number," Gareth pointed out. "And if you look closely at this picture, which is the same one only bigger, you'll see that it is indeed you at the wheel."

They hadn't managed to pick up her vehicle on the Strand where Bianca had been taken, but they had tracked her from Hampstead Heath to the West End.

No answer.

Shrap was glued to the screen.

Gareth changed tack. "You knew your husband was having an affair, didn't you?"

"No."

"I think you're lying. I think you had known for ages, ever since he'd told you about the lap dance. You knew exactly who Bianca Rubik was. You even knew where she lived. Her flatmate confirmed that she'd seen you loitering outside the house. When she asked you if you were looking for someone, you said you'd got the wrong street. Do you remember that?"

That had been a stroke of luck. On a whim, Gareth had called Rona and shown her photographs of both Gregory and Annie Pincher. To her surprise, it had been Annie she'd recognised.

It was all circumstantial evidence, as her solicitor well knew, but it was pretty damning all the same.

"No, I don't."

"What were you doing outside Bianca Rubik's house?"

"I didn't know it was her house. I got the wrong street."

"Where were you going?"

"No comment."

Gareth studied her. "Did it bother you that your husband was sleeping with a stripper? It must have done. A woman of your social standing. What would your friends think if they found out? Not only was he sleeping with her, but he was also paying for her tuition – and that's not cheap."

Still no reaction.

He pushed harder. "Where did they meet? Did they have sex in your house? In your bed?"

Annie slammed her hand down on the table. "Okay, enough."

Shrap nodded, still focused on the screen. Gareth had taken her advice and pushed her until she broke.

"Of course I knew about the affair."

"How did that make you feel?"

"How do you think?" she hissed. "How would you feel if your husband was sleeping with a whore?" Annie shivered.

"When did you find out?" Gareth asked quietly.

"After he told me what had happened at the stag do. I knew he wasn't telling me everything. I can tell when Greg's lying. We've been married for fifteen years. I met him at university. He's the only man I've ever been with and he was screwing a stripper behind my back." She burst into tears.

Sobs echoed around the small office. It had been even louder in the interview room.

"What made you decide to take matters into your own hands?" Gareth asked.

Annie took a jagged breath. "A few weeks ago, Greg said he was going to a team building weekend in the Lake District, but I knew he was lying. I followed him. He went to the club, so I waited outside until closing and I saw them together. He took her to a hotel in Central London, off Piccadilly. I couldn't believe it. He spent the entire weekend with her." She swiped at her eyes. "When he got back on Sunday night, I pretended I didn't know. I asked him about the team building weekend and he even made up some stories to tell me." She scoffed. "If I hadn't known, I'd have been taken in by them. I'd have believed everything."

"Is that when you decided to kill Bianca?"

A small nod.

Devi's voice said, "For the purposes of the recording, the suspect is nodding her head."

"On the night of the third, after your husband was asleep, you left the house and drove to Whispers Gentlemen's Club. Is that right?"

"Yes." Her voice was barely a whisper.

"You waited outside for her."

"She left early," Annie said. "I wasn't expecting her to leave until later."

"But you followed her?"

"Yes, she was acting strangely, like she was following some other guy. At first I thought I might have to call it off and I was about to turn around and go home when the man spotted her. He started chasing her, shouting at her. She took off up the street, running in my direction."

Gareth waited for her to continue. She seemed to want to tell the story now, to get it off her chest.

"I wound down the window and asked if she needed help. She said yes, so I let her in. I didn't have to do a thing. She came to me."

Shrap's jaw tightened.

Gareth knew how she felt. He'd felt the same way during the interview. Annie Pincher was mad. She didn't seem to realise what she'd done or if she did, she didn't care.

"What happened next?"

"I asked her where she wanted to go. She said she had a friend in Southwark, and I could drop her there."

That was new. It was the first time they'd heard about a friend.

"We crossed the bridge and I turned into a quiet side street. I looked at her and thought, you're the bitch who's screwing my husband. That's when I saw red. Up until that point, I wasn't even sure what I was going to do."

"Is that when you strangled her?"

"No, she got out of the car. I watched her walk away and thought, no way. I can't let you live. You're going to destroy my marriage, my life, everything I've built over the last fifteen years."

"So you went after her?"

"I got out of the car. She stopped, surprised, but when she saw the look on my face she started running." Annie's lips turned up in a smirk. "I think that's when she realised who I was. Luckily, I was faster than her. I grabbed her and wrestled her to the ground. I wasn't thinking straight. All I knew was I wanted her gone. I used the metal strap of her handbag to strangle her. I wrapped it around her neck and pulled. It was easier than I thought. It only took a few minutes, and she was gone."

Shrap remained motionless, but Gareth could see her fingers curling into the table.

"At first I thought she was unconscious, but then I checked her pulse and realised she was dead."

"What did you do next?"

"I looked around in case anyone had seen us, but no one had. I only saw one camera, but it was facing the other way."

"What about the old man?" Gareth whispered.

"What old man?"

"The one who saw you kill Bianca."

She frowned, then her forehead cleared. "Oh, you mean the homeless guy. I'd almost forgotten about him."

Shrap's hands clenched into fists.

"What did you do about him?"

"Nothing, at first. I didn't realise he'd seen me until I got back to the car. When I turned around, I saw him leaning over the body. He looked straight at me too, stupid drunk. I knew then he'd be a problem."

"Is that why you went back the following day and set him on fire?"

She scoffed. "I did the guy a favour. He would probably have drunk himself to death anyway. All I had to do was knock him out, pour his own whiskey on him and set it alight. He never felt a thing."

Thank God for small mercies.

Shrap, however, was glaring daggers at the screen.

"How did you find him?" Gareth asked, once he'd recovered from Annie's shocking admission. She'd spoken about Doug like he didn't matter. He'd been so inconsequential that she'd almost forgotten killing him.

"It wasn't hard. I walked up and down the road until I spotted him, and then followed him to the station car park."

"Where you watched him burn."

Annie shrugged. "He was a bum. Nobody cares about them."

Doug was laid to rest in Kensal Green Cemetery a few days later. His headstone read:

At rest, a soldier, a friend, a hero.

"It's a beautiful spot," said Trevelyan, who'd taken time out to attend. There were a handful of other people there, including Budge, and Dicky from the South Bank.

Shrap spotted a middle-aged man with a passing resemblance to Doug. A brother, perhaps. A younger man and woman, possibly his children, although Doug had never spoken about them. They'd cut him off a long time ago.

"Yes," she agreed. "It is."

Although most of the trees scattered around the cemetery had lost their leaves, the ground was covered by a patchwork blanket of rusty browns, burnished oranges and brilliant reds. Autumn confetti to bid Doug goodbye. Her friend was finally at peace.

"It was a good thing you did," Gareth told her as they walked back to the car park. "Justice was served."

"Thanks to you."

After she'd watched that video recording of Annie

Pincher's confession, she'd felt a rage so strong she'd barely been able to contain herself. If she hadn't been in the company of Trevelyan and his partner, she'd have hit something.

"I'm sorry I left so abruptly. I had to get out of there before I exploded."

"I know. I could tell." He flashed her a smile.

"You did an amazing job in that interview, the way you got her to confess like that. To both murders."

"It was easy once she started talking. The thing that scared me the most, was her total lack of empathy. I still don't think she fully grasps what she's done."

"How's Gregory taking it?"

"He's in shock. When we told him, he couldn't believe it. He told us it wasn't possible. Annie wasn't like that."

"Amazing how you can be married to someone for fifteen years and yet not truly know them," murmured Shrap.

Gareth shrugged. "All the more reason not to get married."

She smirked.

"How's Alex?" he asked.

"I don't know. I haven't seen him since he gave his statement." She didn't expect to either.

"Well, thanks to him, the National Crime Agency intercepted the shipment of cocaine when it got to Tilbury. Xhafa was there, along with his henchman, Mikael, and they're both currently in police custody."

"That's great news. Xhafa must have decided to go himself, since Uzi and Thomas were out of commission."

"Or he couldn't find anyone else he could trust on such short notice. Either way, they'll be going away for a good few years."

"Do you think they'll give up the other members of the syndicate?" Shrap asked.

"I doubt it. Not if they know what's good for them. They're tough bastards, I don't expect the NCA will get much out of them."

Shrap tended to agree.

"Any news on Uzi?"

"Sort of." His face lit up. "Forensics found trace DNA evidence in the back of the SUV. It's gone to the lab, but we're hoping it's Petra Burton-Leigh's blood. If it is, then we've got him."

"Good work. Two cases closed."

"Yep. DCI Burrows is the man of the hour again. The Superintendent got invited to tea with the Police Commissioner, so everybody's happy."

"What about you?" Shrap asked.

"I'm just pleased we caught the bad guys and got justice for those poor women, and your friend. It's the least we could do."

She couldn't agree more.

"Oh, and I gave Petra's parents a hard time." His eyes glittered. "Threatened her stepfather with sexual assault charges."

"Good for you."

"It needed doing."

Shrap stopped walking. They'd reached the car park. "Well, thanks for everything." She wanted to spend some time at the cemetery before she made her way back to Waterloo.

"You don't want a lift back?"

She shook her head. "I think I'll hang out here for a bit."

"Okay. It's a lovely day for it."

A moment passed where they gazed at each other, and

then he said, "Oh, I almost forgot. I've got something for you."

"Yeah?"

She watched as he reached into his blazer pocket. Pulling out a folded pamphlet, he handed it to her. "It's a six-week course, especially for veterans. I hope you'll consider it."

She glanced down.

It was a residential intensive treatment programme for PTSD run by an organisation called Combat Stress.

"The charity funds it, so it won't cost you a penny."

"Thanks." She stuffed it into her pocket.

His eyes creased. "Good luck, Shrap."

"And you, Gareth."

He turned and walked to the car, while she stood alone in the cemetery and watched. When he was gone, she went back to Doug's grave, sat down under a tree and pulled the brochure out of her pocket.

She read it through. Sighed. Then read it again.

Shrap leaned back against the tree and closed her eyes. She thought about the friends she'd lost in the field, the men she couldn't save. She thought about Doug. How he'd pulled her back from the edge when she'd wanted to end it all.

Then, she took a deep breath.

Maybe it was time.

AN UNLIKELY SAVIOUR
SHRAP NELSON BOOK 2

When two homeless youths witness a body being dumped in the River Thames, no one believes their story – until one of them goes missing. Shrap, a homeless veteran battling PTSD, takes on the case to find the missing boy and uncover the truth behind the murder.

As Shrap delves deeper into the investigation, she discovers that the victim was a former military police officer with a complicated past. With the help of DC Trevelyan, Shrap must navigate the growing cast of suspects, all while fighting her own inner demons.

But when an attack on her life threatens to derail her progress and the missing boy's life hangs in the balance, Shrap must push through her PTSD to uncover a crime that began long ago in a distant land where the lines between good and evil were blurred.

With the killer always one step ahead, Shrap and Trevelyan

race against time to find the missing boy and bring the murderer to justice.

Can Shrap hold it together long enough to solve the case, or will her own demons consume her?

An Unlikely Saviour is a gripping tale of mystery, suspense, and redemption that will keep you on the edge of your seat until the very last page.

AVAILABLE FROM AMAZON AND KINDLE UNLIMITED.

ABOUT THE AUTHOR

BIBA PEARCE is a bestselling English crime writer and author of the DCI Rob Miller, Kenzie Gilmore and Shrap Nelson series.

Download a FREE mystery novella, or sign up to her mailing list at www.bibapearce.com.